THE BURGUNDIAN'S TALE

A Selection of Recent Titles by Kate Sedley
in the Roger the Chapman Mysteries series

THE BROTHERS OF GLASTONBURY
ST JOHN'S FERN
THE WEAVER'S INHERITANCE
THE WICKED WINTER
THE GOLDSMITH'S DAUGHTER *
THE LAMMAS FEAST *
NINE MEN DANCING *
THE MIDSUMMER ROSE *

* *available from Severn House*

THE
BURGUNDIAN'S
TALE

Kate Sedley

severn House

This first world edition published in Great Britain 2005 by
SEVERN HOUSE PUBLISHERS LTD of
9–15 High Street, Sutton, Surrey SM1 1DF.
This first world edition published in the USA 2005 by
SEVERN HOUSE PUBLISHERS INC of
595 Madison Avenue, New York, N.Y. 10022.

British Library Cataloguing in Publication Data

Sedley, Kate
    The Burgundian's Tale
    1.   Roger the Chapman (Fictitious character) - Fiction
    2.   Peddlers and peddling - England - Fiction
    3.   Great Britain - History - Edward IV, 1461-1483 - Fiction
    4.   Detective and mystery stories
    I.   Title
    823.9'14 [F]

    ISBN 0-7278-6216-2 (cased)
    ISBN 0-7278-9138-3 (paper)

Typeset by Palimpsest Book Production Ltd.,
Polmont, Stirlingshire, Scotland.
Printed and bound in Great Britain by
MPG Books Ltd., Bodmin, Cornwall.

One

It had not been a good year.

To begin with, I was neither as skilled nor as careful a lover as I had thought myself, with the result that, in the late summer of 1479, Adela found herself pregnant yet again. But although this proved a source of worry to us both, and the cause of constant reproaches from my former mother-in-law and Adela's cousin, Margaret Walker, we were all three plunged into mourning when, the following April, the child died within four days of her birth.

Adela's grief, however, went deeper than mine. She already had two sons: five-year-old Nicholas by her first husband, Owen Juett, and almost-two-year-old Adam by me. Our family's only girl, Elizabeth, also five, was my child by my first wife, Lillis Walker. Adela would have liked a daughter of her own. So she unreservedly mourned the lost child, while my misery was secretly tempered by feelings of relief that, for the present at any rate, there was no sixth mouth to feed or back to clothe. But I was unable to hide my emotions well enough to deceive Adela, and as spring once more blossomed into early summer, the atmosphere between us grew increasingly strained.

To make matters worse, as a cold and rainy April turned into an even wetter, chillier May, Margaret Walker caught a rheum that settled on her chest. She needed careful nursing, and my wife repaid her cousin's many past kindnesses by moving her from her cottage in Redcliffe into our house in Small Street, putting her to bed in Elizabeth's chamber and shifting my daughter and a spare mattress into our room to sleep alongside us (arrangements which, however unavoidable,

1

were not conducive to marital harmony). By mid-May, the relationship between my wife and myself was at breaking point, and I decided it was high time I took to the road again instead of peddling my wares in and around Bristol, as I had been doing now for over a year.

I informed Adela of my decision and waited for her protests. Instead, she greeted it with such obvious relief that I realized our marriage was in a more parlous state than I had imagined. Time, indeed, for me to be on my travels! The only decision left to be made was in which direction to go.

But I need not have bothered my head on the subject. As so often in the past, fate was ready and waiting to take a hand in my affairs.

I was busy in the kitchen, restocking my pack and making room for a spare shirt and pair of hose, while Adela brushed my jerkin clean of dirt and dog hairs and my children screamed and charged around the house, completely indifferent to my imminent departure.

'You'll have to take Hercules with you,' my wife declared, turning her attention to my mud-caked boots. 'I can't cope with him and that cur of Margaret's. They hate one another.'

'Hardly surprising.' I rushed to the defence of my canine friend. 'This is Hercules's house.' I stared with dislike at the little black-and-white dog adopted by Margaret Walker when it had been abandoned by its former mistress, and which, for some unknown and utterly ridiculous reason, she had christened Cherub. A less cherubic-natured hound it would have been difficult to find. 'If I take Hercules with me, in a week or two, when I return, that dog will have usurped his place.'

'He'll be company for you,' Adela argued, scraping the last of the dried mud from the soles of my boots and starting to polish them with a piece of soft rag. 'Now, who can that be?' she added irritably as someone banged loudly on the outer door.

She went to answer the summons and returned a few moments later looking worried and followed by a sergeant-at-arms from the castle.

2

He saluted me and asked, 'Roger the Chapman?'

'I'm Roger Chapman, yes.' I eyed the man warily. 'Who wants to know?'

'Your presence is required up at the castle, Master Chapman.' He smiled in what I suppose was meant to be a reassuring way, but one which was rendered sinister by several broken and blackened front teeth. Hercules gave a threatening growl.

'That doesn't answer my question,' I snapped. 'Who requires my presence and why?'

For a moment, the sergeant-at-arms looked as though he might not pander to my curiosity; then he shrugged.

'The King's nephew, John de la Pole, Earl of Lincoln,' was the astonishing reply.

'John de – Who? – What?' I stuttered.

The man repeated the message, adding, 'And also Master Timothy Plummer, Spymaster-General to the Duke of Gloucester and formerly to His Grace the King.'

Timothy! Things began to make a little more sense, although not much. I remembered uneasily that, the previous summer, I had thwarted certain of the spy's deep-laid plans. But that could have nothing to do with this particular summons, surely? I sighed. There was only one way to find out.

'Very well,' I said. 'Shall we get this over with?'

I kissed Adela and squeezed her hand. 'I'll be back. And soon.'

'I certainly hope so.' She looked pointedly at the sergeant. 'You've done nothing wrong.'

But the expression on the rugged, weather-beaten countenance remained noncommittal.

The early-morning streets were as crowded and noisy as ever, the muck-rakers getting in everyone's way as they tried to clear the central drains of yesterday's filth and debris – a thankless task, as people were refilling them as fast as they were emptied. Several friends and acquaintances hailed me, staring with interest at my companion, but I made no attempt to enlighten them as to what was going on. How could I? I didn't know myself.

We crossed the bridge leading to the Barbican Gate and entered the outer ward of Bristol Castle. This presented a livelier scene than usual – a number of supercilious young men, in a livery with which I was unfamiliar, either lounging around sneering at the locals and the building's sorry state of disrepair, or being very busy about nothing in particular. The sergeant-at-arms forced a path between them with a ruthlessness that gladdened my heart, and led me to a chamber on the ground floor of the great keep.

It was a cold, damp little room which would also have been airless but for the fact that there was a crack in one of the inner walls that I could have put my fist through. The floor oozed water from an overflowing sink-hole in one corner, and there was a general smell of decay and corruption. Days when the Bristol dungeons had housed such eminent prisoners as King Stephen and the elder Hugh le Despenser, favourite of the second Edward, had long gone, and the City Fathers were reluctant to spend money (which could be put to far better use feathering their own nests) on the unnecessary upkeep of the castle.

The room's only furniture consisted of a table, at present bearing a flagon and a couple of mazers, and two stools, on one of which, facing the door, sat Timothy Plummer. He rose as I entered and held out his hand.

'Roger, my friend! It's good to see you again.'

I was immediately suspicious. Somebody once said that he feared the Greeks, even when they came offering gifts. I knew what he meant. I particularly feared Timothy Plummer when he was at his most civil and urbane. He waved me to the other stool and poured us both some wine – the best Rhenish, he assured me, rightly confident that I wouldn't challenge him. Whatever it was, it was wine such as I hadn't tasted in years (if ever) and far beyond my pocket. I grew even more uneasy.

'All right, Timothy,' I said, 'what do you want?'

He smiled. 'Blunt as ever! But I suppose it saves time. Just a little favour for Duke Richard, that's all.'

'I see . . . And what exactly does this little favour entail?'

He took a sip of wine and smiled again. 'A visit to London. Nothing that will test your powers of deduction too heavily.'

'Oh, no,' I said firmly. 'I'm not planning on going to London just at present, not even to please Duke Richard, dearly as I love the man.' I wanted to get right away from the hustle and bustle of city life: I had promised myself long spring days of quiet and solitude, watching the rosy-fingered dawn come up over the distant hills, walking knee-high through the early-morning mist and listening to lark song.

Timothy seemed worryingly unperturbed by my adamant refusal.

'A pity,' he remarked cheerfully, pouring me more wine. 'But I'm afraid, Roger old friend, that you have no choice. My Lord of Gloucester has requested your services and I don't intend he should be disappointed. We leave Bristol this afternoon, so you'd better go home and pack anything you might need. A horse will be provided for you – at His Grace's expense, of course.'

'And how,' I enquired coldly, 'do you intend forcing me go with you if I refuse?'

He pushed aside his own mazer and settled forward on his stool, arms folded in front of him on the table.

'There's the little matter of your treasonable activities last summer,' he pointed out, 'helping an enemy of King Edward to escape my clutches. Oh, I know the proof is a bit thin, but I could make things very unpleasant for you, Roger, if I put my mind to it. For you *and* your family. If I made a few enquiries in Marsh Street among your Irish friends, for instance, I feel sure I could gather enough evidence to substantiate a case against you. At the time, I turned a blind eye to what you did because I couldn't see there was anything to gain by charging you. Besides, I like you. We've been friends for years, and you've rendered Duke Richard good service. I'd hate to see you die a traitor's death. Agonizingly protracted and very messy. So, you see, I feel sure you'll be sensible and do as I ask. Or rather, as Duke Richard asks.'

I stared at the spy, so angry with both myself and him that I was temporarily struck dumb. In a futile gesture, I sent my mazer spinning, watching his look of horror as the precious Rhenish spilled across the table top and smiling as he was forced to leap to his feet to avoid being drenched with the stuff.

'You – you – you fool!' he bellowed. 'Wasting decent wine!'

I don't know what might have happened next had the door not opened just at that moment, and a small, self-important page announced, 'The Earl of Lincoln.'

I judged the King's nephew to be about seventeen or eighteen years of age, a very handsome lad of great grace and charm. He must have sensed the tension in the atmosphere, but he ignored it, as he did the spilled wine, smiling gaily at Timothy and clapping me on the shoulder in the friendliest manner possible.

'So! You must be the famous chapman of whom my Uncle Gloucester speaks with such admiration and fondness. Our worthy spymaster has told you, I suppose, that we need you in London to help solve a crime. I've ridden with him from the capital to add my entreaties to his request and also – I must be honest – because I was curious to meet you.' He grinned broadly, joyously. 'And now I have.'

'Your – Your Highness is very kind,' I stammered. 'But I can hardly believe the King's nephew would be eager to meet a common p-pedlar.'

He gave a great roar of laughter at that and once again smote me on the shoulder.

'Good God, man, if we're to talk of being common, there's plenty of plebeian blood on the spear side of my family.' (His father was the Duke of Suffolk, his mother the King's sister, Elizabeth.) 'Why, the founder of our family's fortunes, William de la Pole, was a moneylender from Hull, in Yorkshire. My great-great-grandfather, Geoffrey Chaucer, was the son of a London wine merchant – and if you've ever read any of those tales of his about pilgrims riding to Canterbury, you'll know that he had a truly bawdy sense of humour. His wife, my great-great-grandmother Chaucer, was the daughter of a Picardy herald, one Payne de Roet.' He broke off, aware, perhaps, that he might have denied his royal blood a trifle too enthusiastically. 'Of course,' he added with a self-conscious laugh, 'on my mother's side, the Plantagenets can claim descent from both Alfred the Great and from Charlemagne.'

I gave a brief bow. 'Which proves my point.'

'No, no! Timothy, you've explained our dilemma to Master Chapman?'

The spy had regained his composure. 'Not yet, Your Highness. Roger hasn't long arrived. But he has expressed his willingness to accompany us back to London and to give us the benefit of his extraordinary talent.'

'Splendid!' The earl beamed at us both and I was afraid for a moment that he was going to thump my shoulder for a third time. (I could feel the bruise forming already.) Fortunately, he restrained himself. 'You can explain everything to him during dinner. I've promised to dine with the Constable, and places have been reserved for the pair of you at one of the lower tables.'

'Unnecessary, My Lord,' Timothy answered suavely. 'Roger has invited me to eat with him and his family, but we shall be ready to leave with you and your cavalcade at noon.'

I choked, but no one seemed to notice.

'Good! Good! You'll have more privacy.' Lincoln swung on his heel while his page scrambled to open the door. 'Master Chapman, many thanks. My Uncle Gloucester is looking forward, I know, to meeting you again.'

Adela was relieved to get me back safe and sound, but unhappy at seeing my companion, whom she rightly regarded as trouble.

She and I held conference in the kitchen, while the two elder children entertained Timothy in the parlour, where he proved himself surprisingly adept at playing fivestones, a game at which Elizabeth and Nicholas normally excelled.

'I was going on my travels, anyway,' I argued. 'I might just as well go to London as elsewhere.'

'But you won't be earning any money,' my practically minded wife pointed out. 'And working for the Duke has often proved hazardous. If anything happened, how should I manage without you? I think you should refuse.'

'I can't,' I said and explained why.

Adela was horrified. 'Timothy wouldn't do that to you! He's your friend.'

I shook my head. 'He's a servant of the state first and my friend a very poor second. Don't underestimate him, sweetheart. He's a ruthless man. He couldn't do his job properly if he weren't. I've no choice but to go with him. And it's my own foolish fault that I'm in that position. However, I shall take my pack with me. It's often proved useful for getting my foot inside a stranger's door, and I might make some money as well. Now, shall we eat? It must be nearly ten o'clock.'

At Adela's suggestion, Timothy and I ate alone in the parlour, free from interruption by our three young limbs of Satan and from the querulous demands of the stick-thumping patient upstairs. Using the top of an old leather-bound chest we had recently acquired as a table, we made short work of my wife's meat pasties and gravy, cinnamon tarts and stewed pippins, all washed down with good, strong ale. Rubbing his belly with satisfaction, Timothy was moved to remark that such a meal was enough to make a man think of settling down and getting married himself. But a few seconds later, the sound of Adam throwing one of his tantrums in the kitchen made the spy hurriedly change his mind.

'So?' I asked. 'What's this all about?'

Timothy drank the last of his ale. 'A simple enough case, really. Simple, that is, to a man of your deductive powers.' He noticed my expression and laughed. 'All right! All right! I won't insult you with too much flattery.' Without being invited, he removed himself from his stool to the room's one armchair and leaned back with a sigh of repletion.

'Go on,' I said, valiantly suppressing my annoyance. 'For

a start, what's Duke Richard doing in London? I understood he rarely leaves Yorkshire nowadays, his dislike of the Queen and her family being so intense.'

Timothy settled himself more comfortably, belched loudly and nodded. 'That's true, but in a few days' time, the Dowager Duchess of Burgundy is to pay a visit to the the land of her birth and the whole family – or as many members of it as can be assembled – have been summoned to London to do her honour. The Duke and Duchess of Gloucester's presence has been particularly requested by the King.' Timothy grimaced. 'Easy to guess why, of course. George of Clarence was always Duchess Margaret's favourite sibling. Her first meeting with the Woodvilles and brother Edward since George's death is likely to be awkward, to say the least. Duke Richard, who not only had no hand in that death, but protested vehemently against his brother's attainder and execution, will be the buffer, the pourer of oil on troubled waters, the mediator between the English and Burgundian courts. Young Lincoln and his parents, the Duke and Duchess of Suffolk, will be three others. Also Duchess Cicely has already left Berkhamsted and taken up residence in Baynard's Castle, where the Dowager Duchess Margaret and some of her retinue will be housed. The two women will no doubt have a lot to say to one another in private concerning the Queen and her numerous kinfolk, but the King can depend on his mother to ensure that all her children behave themselves with dignity and propriety in public.'

I interrupted. 'Is this a state visit on behalf of the Dowager Duchess's stepdaughter? Or just a family reunion?'

Timothy pulled another face. 'A little of both, perhaps. The Dowager Duchess hasn't set foot on English soil since her marriage to Charles of Burgundy almost twelve years ago, so in one way, yes, I suppose it is a sentimental journey for her. And there are members of her family – although not, of course, the King and Duke Richard – whom she hasn't seen for the same length of time. But it's also a formal visit on behalf of the Duchess Mary and her husband, Maximilian of Austria, to renew old ties with England –

9

ties that have been somewhat eroded in the last three years since Duke Charles was killed. As you may or may not know – and this benighted city never seems to have any idea of what's happening anywhere else in the world except Ireland – King Louis has wrested back great swathes of Picardy, Artois and the Franche-Comté for the French Crown.'

I flung up a hand. 'Spare me the politics, Timothy! I do know King Edward has done nothing to support Burgundy because he receives a fat annual pension from King Louis . . . Oh, don't pretend to look surprised. I was in France with Duke Richard, if you remember, when the Treaty of Picquigny was signed. So, how does Duchess Margaret's visit affect me? King Edward surely can't be in need of *my* diplomatic skills.'

Timothy shuddered. 'Heaven forfend! You'd be like a bull let loose among the stalls on market day. No, no! But he does want his sister kept sweet and happy during her visit. Or as sweet and happy as possible considering that the young son of Duchess Margaret's favourite waiting-woman has recently been murdered. There's nothing His Highness can do about that, but he and the Duke of Gloucester would at least like to satisfy their sister's desire for vengeance by bringing the killer to justice.'

I was a little confused. 'Wait a moment! Where exactly did this murder take place? In Burgundy?'

'Of course not! Would I be asking for your help to solve it if it had? No. The young man was done to death in London.'

I was even more confused. 'What was he doing in London? I thought you said—'

It was Timothy's turn to hold up his hand. 'Let me explain. I think perhaps I'd better start at the beginning.'

I nodded vigorously. 'I think perhaps you had.'

So Timothy talked. I listened.

Throughout Margaret of York's troubled childhood, when, with her two younger brothers, George and Richard, she had been passed from one noble household to another, sometimes as a guest, sometimes as a prisoner, while her father, the Duke of York, fought King Henry VI for possession of the throne, her closest companions had been twins, seamstresses, Judith and Veronica Fennyman. Some five years older than Margaret herself, the girls had been reared in the York household from birth, both their parents having been loyal servants of Duchess Cicely. But when, in 1461, the widowed Duchess's eldest son had deposed King Henry, avenged his father's defeat and execution and been proclaimed King Edward IV, the twins had at last considered themselves free to leave Margaret's employ and marry.

Judith had done very well for herself, marrying a certain Edmund Broderer, ten years her senior – a man with sufficient income from a thriving embroidery business in Needlers Lane to enable him to live at the Fleet Street end of the Strand. At twenty years of age, therefore, Judith had found herself mistress of a comfortable three-storey house which, if not quite as opulent as the neighbouring dwellings (most of which belonged to members of the nobility), still had a garden running down to its own private water-stairs on the bank of the Thames.

The other twin, Veronica, had been satisfied with finding a husband among her fellow servants, and had married one of Duchess Cicely's grooms, James Quantrell, by whom, the following year, she had had a son, Fulk. Two weeks after the birth, James had been thrown by a wild young stallion he had been trying to tame and trampled underfoot. He had been dead within hours.

The grieving widow and her baby son, invited by Judith and Edmund, had gone to live in the Broderer household, where they had remained for the next six years. No young cousins had arrived to keep Fulk company, and Edmund Broderer's closest male relative remained his cousin's son, Lionel, who lived with his mother in Needlers Lane.

Lionel had been apprenticed early to his cousin, and shown such an aptitude for the embroidery trade that by the time he was eighteen he had been running the business for Edmund almost single-handed, while the older man led a life of leisure. Then, on a wild and stormy March evening in the year 1468, Edmund had disappeared while returning home from one of London's many taverns, his corpse being washed up near Saint Botolph's wharf three weeks later, stripped of clothes and valuables by the water scavengers who made a gruesome living out of the Thames's many casualties. He had only been identified by his wife's intimate knowledge of his body.

In the summer of the same year, Margaret of York, together with a trousseau that had cost the King, her brother, the awesome sum of two and a half thousand pounds, had left England to become the third wife of Charles of Charolais, Duke of Burgundy. Lonely and more than a little frightened – like many a pawn in the royal marriage game before her – she had begged Veronica Quantrell to accompany her as her seamstress-in-chief and, more importantly, as a familiar face and childhood friend. Veronica, in spite of her sister's recent bereavement, had agreed, and for the next twelve years she and Fulk had made their home in the Burguadian court, wherever it happened to be. Veronica had comforted her mistress as Margaret's hopes of presenting her lord with a male heir – with an heir of either sex – slowly faded, and were finally snuffed out altogether with Charles's death. She had become indispensable to the Duchess, and her handsome young son hardly less so. At eighteen, he was Margaret's favourite male attendant.

'Then,' said Timothy, helping himself to more ale, 'just after last Christmas, Veronica died, and young Fulk decided that he must bring the news to his aunt himself. It would seem that the sisters had always kept in touch and remained on good terms.'

In the intervening twelve years, Judith had married twice more; first to a Justin Threadgold, who had been carried off four years later by the plague, and secondly to a man thirteen years older than herself, her present husband, Godfrey St Clair. Still childless herself, Judith had two stepchildren, Alcina Threadgold and her present husband's son, Jocelyn St Clair.

Both these young people were treated as Judith's own,

lavished with affection and everything that money could buy. (She was now a very wealthy woman, thanks to Lionel Broderer's management of the embroidery business.)

'But it's the old, familiar story,' Timothy went on, wiping his mouth with the back of his hand. 'Faced with her own flesh and blood, warmed by the young man's apparent devotion and affection, Judith had barely known him a month before she made him her heir, presented him with extravagant gifts of money and jewels, and allowed herself to become besotted by him . . .' There was a pause before Timothy added grimly, 'Two weeks ago, he was found battered to death in Fleet Street, not two or three hundred yards from his aunt's home in the Strand.'

Two

I laughed shortly. 'Now there's a surprise!'

Timothy nodded gloomily. 'A predictable ending to a predictable tale. But not an unprecedented one. Strange things seem to happen to women of Judith St Clair's age, particularly if they're childless. Suddenly faced with a handsome young man, her twin sister's son, and deeply affected, I suppose, by the unexpected news of that sister's death, she adopted him almost immediately as her own. Her former affection for her stepchildren was overwhelmed by the love she felt for her nephew.'

'So why does Duke Richard need me to solve the crime?' I snorted. 'It seems to me any fool could work out the answer given time and patience. You already have four suspects with very strong motives for wanting the young man dead: Judith's present husband, his son, her step-daughter by her second marriage and the – er – cousin, was it? of her first husband, who runs the embroidery work-shops for her, and who, in the fullness of time, might well have expected some acknowledgement of the fact in Judith's will. It was generally known, I take it, that she had made this Fulk Quantrell her sole heir?'

'*She* may not have said anything about it, but it appears *he* openly boasted of the fact.'

'Well then!'

'It mightn't be quite as simple as that,' Timothy demurred. 'I'm not in possession of all the facts – God knows, I'm just the messenger – but I gather friends of Godfrey St Clair, a certain Roland and Lydia something-or-other, may also be involved. Don't ask me how! Besides, no one else has the leisure to spend on the matter.' His chest swelled importantly. 'By the time we get to London, the Dowager Duchess will already be at sea, and the Earl of Lincoln must set out again almost at once for Gravesend in order to escort his aunt into the capital. I, of course, will be in attendance on My Lord of Gloucester and must be constantly on the alert for any outside forces, any foreign agents, who might pose a threat to the friendly outcome of this visit and England's renewed ties with Burgundy.'

'The French, you mean,' I said drily. 'Such cunning, devious, little bastards – they're everywhere. I wonder you could be spared to come chasing after me.'

Timothy gave me a narrow look. 'You watch that sarcastic tongue of yours, Roger! I volunteered to fetch you because I knew I had the power to make you acquiesce in Duke Richard's request.'

'Not a command, then?'

The spy turned down the corners of his mouth. 'The Duke is sympathetic – unnecessarily so, in my opinion – to the demands of a wife and children. And given your present recalcitrant mood, it would appear to be a good thing that I did come.'

I was not prepared to allow Timothy that much satisfaction. 'As it happens, I was already preparing to leave Bristol and go on my travels for a week or two. So' – it was my turn to shrug – 'I might as well be in London as anywhere.'

I was delighted to note his look of disappointment. But he made no comment apart from asking me where I would choose to stay. 'I daresay a room can be found for you in Baynard's Castle. You've lodged there once before.'

I had indeed; which was how I knew the servants' dormitories to be cramped and overcrowded, some poor fellows sleeping three or four to a bed, others having no bed at all but forced to spend their nights on the draughty floor. Since becoming a house owner I had grown soft and used to my comfort.

'I'll find a room at St Brendan the Voyager in Bucklersbury,' I said. 'I know the landlord, Reynold Makepeace: an honest man, who won't take advantage of a country cousin like me by charging outrageous prices.'

Timothy's face brightened. 'I know the Voyager: it's tucked in among all those grocers' and apothecaries' shops. I also have a nodding acquaintance with Innkeeper Makepeace. But what's even better is that Needlers Lane is a turning off Bucklersbury, about halfway along on the opposite side of the road to the inn. You'll be a mere stone's throw from the Broderer workshops.' He rose and clapped me on the back, the same shoulder favoured by the Earl of Lincoln. I winced. 'And now, if we're not to keep the King's nephew waiting – and I wouldn't advise it, in spite of all his good humour and friendly ways – you'd better make your farewells. We must be at the castle by noon.'

We spent three nights on the road (the young Earl refusing to travel on the Sabbath) and entered London around midday on the sixteenth day of May, which, by coincidence, was the Feast of Saint Brendan the Voyager. Timothy, the least superstitious of men, nevertheless took this as a good augury for my success.

'It's going to prove an easy case for you to solve, Roger. Come and find me at Baynard's Castle this afternoon, when we've both had a chance to settle in. Duke Richard and his Duchess are staying there. They decided against Crosby's Place so that His Grace could be more in the company of his sister. If he's not too busy, he'll be pleased to see you. But he won't be able to afford you much time.'

I didn't take this amiss. I knew from what Timothy had told me during our journey that this rare visit to London by the Duke of Gloucester was not simply to greet his youngest sister, but also to hold urgent talks with his brother concerning Scotland's violation of her truce with England. Egged on, I learned, by the wily French King – who, typically, was also sheltering James III's rebellious brother, the Duke of Albany, at his court – there had been almost daily raids across the Border throughout the past autumn and winter. Four days earlier, the Duke of Gloucester had been

16

appointed the King's Lieutenant-General in the North, authorized, so the Earl of Lincoln had informed us, to levy the men of the Scottish marches, ready for war.

It said much for the Duke's family feeling that, in the midst of all this turmoil and uncertainty, he could find time to worry about Duchess Margaret's probable grief at the death of her favourite's son, and to want to have something done about solving the murder. I could understand why Timothy was so anxious not to let him down, and secretly determined that I would do my utmost to discover the culprit – although I naturally had no intention of telling Timothy this. Let him think me still resentful: it would keep him on his toes.

The Earl of Lincoln left us even before we entered London, making his way to Westminster where the King and Queen and most of the court were lodged. Timothy and I parted company outside St Paul's, he riding south to Baynard's Castle, between Thames Street and the river, I jogging along West Cheap to the Great Conduit, where I took the right-hand fork to Bucklersbury. And here, nestling, as Timothy had said, among the sweet-smelling grocers' and apothecaries' shops, I found the inn of St Brendan the Voyager still with its sign of the saint and his disciples in their skin-covered coracle, being kept afloat by the good offices of a sea monster.

I thought Reynold Makepeace might have forgotten me after more than two years, but he greeted me as though I were his long-lost brother, enquired solicitously after Adela and the children, and generally made me so welcome that I even began to enjoy this unsought and begrudged visit to the capital.

'As luck would have it,' he said, 'you can have the same chamber that you shared with your wife. It was vacated only this morning by a merchant from Nottingham who had business in the city. And when I talk about luck, I mean it. London's seething at the moment with people pouring in to catch a glimpse of Duchess Margaret. Many of the larger, more important inns have been commandeered for members of her retinue. Your guardian angel must be watching over you, guiding your footsteps here.'

The room was exactly as I remembered it – small, but spotlessly clean, opening off a gallery that ringed three sides of the Voyager's inner courtyard. The bed, which took up most of the space, still sported the same goose-feather mattress and down-filled pillows. There were no other furnishings, but my wants were modest, having no luggage except my pack and the cudgel I had insisted on bringing with me despite Timothy's reservations.

'You won't need your cudgel,' he had objected. 'You'll be under royal protection. The Duke's armourer can supply you with any weapons you might need to keep you safe in the London streets.'

But I preferred my own trusty 'Plymouth cloak' and my knife, both of which I was used to handling, and in this argument, the Earl of Lincoln, who had happened to over-hear the altercation, had backed me up.

'Better the weapons you know, Master Plummer, than those you don't,' he had said gaily, but decidedly; and I noted with amusement that Timothy gave in at once. The young man might parade and boast of his de la Pole and Chaucer blood, but he was a Plantagenet at heart, and expected to be treated as one.

The horse that had been hired for me from the Bell Lane stables, in Bristol, Reynold Makepeace readily agreed to house and feed for the duration of my stay in London at a slightly increased cost, to be added to the price of my room. I was happy to agree, and having donned a clean shirt and hose, brushed down my leather jerkin and combed my hair, set out for Baynard's Castle as I had been instructed.

It seemed to me that I had stood in that room only yesterday, instead of nine years earlier. There was no fire of scented pine logs on the hearth, it was true, but everything else was surely just the same: the table against the wall supporting silver ewers and goblets of the finest Venetian glass; the armchairs with their delicately carved backs, depicting birds and trailing, interwined vine leaves; the tapestries, slightly more faded perhaps, showing Hercules's fight with Nereus; and the copper chandelier with its scented wax candles, all lit because of the overcast day and the general gloom of the chamber.

But the dark-haired young man (exactly my own age for, according to my mother, we had been born on the selfsame day) who rose to greet me was older and far more care-worn than he had been on the occasion of our first meeting. Lines of suffering and sorrow were deeply scored into the thin, olive-skinned face. Sadness lurked behind a smile that had once been sweet and gentle, but which, now, could suddenly transform itself into a kind of rictus grin. Once described by the Countess of Desmond as 'the handsomest man in the room after the King', Richard of Gloucester's good looks had been eroded by the twin evils of great grief for the death of his brother, George of Clarence, and his hatred for those he considered responsible for that death, the Queen's family, the Woodvilles.

Then, as he came towards me, he smiled again, and this time his whole face lit up. I realized with gratitude that the man I had known and to whom I had sworn lifelong devotion was still there, inside that shell of suspicion and disillusionment that had hardened around him for his own protection.

'Roger!' The Duke held out a heavily beringed hand, which I knelt and kissed. He raised me, adding, 'It's good to see you once more. Thank you for coming. I know you're married and a father. And also, rumour has it, a householder. You must tell me how that happened, for you'd never accept any help from me. But first, here's someone who wants to meet you.' He turned and beckoned.

A boy, who had been sitting in one of the armchairs, came forward; a tall, smiling, shining – for I can think of no better way to describe him – child of some eleven or twelve years of age.

'My son, John,' the Duke said proudly. 'John, this is Roger Chapman of whom you've heard me speak.'

I bowed. 'My Lord.'

This, I knew, was Duke Richard's bastard son, born before the Duke's marriage to his beloved cousin, Anne Neville. There was also a bastard daughter, Katherine, as much the

19

apple of her father's eye as this bright and lively young man. (I wondered fleetingly about Prince Edward, the Duke's legitimate heir, who, if everything said of him were true, had inherited his mother's fragile constitution.)

The boy grinned broadly. 'My Lord father has been singing your praises, chapman. My cousin, John of Lincoln, insisted on haring off to Bristol just to steal a march and get a glimpse of you before I did. I wanted to go, too, but it wasn't allowed.'

I addressed the Duke. 'Your Grace, I suspect all this under-served praise is a ploy, first to get me to London, secondly to ensure I do your bidding now I'm here.'

Duke Richard smiled. 'You always did have a suspicious mind, my friend. But if you can solve the riddle of a death that will greatly distress my sister, the Dowager Duchess of Burgundy, when she hears of it, I don't mind what you think of me.' He gave his son a little push. 'Off you go, my lad, and make yourself useful to your grandmother if she needs you.' He ruffled the dark hair so like his own and watched with pride and affection as the Lord John made his courtesy to both of us in turn before quitting the room. 'One of the lights of my life,' he said simply as the door closed. 'Now, come and sit down and tell me all that's happened to you in these past two years.'

Half an hour later, he knew as much of my life as I had chosen to reveal; and, being an astute, shrewd man, probably much else that I had hoped to conceal.

'The *bond* of marriage can sometimes be just that,' he said enigmatically when I had finished. 'All the same, I'm delighted you've found a good woman to comfort your bed and bear your children. I'm pleased, too, for your good fortune, and that the money I sent after you last time proved of use in furnishing the house. You obviously rendered this Mistress Ford a great service to be the recipient of such gratitude.' He must have seen me colour up because he chuckled. 'No, no, Roger! I didn't mean that! I give you credit for being a faithful and loyal husband. Now, I'm afraid I must leave you. I'm wanted at Westminster. But I'll send Timothy to you. He'll arrange for someone to show you where the murder was committed and Mistress St Clair's house in the Strand. How you then go about solving our mystery is up to you. But I'm sure we shall see one another again in the days to come.' He pressed my shoulder – the same one – and I valiantly refrained from letting out a yelp of pain. 'I shall, of course, expect to be kept informed of your progress, but otherwise, you won't be bothered. I know you like to work alone.'

I again kissed his hand. When he had gone, I sat down and waited patiently for Timothy Plummer.

In fact, Timothy appeared only briefly before handing me over to a young officer of the Gloucester household named Bertram Serifaber – a stocky, curly-haired young man, as friendly as he was bright and quick-witted.

'I'm to assist you in any way I can,' he told me. 'I'm at your disposal for as long as you need me, and all my other duties are to be subordinated to your demands.' He smiled happily at the prospect and his brown eyes sparkled. 'I'm looking forward to it,' he admitted candidly. 'These state occasions can be a bore. There's such a lot of standing around, just twiddling one's thumbs. Trying to track down a murderer will be much more fun.'

'Only trying?' I teased. 'You should have more confidence in me, my little locksmith.'

He blushed, then quickly forgot his embarrassment and grinned. 'You're right. My father, grandfather and great-grandfather were, or are, all serifabers, but mending and fitting locks didn't appeal to me. When my father did some work in the royal palace at Westminister a year or so ago, I accompanied him, which is how I met Master Plummer. He was in the service of the King at the time, as I expect you know.' I nodded. 'Well, he took a liking to me, thought me bright enough to be trained as a future spy and persuaded my father at least to let me try. Mind you,' my new young friend added with a sigh, 'I didn't bargain on Master Plummer returning to the Duke of Gloucester's household and having to go with him to Yorkshire.'

He spoke the last word with the kind of scorn reserved

21

by all Londoners for anywhere outside the capital, but I was used to that. My lips might have twitched, but I hid my amusement and said bracingly, 'Well, you're back home now.'

'But not for long. It'll be Scotland next,' he added gloomily, 'if all the rumours are true.' Then what was plainly his natural buoyancy shone through and he gave me a blinding smile. 'However, anything's better than locksmithing, and you do get to see a bit of the world. And now that I'm trying – oops! sorry! – *going* to solve a murder with you, perhaps I'll be noticed by the King and My Lord of Gloucester and Duchess Margaret.' He didn't add, 'Things are looking up!' but the words were implicit in his general demeanour. He was an optimist and nothing could alter that fact.

'Then we'd better make a start,' I suggested. 'As we're not far from Fleet Street, you can show me first where this Fulk Quantrell was murdered.' I had a moment's misgiving. 'You do know all about this killing, I suppose? Master Plummer has explained everything to you?'

Bertram Serifaber nodded vigorously. 'He's told me all that he knows, yes. But it's not very much now, is it?'

I laughed and agreed.

We left London by the Lud Gate, under the raised portcullis, past the guards whose job it was to turn back any lepers who tried to enter the city, and across the drawbridge that spanned the ditch. I had forgotten how much bigger, dirtier and noisier London was even than Bristol, the second city in the kingdom; and long before we reached our destination my head was aching from the incessant cries of the street vendors, the chiming of the bells and the effort of pushing my way through the jostling crowds. The screech and rattle of carts, many driven at breakneck speed, was the inevitable prelude to being splashed with mud and refuse from the central drain. I cursed loudly and openly wished myself at home; but at the same time, there was a vitality, a sense of urgency about life in London that I secretly found exhilarating.

I remembered Fleet Street from my previous visits to the capital: a road leading from the Lud Gate at one end and merging into the Strand at the other. The River Fleet ran at right angles to it, as did Shoe Lane and the Bailey, and the houses that flanked it on either side were three-storeyed dwellings of fair proportions, home to the well-to-do, but nothing like as opulent as the nobles' mansions in the neighbouring Strand.

'It was here,' my companion said eagerly, darting ahead of me as we approached the turning to Faitour – or Fetter, as my London friend pronounced it – Lane. 'Between here and Saint Dunstan's Church. According to Master Plummer, the man had been felled with a blow to the back of his head and then finished off with several more. He'd been robbed of everything of value.'

I reflected that this was hardly surprising. A number of the faitours – or beggars, vagrants, vagabonds, scroungers, whatever you prefer to call them – after whom the lane was named, were even now skulking around in doorways, rattling their tin cups or displaying their war wounds (ha!), waiting for the largesse they felt to be their due to rain down upon their undeserving heads.

'I assume this murder happened at night,' I said, provoking an incredulous glance from Bertram.

'Yes, of course! Didn't Master Plummer tell you *anything*? I thought you'd know more than I do.'

'Master Plummer has left me in your more than capable hands,' I answered smoothly, but feeling a fool just the same. I determined to have a few well-chosen words with Timothy the next time I saw him. Nevertheless, I acknowledged that my ignorance was partly my own fault: I should have asked more questions, instead of wallowing in the ease and luxury of a journey undertaken in the company of a royal earl.

I surveyed the scene of the crime. The church of Saint Dunstan-in-the-West stood maybe fifty yards or so from the entrance to Faitour Lane, at a point where there was a small dog-leg turning in the road. On the walls of at least two of the houses, and on a wall of the church itself, were cresset holders which, judging by the smoke-blackened stonework and plaster behind them, were frequently used.

But I reckoned the flames of the cressets might cast more shadows than light under certain conditions, as well as being put out altogether in rain or high wind. Besides, there was plenty of protection to be had by a would-be killer in the narrow doorways of the houses, and a way of escape up Faitour Lane itself to the village of Holborn. All in all, I didn't think a murderer would have had much difficulty in getting away unnoticed and undetected.

I wondered if the local brotherhood of beggars had been questioned as to anything any one of them might have seen or heard that night, but guessed that, even if they had, the interrogation would have yielded nothing. Communities, particularly those that live by their wits or by preying on other people, stick together. They live by a code of which the cardinal – probably the only – sin is betrayal.

I knew from Timothy that there had been an enquiry of sorts, but the Sheriff's officers had been needed elsewhere to root out those Frenchmen thought to be lurking around every corner of every London street, just waiting to disrupt the Dowager Duchess's visit. I had tried to persuade Timothy, during one of our convivial drinking sessions on the journey from Bristol, that such fears were probably unjustified. I pointed out that King Louis was already master of the situation on account of the seventy-five thousand crowns he paid yearly to King Edward. Surely, I argued, that was a sufficient inducement to preclude any serious English assistance to Burgundy against the French, particularly as the King had a very expensive wife and, in the Woodvilles, as rapacious a set of in-laws as any ruler in Christendom.

But Timothy had remained unconvinced. He had reminded me sharply that it was *my* job to discover the identity of Fulk Quantrell's murderer while he and every other officer of the law busied themselves about the safety of the realm. In the face of such blinkered obstinacy I had given in gracefully, but I should have questioned him more closely about the crime.

So here I was with very little information to aid me in my search. I looked thoughtfully at the faitours, who either whined for alms or, when they had assessed my social

24

standing and probable worth, gave me back stare for stare, poked out their tongues and made other obscene gestures which I am too much of a gentleman to describe. But I decided they could wait. They would still be here whenever I was ready to speak to them.

'Very well,' I said to my companion. 'Now you can show me the house in the Strand where Mistress St Clair and her husband live; then we'll retrace our footsteps back to the city, to Needlers Lane.'

At my request, we walked the whole length of the Strand as far as the Chère Reine Cross, because I wished to renew my acquaintance with this part of London-Without-the-Walls, where the tentacles of the city were creeping further and further into the countryside between the capital and Westminster. Then we walked back again.

On our right were some of the finest houses in and around London – magnificent four-storey affairs with well-tended gardens running down to their own water-steps and landing stages on the Thames. Mansions, I suppose, would not have been too strong a word for many of them. Here, the great palace of the Savoy had once stood before it was destroyed during the insurrection of the peasants almost a hundred years before.

At the Fleet Street end, however, were three smaller houses; still handsome, but modest by comparison with the rest: they lacked a storey and were narrower in width. Nevertheless, the gardens were just as pleasant, and the overall impression was of money, possibly hard-earned, but plenty of it and well spent.

'I think Master Plummer said one of those three belongs to Mistress St Clair.' Bertram rubbed his nose apprehensively. 'But I'm not sure which. The middle one, I think.'

'Don't worry. We'll soon find out.' I smiled at him, not displeased that he seemed a little wary of my displeasure. (I judged him to be a youth who could easily get too cocky.) 'But first we're going to pick up my pack and cudgel at the Voyager and then we'll pay a visit to Needlers Lane.'

Three

In the event, I paid the visit alone, leaving young Master Serifaber to kick his heels in the ale room of the Voyager until my return.

Upon reflection, I had decided that it might be as well not to advertise – at least, not immediately – the Duke of Gloucester's interest in this affair, which my companion's blue and murrey livery, together with the badge of the White Boar, most certainly would do.

'Just to begin with, I'll spy out the lie of the land on my own,' I told him.

'I've been instructed to help you,' Bertram complained fretfully. 'After all, *I'm* supposed to be the spy.'

'You're a novice at this game, my lad,' I retorted, 'and don't you forget it. You're here to do my bidding. And if I have any nonsense, you'll find yourself back at Baynard's Castle quicker than you can blink. I don't think Master Plummer would be very pleased about that, do you?'

He grumbled mutinously under his breath, but was forced to cave in.

I patted his shoulder. 'I can't conceal Duke Richard's involvement for long,' I consoled him. 'Then you shall live in my pocket.'

He grinned at that and took himself off to sample Reynold Makepeace's best ale with the money I had given him as a bribe for his good behaviour. I crossed the road and turned into Needlers Lane. A quick enquiry of a passer-by elicited the fact that Broderer's workshop was on the right-hand side, at the far end, where the street we were in joined Soper Lane.

It wasn't difficult to find. Not only was it the largest workshop in the vicinity, but it had an imposing sign above the door, bearing the somewhat faded, but still readable legend 'EDMUND BRODERER' in red paint. I hitched up my pack and went inside.

I knew nothing about embroidery, but I didn't need to in order to understand that this was a thriving business. A first, cursory glance suggested that there were at least ten or twelve people in the room, and all hard at work. Along one of the walls, great panels of silken mesh were stretched on wooden frames. Two men in white linen aprons were busily plying their needles in and out of the net in a kind of cross stitch, which gradually formed patterns of birds and beasts and flowers. Occasionally, one or the other of them would refer to a coloured pattern, drawn on a piece of parchment and nailed to the upright between the frames. But for the most part, they seemed to need no guidance, knowing instinctively what to do next.

Three women were working at a horizontal frame just in front of me, laying strands of gold and blue thread across a piece of crimson silk, then stitching the strands in place to form a solid block of colour. (This process I eventually learned is known as 'couching'. There's also another process called 'undercouching', but we won't go into that.) Two young women were being instructed by a grey-haired matron in the art of appliqué work; while yet another, middle-aged woman was sewing tiny prismatic glass beads into the centre of embroidered velvet medallions which, in their turn, were being stitched to the sleeves of a dark-green silk dalmatic. And at a long trestle to my left, a bevy of much younger girls were busy embroidering the smaller items such as purses, orphreys, belts and ribbons. A veritable hive of industry.

As I stood staring about me, a second door at the other end of the workshop opened and a man entered carrying a small metal box, iron-bound and double-locked. This, I guessed, most likely contained pearls and other precious gems which, as I could see from several of the richer garments hanging up around the room, were used for decoration. The man put the strong-box down on the end of the trestle, said something to one of the girls, looked up and saw me.

He frowned. 'Who are you?'

I could see by his expression that he wasn't really annoyed, but his voice had a harsh timbre to it that made him sound as though he might be, and was probably good for discipline. He could have been any age from the late twenties to mid-thirties, and was indeed, as I discovered subsequently, not long past his thirtieth birthday. He was of middling height, the top of his head reaching just above my chin, sturdily built, but with surprisingly delicate, long-fingered hands – a great asset, I imagined, in his chosen calling. Apart from a slightly bulbous nose, his features were unremarkable: blue-grey eyes and hair of that indeterminate fairish brown so prevalent among my fellow countrymen.

Before I could reply to his query, he had noticed my pack. 'A chapman, eh?' he went on. 'Looking for offcuts to fill your satchel, I daresay. You won't find many here. The owner likes the last scrap of material, be it silk, velvet or linen, and the last inch of thread to be accounted for.'

I didn't want to start by lying and playing the innocent, so I resisted the temptation to ask if the owner were Edmund Broderer and merely said, 'It's not your business, then.' I didn't even make it sound like a question, but the man naturally took it as one.

'No.' His tone was curt. 'I'm Lionel Broderer, as anyone around here will tell you. My cousin-by-marriage is the owner. The business was left to her by her husband.'

'That would be the man whose name is over the door of the workshop?'

'That's right. He died twelve years ago this summer and I've run the place for Judith ever since.' He stopped and the frown reappeared. 'Not that it's your affair. But you're welcome to take a look around. If you see anything that might do for your pack, point it out and I'll say whether or not it's for sale. If it is, we'll fix a price.'

'Fallen on hard times, has she, this cousin of yours?' I enquired, as he led me towards the trestle where the smaller items were being worked.

Lionel Broderer made a noise which could have been interpreted as a snort, but which he turned into a cough.

'Not at all,' he answered. 'Just careful.'

'Wealthy, then,' I suggested.

This time he made no attempt to hide his exasperation, but whether with me or with Judith St Clair, I wasn't certain. But it got me a reply.

'She's married twice since my cousin died. Although, as far as I know, neither husband had, or has, much money.

I paused to watch one of the girls do what, in the trade, is known as 'pricking and pouncing', (again, a term I got to know later). She laid a long, thin strip of parchment, on which was drawn a pattern of oak leaves and acorns, along the length of a silken girdle. Then, with her needle, she pricked the outline of the pattern on to the silk.

I looked up to see the dawning of suspicion in Lionel Broderer's eyes.

'Who are you?' he asked for a second time. 'You're not from these parts.'

'Somerset born and bred,' I declared proudly. 'Wells is my home town, but nowadays I live in Bristol.'

'Married?'

'A wife and three children.'

The embroiderer nodded. 'Yes. You look leg-shackled.' (I wished people would stop saying that!) 'Now me – I've had the wit to remain single.' But his tone held that hint of wistfulness I've often noticed in the unmarried when they boast of their untrammelled state. 'Anyway,' he continued more briskly, 'you still haven't replied to my question.'

'I've told you who I am,' I parried. 'A chapman up from Somerset, peddling my wares around your glorious city. You can take a look in my pack if that will help to convince you.'

'Oh, I'm not doubting your word. I just don't think you're telling me all the truth.' He was quick on the uptake, this one, and a lot sharper than he looked.

'Why would you think I'm hiding something?'

'Because of the murder of my cousin's nephew?'

He didn't bother to lower his voice and I was aware of tension throughout the workshop. Nobody stopped working, but there was a deafening silence as though everyone had suddenly sprouted ten-foot-high ears.

Lionel Broderer went on, 'You don't look at all surprised by this information, Master Chapman, so can I assume that you knew it already?'

I stalled for time. 'Why should I be surprised? People get murdered every day, especially in large towns and cities.'

'So they do,' he agreed affably. 'But they don't all have royal connections.'

I raised my eyebrows with what I hoped was an incredulous smile, but he wasn't fooled for a minute.

'My cousin's nephew came here from Burgundy and was a great favourite of the Dowager Duchess – a lady due within London's walls by this time tomorrow afternoon on a visit to her brother, King Edward. But I hardly think I'm telling you anything that you didn't know before.'

'A country pedlar? What should I know?' I was still hedging.

Lionel Broderer sighed wearily. Then he produced a small key from his pouch, unlocked the metal box, dipped in his hand and let a shower of needle-thin gold discs cascade through his fingers. I recognized those discs. Each was pierced with a tiny hole near the rim, and they were used for sewing on clothes so that the garments shimmered as their wearers moved. Two years earlier I had seen ones just like them being made.

Something of my thoughts must have shown in my face because the embroiderer laughed and nodded. 'That's right! I bought these only yesterday from Miles Babcary's shop in West Cheap. He naturally asked me about the murder, having an interest in it beyond the ordinary . . . Do I need to go on?' I didn't answer, so he continued with growing impatience, 'Miles Babcary's late wife was a cousin of Jane Shore, the King's favourite mistress. Therefore, when

Miles's daughter was accused of murdering her husband, it could have proved embarrassing for everyone concerned. But the mystery was eventually resolved by a West Country pedlar working for His Grace, the Duke of Gloucester . . . You acknowledge the similarities, chapman? More than a coincidence that you've turned up here this afternoon, wouldn't you say?'

I knew when I was beaten. As soon as Lionel mentioned the goldsmith, Miles Babcary, I accepted that further prevarication would be useless.

'All right. I admit it. I am working on behalf of Duke Richard. He feels that his sister will want the killer of your cousin's nephew found.'

'And he's brought you up from Bristol to discover him. Or her.' The embroiderer locked the box again, returned the key to his pouch and regarded me without rancour or even dismay. 'Why didn't you say so from the first? Did you think I wouldn't want this murderer caught? Until he is, I move, eat and sleep under a cloud of suspicion, along with all the rest of us who had good reason to wish Fulk Quantrell dead and buried.'

'That's honest.'

'Why shouldn't I be? I didn't do it. I need to clear my name. It worried me when the Sheriff's men made no further enquiries. Now I understand why. His Grace of Gloucester wanted someone he could trust to make them. Someone who would discover the truth.'

'You flatter me,' I said, but absently. I was watching him carefully, unable to decide if Lionel Broderer were an innocent or an exceedingly disingenuous man.

He shook his head. 'Not if all Miles Babcary told me is true.' He glanced about him, suddenly seeming aware of all his interested listeners. 'We can't talk here,' he protested. 'I live nearby, just opposite the workshop, with my mother. But she's out at present. It's only a step if you'd care to accompany me.'

I experienced a pang of conscience when I thought of Bertram, patiently awaiting me in the ale room of the

Voyager, but came to the conclusion that it would do him no harm to learn his place. And he had, in some respect, been foisted on me.

The house Lionel Broderer shared with his widowed mother was a neat two-storeyed dwelling, between a draper's on one side and an ironmonger's on the other. What had once been a ground-floor shop had now been converted to an entrance hall and a kitchen. This allowed more room on the upper floor for a reasonably spacious parlour and two bedchambers, while a small yard at the back contained a lean-to privy and a flower border or two, surprisingly well maintained. A plot of earth planted with a wide variety of herbs suggested that Dame Broderer was fond of cooking, a fact to which the well-nourished body of her son could testify. Everywhere and everything indoors was swept and dusted, indicative of a tidy nature. Lionel might not be married, but in one respect he had no need to be; and as for the other, I had already, in a few hours, seen more whores touting for business on the streets of London than I saw in a week at home.

'All that a bachelor could desire,' I said, taking a proffered seat in the parlour after I had proudly been shown the rest of the house and garden. I reflected that my host had some womanish traits, probably the result of being the pampered only child of a doting mother. Or was that simply a blind, masking a more violent and passionate nature?

I refused his offer of wine. Some of the church bells were already beginning to toll for vespers, and there would be nothing much else to do after curfew except sample Reynold Makepeace's ale. I might as well keep a clear head while I could.

'What do you want to know?' Lionel Broderer asked, settling himself in the parlour's second armchair, opposite mine. (Good furniture, I noted admiringly, comparing it with my own somewhat ramshackle possessions. Whatever faults Judith St Clair might have, she had not stinted on her foreman's wages.)

I recited as briefly as I could what I had learned from

Timothy Plummer: the circumstances that had shaped the present household in the Strand, and also those which had brought Fulk Quantrell from Burgundy some months ahead of his royal mistress. 'I was told that Mistress St Clair grew very fond of him.'

Lionel's mouth had thinned to an almost invisible line. His face was bleak. 'I've never seen anyone become so completely enslaved in so short a time. Oh, he was a handsome devil, all right. And it wasn't just Judith who was a victim of his charm. All the women seemed to go down before him like ninepins. Alcina – that's Alcina Threadgold, Judith's stepdaughter from her second marriage – was as good as betrothed to Brandon Jolliffe, but once she'd clapped eyes on Fulk, poor old Brandon thought himself lucky if she so much as gave him the time of day.' Lionel spoke with a bitterness that made me eye him suspiciously. Did he harbour secret feelings for Alcina?

'Who's Brandon Jolliffe?' I asked.

'The son – the only child – of Lydia and Roland Jolliffe. They're friends of Godfrey St Clair and live in the Strand, next door to him and Judith.'

'They weren't happy then with Fulk's arrival?'

Lionel looked even grimmer. 'Well, Roland Jolliffe certainly wasn't. But if you ask me, it wasn't simply on account of his son being jilted.' I raised my eyebrows and he went on, 'I've always suspected – although I've no proof, you understand – that there was more than common friendship between Fulk and Mistress Jolliffe.'

'You mean she was his mistress?'

'I'm not saying that. But I'm very sure she would have been willing enough had he asked her. I've seen the way she looked at him when she thought her husband wasn't watching.'

'And you think Roland Jolliffe suspected his wife's feelings for this Fulk Quantrell?'

'I can't be certain, but I shouldn't be at all surprised. He's not nearly such a blockhead as people take him for. Not nearly so complaisant, either.'

33

'A jealous husband then, you reckon?'

Lionel nodded. 'Roland Jolliffe's one of those big, quiet men who doesn't say much about anything. Doesn't wear his heart on his sleeve, as the old saw goes; but he's devoted to Lydia. And he's the sort who'd never blame her if she ever did play him false. In his eyes she'd have been seduced, led astray, by the man.'

I smiled. 'You seem to know a lot about someone who, according to you, doesn't say much or show his emotions.'

'I keep my eyes and ears open,' Lionel retorted briskly. 'I know, for instance, that there were quarrels between the two women, Alcina and Lydia Jolliffe.'

'About Fulk?'

'That would seem the obvious answer. They were quite friendly before he arrived – well, as friendly as a girl of eighteen and a woman of forty are likely to be. But after a few weeks of his company, whenever they were in a room together it was worse than a couple of cats tied up in a sack.'

'What about Mistress St Clair? Did she notice nothing of all this?'

Lionel paused to scratch himself in various intimate places. The warmth of the afternoon was making his fleas active. Mine began hopping about in sympathy.

'Judith was so besotted by her nephew that even if she did notice, she didn't care. He could do no wrong in her eyes.'

'And her husband and stepson? What were their feelings, do you know?'

My companion gave a short bark of laughter. 'They didn't like it. Of course they didn't! Especially Jocelyn. When Judith married his father, she more or less adopted him, just as she had Alcina. They were her co-heirs and she treated them as if they were her own. Mind you,' he added reflectively, 'Alcina may have had her nose put out of joint. She was sixteen when Judith married Godfrey two years ago, and she'd been the only heir since she was eight. But if she resented Judith's adoption of Jocelyn, she never showed it.

In fact, the pair of them seem to be the greatest of friends – more like brother and sister than many true siblings.' Lionel pursed his lips. 'Although I fancy that doesn't please Godfrey. I feel sure he'd like them to marry, then they and their children would inherit all Judith's money when she dies. He was always complaining that Alcina is far too good to throw herself away on Brandon Jolliffe.'

'So Fulk Quantrell proved a stumbling block to *his* plans, as well?'

Lionel shrugged. 'Possibly, if I'm right about what he wants. And I think I am. Alcina made no secret of her passion for Fulk.'

There was a moment or two's silence. Then I asked abruptly, 'And you? What grudge did you bear him? Surely you expected to inherit something if your father's cousin should die?'

He reddened and I thought he was going to bluster and make denials. But he seemed to think better of it, and grinned instead. 'I had Judith's promise that if she died before me – which, mark you, is by no means certain with only nine years between us – the workshop would be mine. She told me it was the least she could do after I had run it so success-fully for her all these years. And I know for a fact she meant what she said. She showed me her will. Her old will, that is.'

'She made a new one?'

'Oh, yes! Within a fortnight of Fulk's arrival. Everything – all her money and the workshop – was to go to him. She said nothing, but he made no seceret of the fact. Why should he? He was cock of the dunghill and he couldn't stop crowing.'

'Did Mistress St Clair give any of you any reason for what she'd done? Or didn't you ask?'

'Jocelyn and I both tackled her and both of us got the same answer. Fulk was her nephew. She'd nursed him as a baby, when he and his mother lived with her and my cousin. His mother was her twin. He was her own flesh and blood. I pointed out that he always had been, but she hadn't let it worry her for the past twelve years. She said she hadn't seen him since he was six. Now that she had, her feelings towards him had been reanimated and she realized how much she loved him. The truth is,' Lionel added viciously, 'he buttered her up and told her anything she wanted to hear almost from the first day he arrived: how young she was for a woman of thirty-nine – his mother, her twin, hadn't aged half as well; how often and how fondly his mother and Duchess Margaret had talked about her and wished she were with them in Burgundy; how his mother had spoken of her sister with her dying breath. Oh yes! He quickly realized that Judith would swallow any lie that flattered her and bolstered her ego.'

'And what were Mistress Alcina's feelings about her stepmother changing her will?'

'Oh, she didn't care. She thought Fulk was going to marry her, you see. She counted on inheriting everything through him.'

I stirred in my chair and sighed. With so many people to suspect of murdering Fulk Quantrell, it was a relief to be able to rule out Alcina Threadgold as well as Judith St Clair.

But I wasn't going to be let off the hook that easily. A voice spoke scathingly from the parlour doorway. 'He wasn't going to marry her! You know very well he wasn't! You were present when he told her so!'

'Mother!' Lionel rose from his seat and hurried across to give his parent a dutiful peck on her cheek.

Dame Broderer, I thought, as I, too, got to my feet, was not at all what I had expected. I had envisaged a much older woman, not the fashionable, well-preserved dame I saw in front of me. She must have been little more than a child when she gave birth to her son.

She seated herself in Lionel's chair and waved me back to mine.

'Now,' she said, eyeing me up and down, 'who is this? Apart, that is, from being a pedlar and an extremely handsome young man.' I did my best to look modest. 'Lal! An explanation, please! You know I don't like strangers in my house without knowing who they are or what they're doing here.'

Lionel told her as briefly as he could, helped by the fact that she refrained from interrupting him with pointless questions or exclamations. She simply sat, regarding me steadily with a pair of fine blue eyes, of which her son's were a pale and smoky copy.

When he had finished, she gave a satisfied nod. 'Yes, I've heard Miles Babcary tell that story about the pedlar as well. So! That was you, was it, Roger Chapman? Then I trust you'll discover the truth of this sorry affair. It's high time someone did. There are too many people whispering behind their hands about my boy. Not, of course, that he's the only one. Brandon Jolliffe and his parents, Godfrey and Jocelyn St Clair – they're all being pointed at as potential murderers.'

'But not Mistress Threadgold?' I queried.

Dame Broderer snorted. 'She's escaped the worst of the gossip so far because most people assume she was going to marry Fulk Quantrell. Therefore, in due course, all Judith's money, not just half, would have come to her through him.'

'A reasonable assumption,' I prompted her as she paused.

'Indeed! If it had been true.' Dame Broderer turned on her son. 'Lal, for heaven's sake pull up a stool and stop looming over me. You're blocking the daylight.'

Somewhat to my surprise, Lionel made no objection to this reprimand, but did as he was bidden. However, his broad grin indicated an amused tolerance of his mother and her ways rather than intimidation. They understood one another, this pair.

'Are you saying,' I asked, 'that Fulk Quantrell *wasn't* going to marry Alcina Threadgold?'

Dame Broderer leaned back in her chair. 'The evening he was murdered, Fulk came round to the workshop to nose and poke about. He had taken to doing that as though he already owned the place. On this occasion, quite by chance, I was also present, collecting a new girdle that I had had embroidered. He hadn't been there five minutes when Alcina came in, obviously in a towering rage. She immediately started shouting at him, in front of everyone, that he was a liar and a cheat. She'd given him everything and in return he'd promised her marriage.

'Well, Fulk let her rant and rave for a moment or two, then he turned on her, even more furious than she was. He yelled that he had *never* promised to marry her; that he wouldn't marry her if she were the last woman on earth. And finally he told her that he couldn't marry her: he was already betrothed to one of Duchess Margaret's tiring-women, back in Burgundy.'

Four

'What happened next?' I asked.

Dame Broderer shrugged. 'Fulk stormed off without giving Alcina a chance to reply, and she burst into a flood of tears. As you might expect. Lionel and I tried to comfort her, but she wanted none of us. Shook us off and went after Fulk.'

I raised my eyebrows thoughtfully. 'And that was the night Master Quantrell was murdered?'

'It couldn't have been Alcina,' Lionel said quickly. 'She had no weapon with her. And she doesn't have the strength to beat a man's head in.'

I saw Dame Broderer give her son a look in which pity and affectionate contempt were blended in equal measure. My hunch had been right then: he did entertain more than friendly feelings for his cousin's stepdaughter.

'Anger can give people, even women, an extraordinary strength,' I pointed out. 'As for a weapon, Mistress Threadgold might have picked up anything anywhere. I expect London, like Bristol, has its fair share of animal bones – big ones – to be found in the central drains. Also, all sorts of rubbish is mixed in with the rotting carcasses and vegetables; bits of old planking, broken walking sticks and cudgels – in fact anything at all that our good citizens have no use for.'

Lionel glowered and his mother laughed.

'I've told him that, chapman. But my son is sweet on Alcina and won't hear a word against her. It's no good trying to deny it, Lal! Our friend here can put two and two together with the best of us. Probably better than most of us, if all that Miles Babcary says is true.'

I let this flattery pass without acknowledgement. 'What did *you* do, Mistress Broderer,' I enquired, 'after the two young people had left?'

'I came home. Lionel stayed on to lock up the workshop for the night, as Jeb Smith and Will Tuckett will testify.'

Lionel looked surly. 'I can answer for myself, thank you, Mother.' He turned to me. 'But she's right, chapman. Ask either Jeb or William. I was the last to leave. I always am. I like to make sure that all the candles and wall cressets have been properly doused. I wouldn't trust the job to anyone else.'

I stroked my chin. 'I understand from Master Plummer that the murder took place around a fortnight ago, which would put it at the beginning of the month. Was it still light when you locked up the workshop?'

Dame Broderer opened her mouth to speak, but thought better of it and shut it again.

'Not as light as it might have been,' Lionel admitted after a pause. 'In fact it was near enough dusk. We were working on a particularly intricate wall hanging for York Place. That's the Archbishop of York's house, near the Chère Reine Cross. It was wanted in time for Duchess Margaret's visit, starting tomorrow. Jeb Smith and Will Tuckett were anxious to get it finished that evening, so they stayed on. I gave them a hand. The others left just after Mother arrived to pick up her girdle.'

'Always anxious to get off home,' Dame Broderer grumbled, although it was a grumble that slid easily into a chuckle. 'But after all who can blame them? I was the same at their age.' She noted my glance of curiosity and added with perfect frankness, 'Yes, I was once an embroidress in the Broderer workshops. It wasn't my good fortune, however, to attract the attentions of its owner, at least not then. By the time Edmund did cast his eyes in my direction, it was far too late. He was married to Judith and I was the relict of his much poorer kinsman, his cousin Jonathan.' She added with a sigh, 'Married at fifteen, a mother at sixteen, widowed at twenty. That, briefly, is the story of my life.'

I gave what I hoped was a gallant bow. 'But you must

have had many opportunities to marry again since your husband's death.'

'Oh, I'm not lucky in love,' she said and rose abruptly, smoothing down her skirts. 'It must be past supper time. Will you stay and eat with us, Master Chapman?'

I shook my head. 'Thank you, mistress, but no. I must return to the Voyager. I've left a young friend there, kicking his heels.' And I explained about Bertram Serifaber. 'He'll be wondering what has happened to me.'

'What will you do now?' Lionel asked. 'About the murder, I mean.'

Before I could reply, Dame Broderer said firmly, 'He needs an introduction to the household in the Strand. But tomorrow, everyone will be abroad to see the state entrance of the Dowager Duchess into London. Judith won't miss that. She might even be summoned to wait on Her Highness as an old friend and retainer of the Princess. So call here the day after tomorrow, chapman, and I'll take you to see Judith and Godfrey then.'

I was tempted to refuse: I have always liked to do things in my own way and my own time. But the dame's offer would cut many corners, and I knew that Duke Richard would like this murder solved as soon as possible for his sister's sake.

'You're very kind.' I picked up my pack from where I had dropped it beside my chair, bowed once again to them both and took myself back to the Voyager.

'Well, I call that very underhand and sneaky,' Bertram declared somewhat indistinctly, as we ate an excellent supper of stewed neck of veal with leeks and cabbage. 'I'm the one who's supposed to be helping you with this case, not some old woman.'

'Dame Broderer is only in her forties,' I reproved him.

'That's what I said: old.'

'And,' I went on severely, 'she's a very well-looking woman for her age.'

He would have continued the wrangle, but I suddenly

realized how tired I was, how long and busy a day it had been. I had risen at the crack of dawn to continue our journey into London; I had been to Baynard's Castle to meet the Duke and to the Broderer workshops and Lionel's home. And even though it was still light, I was ready for my bed. Home, my wife and children seemed as distant from me as the moon. I needed to be quiet, to reorientate my thoughts and let my spirit get in touch with theirs again. So, to Bertram's great indignation, I suggested he return to the castle as soon as he had finished eating, and inform Timothy Plummer of such progress as I had made so far.

'Come back early in the morning,' I said, 'and we'll go to see Duchess Margaret's entry into the city together.'

'I may. I may not,' was his lofty parting shot.

But I knew that he would.

I slept badly. I was lonely. Not for the first time in my life, my own company proved to be no satisfaction. I missed Adela. I missed the children. I even missed Adam. I wondered if I were sickening for something.

I awoke, bad-tempered and unrefreshed, to an inn and a city already humming with life and the anticipation of pageantry and spectacle. And by the time I had finished a breakfast of oatcakes and honey, cold boiled mutton and a mazer of ale I, too, was beginning to relish the prospect of seeing a bedecked and bedizened London, ready to welcome home one of its own. Margaret of York had been young, pretty and popular when she had left for Burgundy twelve years earlier. She might now be older, staider, wiser, even plainer, but she would receive the same rapturous applause.

'The procession'll be coming through the Ald Gate,' Bertram informed me, arriving just as I was finishing my meal. 'Cornhill, the Poultry, Stocks Market, past the Grocers' and Mercers' Halls, where the Duchess will be greeted by some of the Guildsmen, then along West Cheap – more greetings, and probably gifts from the goldsmiths: they're an ingratiating lot – St Paul's, the Lud Gate and along the Strand to Westminster, where the King and all the royal family will be waiting to greet her. Not the Prince of Wales, of course. He lives at Ludlow.' Master Serifaber wrinkled his nose in indignation 'You've had boiled mutton!' he accused me. 'Not fair! All I had was a pickled herring.'

I laughed. 'Yes, that sounds like the kind of breakfast I remember at Baynard's Castle. The Duchess of York isn't the most generous of providers, if I remember rightly.'

My companion poured the remainder of the ale from the jug into my mazer, and drank. 'Duchess Cicely', he said feelingly, 'expects everyone to lead the same sort of ascetic, religious life as she does at Berkhamsted. I'm glad I don't belong to her household. Thank heaven Duke Richard is more liberal in his ideas. That's one thing to be said for living in Yorkshire: plenty of good food.'

He sniffed again, piteously, so I ordered him a plate of boiled mutton and some oatcakes. When, finally, he could make himself understood once more, he enquired, 'Where do you want to watch the procession? West Cheap or Westminster? Duke Richard, Duchess Anne, Duchess Cicely and all their followers – *hundreds* of 'em: I couldn't be bothered to count – rode to Westminster very early this morning, so Fleet Street and the Strand should have cleared a bit by now.'

'I'll abide by your decision, lad. Whichever you recommend.'

'Well . . .' Bertram ran his tongue around his teeth, making sure that he had found every last scrap of meat. 'Westminster will be just about as crowded as West Cheap, but with my livery I can probably find us both a place among my lord's retainers.' He patted his chest importantly.

'Then Westminster let it be.' I got to my feet. 'At the same time, we can go over the ground again that Fulk Quantrell must have covered the night he was killed. Now, if you've finished trying to scrape the bottom out of that plate, we'll make a start.'

But I had been foolishly optimistic in imagining that our walk to Westminster would provide us with an opportunity to discover any more concerning the Burgundian's death. The whole journey, beginning in Bucklersbury, on through

43

West Cheap and continuing beyond the Lud Gate, was a nightmare of people pressing in on us from every side. On at least three occasions the crowds were so thick that we were unable to move for several minutes. The first time, it was even difficult to breathe.

It was a pickpocket's dream of paradise and I congratulated myself that I had the bulk of my money in a pouch strapped around my waist under my shirt and breeches. Mind you, it was a grave disadvantage when what few loose coins I had had been filched and I wanted to buy a meat pie or a jellied eel from a street vendor. These persistent gentlemen (and – women) were as numerous as their criminal associates, and indeed, quite often they worked together, the vendor distracting the customer's attention while the thief relieved him of his purse. However, either my commanding height and size or the Duke of Gloucester's blue and murrey livery, worn by Bertram, or perhaps both, gave us a freer passage through the throng than we might have otherwise expected.

In West Cheap, two arches of marguerites, each beaten gold flower-head trembling on its fine wire stalk, had been raised. A choir of 'angels' – local boys, reluctantly recruited, whose mothers humiliated them by constantly shouting advice and instructions from the crowd – waited to greet the illustrious guest. A little further on, the more professional choristers of St Paul's jostled for position, each one hoping, I presumed, that the beauty of his singing might recommend him to the Duchess and earn him a place at the Burgundian court. The Lud Gate was decorated with shields of stiffened paper displaying the red cross of Saint George and the white rose of York. People were dressed in their Sunday clothes, and everywhere there was a general atmosphere of carnival and holiday.

Bertram and I were not the only two making for Westminster, in the belief that it offered a better vantage point for viewing the Duchess than the overcrowded roadway of West Cheap. The thoroughfare out of London was packed with citizens sweating in a burst of sudden warmth. Typically, May had decided to stop imitating January and

44

was pretending to be July instead; in short, the weather was showing all the usual vagaries of an English spring.

As we walked, or rather pushed our way, along Fleet Street, I glanced in the direction of Faitour Lane, but there was, of course, nothing to be seen. The beggars congregated in the alley's mouth were rattling their tin cups, baring their sores and trusting that a suitable display of enthusiasm for the Londoners' princess would loosen their fellow citizens' purse strings.

We at last managed to move on into the Strand. The going was easier here, where the road was wider and the smell of the open countryside counteracted the stench of the city. The gardens of the great houses on either side were also beginning to bloom in earnest, and the faint breeze blowing inland off the river brought a hint of summer trailing in its wake.

Bertram indicated the three smaller dwellings to our left, just beyond the Fleet Sreet bridge. 'I was right. The middle one does belong to Godfrey and Judith St Clair. I asked Master Plummer last night. The one on its left, as we face them, is Master Joliffe's house.'

'And to its right?'

My companion shook his head. 'I didn't ask, and Master Plummer didn't say. No one of importance, I daresay. At least, nothing to do with the murder.'

I stared long and curiously at Godfrey St Clair's house, being roundly cursed by the people whose progress I was impeding, but there was no sign of life. Master, wife and servants were all abroad, waiting for the Duchess's arrival. And at that moment, the faint and distant sound of cheering suggested that she had at last made an appearance at the Ald Gate.

'We'd better hurry,' Bertram urged, tugging at my elbow.

Quite a few people now stayed where they were, lining both sides of the Strand, but we battled on to Westminster.

'Watch out for pickpockets,' Bertram said as we passed through its gate.

But I had no need of his advice. I knew this place of old. The London thieves and cutpurses, fast and nimble-fingered though they might be, were mere novices compared with those who frequented Westminster. The latter would take anything that was portable and in such quick time that the unwary stranger found himself stripped almost naked before he had been five minutes inside the walls. The Flemish merchants who thronged its streets were little better, picking on the small and weak and forcing sales of their wares at knife-point.

Today, however, unlike its larger neighbour, the city of Westminster was quieter than usual, an air of enforced calm pervading its streets. For this, the presence of a substantial number of armed men was responsible. Officers of the King's household were patrolling every alley and byway, and had been doing so since dawn judging by the bleary-eyed look of them. The cookshop stalls that normally proliferated around Westminster Gate had been moved elsewhere, much to the annoyance of owners and customers alike.

Before we had been there many minutes, a royal messenger arrived in a flurry of sweat and horse's hooves, disappearing inside the palace, presumably to announce that the Duchess was on her way. The crowd buzzed with anticipation, and Bertram dragged me round into Westminster Yard and thence into the great hall where the royal family was beginning to assemble.

The Duke and Duchess of Suffolk, Lincoln's parents, had already taken their places – he an aggressive-looking, bull-necked man, totally unlike his eldest son, she a proud Plantagenet with something of the appearance of her late brother, the Duke of Clarence, about her. The King's two stepsons, the Marquis of Dorset and his younger brother, Lord Richard Grey, were glancing about them and occasionally whispering together behind their hands. (I don't know that I should have recognized them if Bertram hadn't reminded me who they were.)

After that, the hall began to fill up faster than I could take note of who was and was not present. Nobility and clergy, the great and the not so great, the good and the definitely not so good, crowded around the empty thrones at the far end of the hall. Bertram, as he had promised, had managed to squash me in among the lowliest ranks of the Gloucester retainers to the left of the door. My ribs felt as though they might crack beneath the pressure of other bodies. My bad mood was returning.

Foreign dignitaries and their attendants arrived just before the bulk of the royal party, by which time I had given up even trying to guess or remember who was who. I had just decided that there were far too many high and mighty pomposities in this world who served no useful function, when a louder fanfare than normal assaulted my already protesting ears. This, however, finally heralded the entrance of the King and his immediate entourage.

Duchess Cicely, matriarchal in royal purple and stiff-necked with Neville pride, preceded the Duke and Duchess of Gloucester, both of them resplendent in cloth of gold and silver, the Duchess looking so fragile that it seemed a puff of wind could blow her away. The six-year-old Duke of York walked with his slightly older duchess and was followed by four of his sisters, Elizabeth, now a lovely young woman of fourteen, Mary, Cicely and Anne. The baby, Katherine, born the previous year, was carried in the arms of her nurse. And then, finally, King Edward, wearing the insignia of the Golden Fleece, and Queen Elizabeth entered the hall.

I was shocked on two counts – well, perhaps not shocked, but certainly surprised, to see that the Queen was pregnant yet again; not far gone as yet, but showing enough belly to leave little room for doubt. Elizabeth Woodville – Lady Grey, as she had been when the King married her all those years ago – must, I reckoned, be well over forty, her two first-marriage sons being themselves married men. But it was really King Edward who commanded my attention, and, in his case, shock at his appearance was too mild a word to describe my emotions.

When young, this magnificent, golden-haired giant had been dubbed 'the handsomest man in Europe'. Even when I had first set eyes on him five years earlier, it had still been possible to understand why, although the effects of drink and dissipation were already beginning to make themselves apparent. But now his features had coarsened and thickened out of all recognition. His height (much the same as mine) was of course the same, but his girth weighed him down and made him round-shouldered. His jaw hung slack and heavy and his complexion was moist and pale, like uncooked dough. But then he smiled at someone in the crowd, and I could see that the old charm and humour still wove their magic. My instincts warned me that here was a sick man; but I was unwilling to accept the evidence of my eyes and dismissed the thought.

After the King and Queen were seated on their thrones, there was a delay while we all awaited the arrival of the Duchess, whose progress had no doubt been hindered by the cheering crowds. I caught a glimpse of Timothy, standing not far behind Duke Richard's chair and, from time to time, signalling vigorously to other men stationed at various strategic points around the hall. I wondered what they thought would happen. Did they seriously expect the French ambassador to leap forward and attack Duchess Margaret with his poignard? Or was it, as I suspected with my usual cynicism, self-importance for its own sake?

Suddenly I found Timothy directly behind me, panting heavily after having forced his way through the press to my side of the hall. He dug me painfully in the ribs. Before I could protest, he hissed in my ear, 'Directly in front of us. Front row. Black gown, heavily embroidered. Judith St Clair. The man on her left is Godfrey.'

I craned my neck, trying to get a better view across the intervening two ranks, but the women's hennins with their floating scarves made it impossible to see anything from where I was standing. It was like peering through a forest of flags all flying from the tops of steeples. (And it confirmed me in my belief that the current crop of women's fashions were being designed by madmen.)

'I can't see—' I was beginning, but just at that moment the trumpeters went wild with a fanfare that made even my teeth hurt. Timothy gave a strangled cry and set off to fight his way back to his official position, while I suppressed a desire to burst out laughing. All the same, I had managed to catch a glimpse of a heavily embroidered black sarcenet sleeve and a white hand resting on a wrist cuffed in black velvet. At least I knew roughly where to look for my quarry once the present ceremony was over. Moreover, two people in deepest mourning stand out in a crowd of popinjays.

My travelling companion of the last three days, the young Earl of Lincoln, resplendent in white and gold, proudly led his aunt towards the thrones at the far end of the hall. As she passed, I saw enough of the Dowager Duchess to realize that the slender, vibrant, twenty-two-year-old girl, who had set sail for Sluys twelve years previously to become the third wife of Charles of Burgundy, was now a matronly woman in her mid-thirties with a thickening waistline. But she was still attractive enough, with her pale skin and Plantagenet red-gold hair, to send the waiting crowds into a frenzy of adoration. Their cheers rolled in through the open doorway, and probably drowned out the King's initial greeting to his sister. (I saw her lean closer to him, as though she had difficulty hearing.)

Edward had risen at the Duchess's approach and embraced her lovingly. Then, after greeting the Queen and making suitable obeisance to her mother, Margaret was passed from one sibling to another, one in-law to another, rather, I reflected irreverently, like a bolster full of feathers.

I touched Bertram on the shoulder. 'Let's get out now,' I whispered, 'before everyone has the same idea.'

We weren't far from the door, and managed to inch our way outside without attracting too much notice. Once in the fresh air, we took deep breaths and stretched our cramped muscles. I drew Bertram into the shelter of the Abbey.

'When the crowds begin to disperse,' I said, 'look for a couple in mourning. That'll be Judith and Godfrey St Clair.'

My companion nodded. 'I wondered what Master Plummer was whispering to you about.'

It was a lengthy wait. It was not until the good and the great, led by King Edward and the Dowager Duchess Margaret, had processed from the hall into the palace –

'Banquet,' Bertram informed me tersely – that the less important guests who had been invited to the welcome ceremony were permitted to leave. Even then, there was an order of departure to be observed. But, at last, among the many-hued silks and velvets emerging into the uncertain May sunshine, I saw two sable-clad figures walking decorously side by side.

Judith St Clair was a woman of around the same age as Mistress Broderer; perhaps, to be fair, a few years younger. She was good-looking and knew it: that was obvious in the upright stance and the proud carriage of her head. At some time in her life she had been taught to set a value on herself, probably by the woman I had so recently been watching, Margaret of York, when Judith and her twin had been in the Duchess's employ. She had no one distinguishing feature that made her instantly recognizable, and yet, oddly, I felt that I would know her again if I had to pick her out in a crowd.

Her husband was considerably older, painfully thin and already beginning to stoop. He had once been dark-headed, but was now going grey and would soon be greyer, a fact to which the abundance of white hairs among the black could testify. There could not have been a greater contrast between husband and wife: the one frail and shambling, the other vigorous and purposeful, even in grief.

I was just about to accost them, when a man wearing the Gloucester livery stepped into my path.

'Serifaber,' he said, addressing Bertram, 'is this the pedlar?' He jerked his head in my direction.

'I'm Roger the Chapman,' I answered with dignity. 'Who wants to know?' Although, of course, I could guess.

The man shifted his gaze to me and stared for a moment, much as he might have considered something rather unpleasant that had just crawled out from under a stone. 'His Grace, the Duke of Gloucester,' he condescended to say at last. 'He commands your presence at Baynard's Castle again this evening. After supper. You' – he flicked an equally disdainful glance at Bertram – 'will accompany him.'

Five

Of course, by the time the Duke's messenger had taken himself off, with a flourish that would have done justice to a preening peacock, Judith and Godfrey St Clair had disappeared; and although I immediately set out in search of them, they had vanished. In all that vast multitude I could see no one dressed in black. Bertram was no wiser as to where they had gone, and was more concerned with the fact that he was to conduct me to Baynard's Castle that evening.

'We'd better set out as soon as we've finished supper,' he decided. 'We don't want to keep the Duke waiting.'

'I don't suppose he'll return from Westminster that early,' I argued grumpily. 'These state banquets can go on for hours. And afterwards, people need a chance to recover.'

'Not the Duke,' Bertram disagreed. 'Eats and drinks very sparingly. An abstemious man.'

'I'm aware of that,' I snapped, annoyed that he should think himself better acquainted with Duke Richard than I was. I had known the man on and off – more off than on, admittedly, but well enough – for years. 'All the same,' I added, 'he won't be able to leave the banquet until the King does.'

We made our return journey, together with the rest of the crowds, along the Strand towards London. By dint of much shoving and pushing, I managed to keep us both on the right-hand side of the road; and as we approached the Fleet Bridge, I grabbed the wrist of my nearest neighbour.

'Do you know who owns that house?' I asked, nodding towards the third of the three smaller houses.

The man shook his head. 'Sorry, friend! I'm from Clerkenwell.'

But I didn't give up. I just stood there, getting roundly cursed for my pains, asking anyone willing to humour me the same question. My chief hope was that Judith and Godfrey St Clair would turn up, but there was no sign of them.

Eventually, I got an answer. I had stopped a woman for no better reason than that her black homespun gown and hood suggested that she too might be in mourning. And, as it turned out, I was right.

'Why do you want to know?' she demanded. 'Who are you?' She caught sight of my companion's livery and modified her tone somewhat. 'Are you with him?'

'I am. He's a member of the Duke of Gloucester's household.'

'I can see that,' the woman replied tartly. 'But you still haven't answered my questions.'

She was small, in height only up to my shoulder, thin as a whippet, with a sallow complexion made even sallower by her sombre clothes. She wasn't old, but nor was she in the first flush of youth. If pressed, I would have said she was somewhere in her middle thirties. Her eyes were her most arresting feature, being so dark in colour that they seemed to be all pupil.

'And you haven't answered mine,' I retorted, nettled. 'Do you know who this house belongs to or not? I've been told that the middle one is the property of Judith and Godfrey St Clair, and the one to its left is the home of a certain Lydia and Roland Jolliffe.'

The woman regarded me silently for a moment or two, then her thin lips cracked into a quirky half-smile, half-grin.

'Mmm. You've been told a great deal, haven't you, master? I wonder who by.' When I failed to volunteer the information, she went on, 'As it so happens, I'm Paulina Graygoss, housekeeper these many years to Judith St Clair. The house you're enquiring about belongs to Martin Threadgold, bachelor. His younger brother, who died six years ago, was my mistress's second husband. Are you satisfied now?' And she moved towards the door of the middle of the three houses, producing a key from the pouch attached to her girdle and inserting it into the lock. Then she turned and looked over her shoulder.

'You still haven't answered my second question,' she reminded me. 'Who are you?'

Before I could think of a suitably vague explanation, Bertram huffed importantly, 'This is Roger Chapman. He's an agent of my master, the Duke of Gloucester.'

'Ah!' The housekeeper subjected me to a long, curious stare, then laughed. 'Dear me!' she said enigmatically before going inside and closing the door behind her.

'What do you suppose she meant by that?' Bertram demanded anxiously.

I didn't reply. I was busy thinking what a tight little enclave these three houses represented. Judith and Godfrey St Clair, his son and her stepdaughter in the middle, Alcina's uncle (and Judith's erstwhile brother-in-law) on one side and the Jolliffes, described by Mistress Broderer as friends of Godfrey St Clair, on the other. And into this close-knit, almost incestuous community, linked by various threads of kinship, liking and would-be kinship, had come the stranger, the outsider, Fulk Quantrell, good-looking and no doubt exotically foreign after twelve years at the Burgundian court. Small wonder he had created havoc . . .

'You haven't heard a word I've been saying,' Bertram complained as we crossed the Fleet Bridge and were borne along on the tide of people all making for the Lud Gate.

There was some truth in his accusation, but I had suddenly recollected that I had had no dinner. Judging by the sun, it was well past noon and my belly, perfectly quiescent until that moment, immediately started to rumble, reminding me that food was at least two hours overdue.

'Let's get back to the Venturer,' I said, 'and see if Reynold Makepeace can find us something to eat. We'll talk all you want to then and I promise I'll listen.'

After an excellent meal, we spent the rest of the day indoors, avoiding the holiday crowds who still thronged the streets. The noise of their revelry reached us like the muted hushing of the sea on some distant shore, as we stood leaning over the gallery palings, staring into the Voyager's almost deserted inner courtyard. From time to time Reynold Makepeace brought us each a stoup of ale, having given his potboys a few hours freedom to go and see the sights, like the kind and generous master that he was.

By supper time the inn was busy again as people returned, tired and happy and full of the day's events, eager to be fed before braving the streets once more in order to sample whatever jollifications were being provided by the various guilds. Bertram would have set out for Baynard's Castle as soon as we had put paid to a dish of brawn in mustard sauce, a cold pigeon pie, a platter of pear-and-apple fritters and several more beakers of ale. But I insisted on letting my food settle before mixing with members of the nobility, having no wish to fart and belch all evening in competition with my betters. (Heaven only knew what they had been stuffing themselves with all day!) So the church bells were ringing for compline before we left the inn.

At my insistence, we avoided the main thoroughfares, making our way by lesser-known alleyways until we reached Thames Street, where we got held up by a score or so of young people dancing round a maypole – an innocent enough pastime, but one which would obviously lead to far more lecherous activities as the evening progressed. Two of the girls entwined themselves in a highly erotic manner around Bertram and myself, advances which we reluctantly declined for different reasons. On my part, I pretended it was because I was a faithful and loving husband; but deep down, it was really because I was afraid of what noisome disease I might catch if I allowed my natural inclinations to run away with me. Bertram's reason, I suspected, had far more to do with the fact that he was wearing the Duke of Gloucester's livery than from fear of acquiring a dose of the pox. (I decided I must have a quiet word with the lad. He was still somewhat wet behind the ears.)

This diversion meant that the May day was closing in before we presented ourselves at the main entrance to Baynard's Castle. Even so, we were kept kicking our heels for at least half an hour in an ante-room of Duke Richard's private apartments before he was finally ready to receive us. Receive *me*, to be precise. The Duke dismissed Bertram with a kindly pat on the shoulder. 'Report to Master Plummer and then get some sleep,' he advised. 'It's been a long day.'

My companion had no choice but to obey, but I could see he wasn't pleased. Not that the Duke noticed. Indeed, with great dark circles under his eyes, he looked too tired to notice very much at all; and I guessed that a whole day spent being polite to the numerous members of the Queen's family had placed an intolerable strain on his already over-burdened spirit and natural goodwill. Certainly the smile he gave me was an effort that showed in every muscle of his face, and I was seized by the sudden fancy that there was a shadow on his spirit like an indelible stain . . .

Such nonsensical imaginings only demonstrated that I, too, was fatigued almost to the limit of endurance. I took myself in hand.

The chamber into which I had been shown was one I had not seen before. Logs burned brightly on the hearth, for the warm day had given way to a chilly evening, and there were woven rugs on the stone floor instead of the usual scattering of rushes. Tapestries – Moses in the bulrushes, Joshua before the walls of Jericho – glowed against the walls, cushions covered with jewel-bright silks and satins adorned the beauti-fully carved armchairs, and a broad-seated settle was drawn up in front of the fire. There was a profusion of scented wax candles, some in a silver chandelier suspended from the middle of the ceiling, others in silver candelabra and in wall sconces.

The Duke, who had changed the day's formal attire for a long, loose gown of dark-green fur-trimmed velvet and soft slippers, also made of fur, poured wine into two Venetian glass goblets and handed one to me. (I immediately broke into a sweat in case I should drop it. My hands felt as big as shovels.) Then he filled a third, holding it up to the light. Misted by the glass, the liquid gleamed pale and tawny; amber silk shot through with a weft of gold.

'The Dowager Duchess will join us in just a moment,' he said.

In fact she joined us almost at once, a small page preceding her into the room in order to hold the door open, and then taking himself off with a skip and a hop that suggested his duties were finished for the day. (No doubt another lackey would materialize when the Duchess wished to leave. Such is the smooth passage through life of our superiors.) She had also shed the heavy cloth-of-gold dress and jewel-encrusted mantle that she had worn for her entry into London and was clad instead in a simple blue silk gown that enhanced the colour of her eyes, and which made her appear far less matronly than her finery had done. Her abundant hair was loosely confined in a silver net. A huge ruby ring on her wedding finger was her only adornment.

It was when she glanced in my direction that I realized she had recently been crying. Her eyes were still moist and there were traces of tears on her cheeks. She beckoned me to approach, and when I did so, she extended a plump white hand which I duly kissed.

She smiled faintly at her brother. 'How very sensible of you, Dickon, to choose such a handsome young man as your investigator. You remembered my weakness.'

The Duke laughed with genuine amusement. 'My dearest Margaret, I've known Roger Chapman for a number of years now, and have received many services from him, but I can honestly say that his looks have never been a consideration.' He turned and indicated the settle. 'Sit down, Roger.' He himself sat in the other armchair on the opposite side of the fire to his sister. 'I've told Her Highness all about you. She wanted to meet you. Hence this summons.'

The Duchess nodded eagerly. 'I knew nothing of my dear Fulk's death until my nephew, Lincoln, informed me of it when he met me yesterday at Gravesend. I've hardly had time to take it in. Indeed, it didn't even seem possible until I spoke to Judith St Clair an hour ago.' She drew a deep breath. 'We shed a few tears together. Judith was unaware

56

of your investigation. She hasn't met you yet.' The Duchess ended on a note of reproach.

'Roger himself only arrived in London yesterday,' Duke Richard told her sternly. He raised an eyebrow. 'But *do* you have anything to report, my friend?'

'Very little as yet, Your Grace.' I tried hard not to sound apologetic. What did they expect? Miracles? 'However, I have spoken at some length to both Lionel Broderer and his mother.'

The Duke looked impressed, the Duchess merely puzzled.

'Lionel Broderer? That would be some relation of Judith's first husband, I take it?'

I bowed assent (which is quite a difficult thing to do when you're sitting down). 'Edmund Broderer's cousin's son,' I explained. 'He has run the embroidery workshop for Mistress St Clair ever since his cousin's death, and run it very successfully. He has made her a wealthy woman in her own right, irrespective of anything her second husband might have left her.'

'Oh, you mean Justin Threadgold!' The Duchess was dismissive. 'According to Veronica, he was not a wealthy man, and what little he had he probably left to his daughter. Nor, I fancy, is Godfrey St Clair particularly plump in the pocket. What he brought to the marriage, as far as Judith is concerned, is an old family name and noble connections. He is, I believe, distantly related to Lord Hastings on his mother's side.'

I had to think for a moment who Veronica was, then recollected that she had been Judith's twin sister and Fulk Quantrell's mother. She had died recently, shortly after Christmas.

'So the fortune,' Duke Richard put in quietly, 'is Mistress St Clair's, inherited from the first of her three husbands and enlarged by the industry of this Lionel Broderer. Does that make him the chief suspect for Fulk's murder, do you think?'

'He must have had expectations,' I admitted. 'But there are others, as well, who had excellent reasons for killing

57

Master Quantrell once his aunt made her intentions concerning him known. And very foolish intentions they were, if Your Highness will pardon my frankness.'

'Oh, I know! I know! And so I told her.' The Duchess sipped her wine. 'Indeed, I think – I'm sure – she knows it herself now, in spite of all her excuses. But I should hesitate to condemn her folly too strongly.' The blue eyes filled with tears. 'Fulk was a most charming young man. I remember that as a child he was enchanting. He could wrap all my ladies around his little finger.' She smiled ruefully. 'Including me. And as he grew older, he was no less popular. To his aunt, who had not seen him for twelve years, he must have seemed hardly lower than the angels. And bringing, as he did, the news of his mother's death, comforting his aunt as he must have done . . .' The Duchess's voice became suspended. 'Need I say more?' she added after a pause. 'Judith admitted to me that she was in thrall to Fulk from the very first moment of seeing him.'

I thought this over for a minute or two. The Duke made no comment, but stared into the heart of the fire. A shower of sparks flew upwards like stars in the black night sky.

I addressed the Duchess. 'Can Your Highness tell me what this Fulk Quantrell was really like?'

'I've just told you! Weren't you listening?' Her indignant look appealed to her brother, who ignored it.

'With respect, Your Highness,' I said firmly, 'you've told me what this young man was like only on the surface – about his fascination for women. But underneath, did he have a streak of cruelty? Of greed? Did he ingratiate himself with those who could advance his interests and abandon them when they could no longer be of use to him?'

'No!' The blue eyes flashed with anger. 'He was like his mother, gentle and kind. He had a beautiful singing voice and was always near at hand whenever I needed him. How dare you suggest otherwise? You didn't know him! Who has been poisoning your mind against Fulk? If this is your attitude, I would much rather you had nothing to do with solving his murder. Richard!'

58

The Duke stirred in his chair and slewed round to look at her.

'My dearest sister, calm yourself. Roger is right to ask such questions. As you say, he knows nothing of Fulk Quantrell. Therefore, he has to find out. And how can he find out if he doesn't ask the people who knew the lad best? Just answer him. Tell him the truth.'

I nodded agreement, smiling blandly; but, personally, I considered the Duchess had already revealed more than she would have wanted me to know. Her furious defence of the dead man suggested that he was far less perfect a character than she would have me believe. She, too, had been under his spell, and had deliberately ignored the flaws in his nature. And if what Lionel Broderer and his mother had said of Fulk were true, then he could have been a very unpleasant and ruthless young man. On the other hand, the Broderers were undoubtedly biased against the favourite.

The Duchess pouted, looking mutinous, and I could see what she had been like as a girl: pretty, used to getting her own way, petted by her older brothers and finding a close, kindred spirit in the brother next to her in age, George of Clarence; the pair of them both handsome, both conscious of their own importance and their place in the scheme of things. Both spoiled. But, also like the late duke, Margaret of York could just as suddenly dispel the impression of conceit and arrogance with a self-deprecatory laugh. Or, as now, with a smile.

'Forgive me, Master Chapman! Of course you need to ask questions about Fulk's true character. So, yes, he had faults, but then, who doesn't? He would have been unbearable had he been too perfect. But in general he was a good boy, a loving son to his mother, kind and in tune with the world around him.'

I considered this. 'You don't think then that he could have brought any pressure to bear on his aunt to persuade her to alter her will in his favour?'

The Duchess grew indignant again, even more so than before. 'What sort of pressure are you suggesting?'

'Could he have played on her love for her sister? Mistress St Clair must have been deeply shocked and distressed by news of that sister's death. She might even have felt guilty that she hadn't accompanied you and Mistress Quantrell to Burgundy after her first husband's death.'

The Duchess's anger evaporated. 'No, no!' she said gently. 'However upset Judith may have been by Fulk's tidings, she would never have let anyone force her into something she didn't want to do. Judith has always been very strong-willed. When I left for Burgundy, twelve years ago, I did my best – and so did Veronica – to persuade her to accompany us. We told her that with Edmund Broderer dead, she had nothing to keep her in England. (There were no children of the marriage.) She resolutely refused. She said she couldn't go back to being a seamstress after being mistress of her own establishment.'

'An understandable point of view,' Duke Richard murmured, still staring into the heart of the fire where the flames, blue and red and orange, licked the bark of the pine logs, filling the room with a thick and heady scent. He leaned forward, throwing two more logs from the pile at the side of the hearth on to the blaze.

'You should have summoned a lackey to do that,' the Duchess reproved him sharply. 'Understandable? Perhaps, but Veronica said that during the six years she and Fulk lived with Judith and her husband, her sister never ceased to complain about the smallness of the house – don't forget that the twins had been used to living in palaces – the smell from the river and the dampness and chill in winter. I expected her to be as eager as Veronica to accompany me to Burgundy.'

Duke Richard regarded the Duchess thoughtfully, but said nothing. It was left to me to point out that there was all the difference in the world between being dissatisfied with one's lot and exchanging independence for a life of service.

'Veronica didn't think so,' was the indignant rejoinder.

'But she hadn't been independent,' the Duke demurred, once again entering the fray. 'After a very brief marriage,

60

she had lived for six years on her sister's and brother-in-law's bounty. She had simply exchanged one form of servitude for another.'

'I'm sure you do Judith an injustice, Dickon! She would never treat her sister like a servant.' The Duchess was outraged.

Her brother smiled and again refrained from stating the obvious; that being the poor – or poorer – relation in an affluent household like the Broderers' was almost bound to entail some form of subservience.

'Did Mistress St Clair offer you any particular reason for declining your request?' I asked, choosing my words with care. It was plain that even after twelve years, Judith's refusal still rankled with her former mistress, who had been used for most of her life to commanding loyalty amongst those she regarded as 'her' people.

The Duchess grimaced petulantly. 'Oh, the usual high-flown nonsense about owing it to her late husband to carry on his work. Although it seems now that this young cousin of his was perfectly capable of doing so without Judith's assistance.'

At this, Duke Richard suddenly forced himself up and out of his chair, as if he had taken about as much as he could stand.

'My dear,' he said, and his voice was tight with suppressed irritation, 'you're being unreasonable.' He forced a smile. 'You talk as if Mistress St Clair had no duty to anyone but yourself.' He went over to his sister's chair and took one of her hands in both of his, raising it to his lips. 'Now, it's late and we are all tired. It's been a very long day. You must be exhausted after all your exertions. You were the brightest star of every event and everyone loved you. But you must get some sleep so that you can dazzle us all again tomorrow.'

I had never thought of the Duke as an accomplished courtier, but he certainly knew how to handle the Duchess, who was positively purring like a cat that had been given a dish of cream. I guessed she had always been susceptible to flattery, and the mature woman was no different from the girl. It made me wonder how accurate her assessment of Fulk Quantrell's character really was. Had he truly been the charming and affectionate boy she had portrayed in speaking of him to me? Or did he simply understand how to ingratiate himself with a lonely, childless woman, the victim of a loveless marriage?

The Duke opened the door and shouted for a page, who was instructed to see me safely out of the castle. The Duchess again graciously proffered her hand for me to kiss, but said acidly that she trusted I would have discovered the identity of the murderer of her dearest Fulk before her return to Burgundy in seven days' time. (Her tone implied a doubt and a mistrust of my abilities that annoyed me.) Duke Richard, on the other hand, much to my astonishment and also to that of his sister, embraced me like a friend.

'Take care, Roger,' he said. 'Loyalty such as yours is a difficult commodity to come by nowadays.'

My mind was still reeling from this unlooked-for demonstration of royal affection when the last of a series of doors and gates clanged shut behind me and I found myself out in the London streets, making my way back to the Voyager.

I walked to Thames Street, then climbed St Peter's Hill into Old Fish Street. It was dark by now. The evening's revelries seemed to have finished and there were very few people about. A three-quarter moon lent a ghostly radiance to the still, grey scene, and the only creature moving, apart from myself, was a scrawny black cat, sitting in the lee of St Mary Magdalen Church, and unconcernedly tidying its whiskers. A couple of drunken revellers passed me as I turned into Cordwainer Street and made my way north towards Budge Row. From there it was merely a few strides left into Soper Lane, then right by the Broderer workshop into Needlers Lane, and I was almost home.

As I passed the Church of St Benet Sherehog, I could see the opening into Bucklersbury only yards ahead of me. I began to whistle in my usual tuneless fashion under my breath . . .

Someone jumped me from behind, coming out of the

church porch with all the speed and ferocity of an arrow just released from the bow. I went down like a felled tree, stretching my length on the ground, where I was pinned by my assailant sitting astride my back, his bony little knees gripping my upper arms. A head was lowered next to mine and a blast of garlic-laden breath hit the side of my face.

'Mind your own business, chapman, if you know what's good for you,' hissed a voice in my ear. A very Welsh voice. 'This is just the first warning. So go back to Bristol, there's a good boy!'

Then, just as suddenly as he had arrived, my attacker had gone, his footsteps echoing hollowly in the empty street as he ran towards Soper Lane.

Six

I lay where I had fallen for perhaps a minute. I had been winded and needed to recover my breath.

Except for a sore cheek, where I had scraped my face along the ground, and some scratches to my hands, I wasn't really hurt. But my pride was deeply wounded. My head had been so full of my meeting with the Duke and Dowager Duchess that I had grown careless, ignoring my own first rule of survival: always be on your guard – which isn't to say that I had never been ambushed before, but, generally speaking, on those occasions I had been unlucky. Tonight, however, I hadn't even considered the possibility that I could be in danger or that I might have been followed from Baynard's Castle. Yet I should have done. Somewhere in London lurked the murderer of Fulk Quantrell, and I was doing my best to uncover his – or her – identity.

As I heaved myself into a sitting position and probed cautiously for any bodily damage that might so far have escaped my notice, I went briefly through the people who knew of my presence and, above all, my purpose in the capital. I could forget all members of the royal family along with Timothy Plummer, Reynold Makepeace and Bertram Serifaber. That left Lionel Broderer and his mother, Judith St Clair's housekeeper and Judith St Clair herself, who had been told of my visit by the Dowager Duchess. So, possibly, Godfrey St Clair was also aware of my existence.

But the voice that had hissed its warning in my ear had been male and Welsh. Not that the last fact meant very much. The lilting cadences of my near neighbours across the Bristol Channel are some of the easiest to fake, and I hadn't been in any condition to listen to it carefully . . .

'Master Chapman! Are you all right? Mother and I saw what happened. I tried to intercept the man who attacked you, but he was running too fast, and he had his hood pulled right over his head, hiding his face.'

It was Lionel Broderer, kneeling beside me in the dust. His face was nothing but a blur as the moon disappeared behind a cloud, but I recognized the voice with its harsh timbre, and his compact figure. 'Here! Let me help you to your feet.'

I should have been grateful for his assistance, but I was feeling too much of a fool to appreciate his sympathy. I shook off his supporting hand.

'I'm well enough,' I answered brusquely. 'A bruise or two. Nothing more.'

He proceeded to make matters worse. 'You shouldn't be walking abroad in the streets at night without a cudgel.'

I restrained the impulse to shout at him, but it was an effort. 'I was summoned by His Grace of Gloucester to Baynard's Castle and I felt a cudgel would have been out of place. In any case, I doubt if it would have helped me much. I was surprised.'

He nodded understandingly. I could cheerfully have hit him. 'Yes. Mother and I had just returned from West Cheap, where members of the Mercers' Guild were doing a re-enactment of the Lady Margaret's marriage to Charles of Burgundy, twelve years ago at Damme. We came back down Soper Lane, and just as we rounded the corner, we saw you jumped on by this man who came out of St Benet Sherehog's porch.'

'How did you know it was me?'

Lionel chuckled. 'How many other men of your height and girth are there in this part of London?'

By this time Mistress Broderer had joined us. 'Is he all right, Lal?' she enquired.

'A trifle winded, that's all,' I snapped. 'Nothing so wrong with me that I can't answer for myself.'

I was immediately ashamed that I had allowed my bad

temper to get the better of me, but while Lionel looked affronted, his mother merely laughed.

'Feeling sore, are you? In more ways than one? Well, I suppose that's only to be expected.' Her sympathy was tinged with a mockery that she couldn't quite conceal. 'Come back to the house with us and have some wine.'

I thanked her, but refused. 'I'm so near the Voyager now that I'll go on. I need my bed.' And I thanked both of them again, over-profusely, to compensate for my previous rudeness.

But my refusal was not entirely due either to tiredness or to embarrassment at what had happened. I suddenly found myself wondering if Lionel Broderer could have been my assailant. He had been close at hand.

I was still considering the idea while I stripped and rolled between the blankets, nestling into Reynold Makepeace's goose-feather mattress. (I had gone straight to my chamber, avoiding the ale room, where a crowd of indefatigable merrymakers continued to drink the Dowager Duchess of Burgundy's health.) I tried to recall the voice which had whispered in my ear and to match it with Lionel's, but the difference seemed too great for probability. And yet . . . And yet I couldn't have sworn that they weren't one and the same. Welsh tones are usually soft and soothing. This voice had been neither of those things, just low and sibilant.

I repeated the words over to myself: 'Mind your own business, chapman, if you know what's good for you. This is just the first warning. So go back to Bristol, there's a good boy!' Boy. Boyo. A Welsh term of address as I well knew from hearing it so often along the Bristol Backs.

I could feel sleep beginning to engulf me, and decided that the problem would have to wait until the morning. I groped for the reassuring feel of my knife beneath my pillow and felt for my cudgel, which I had placed along-side me on the bed. Only then did I close my eyes and allow my mind to drift.

*   *   *

After nine years I had at last trained myself to sleep through the night and not wake in the small hours for the service of matins and lauds, as I had had to do when a novice at Glastonbury. (It had been a habit greatly deplored by Adela.) And that particular night, worn out by the previous day's events, I had slept even more soundly than usual – with the result that, when I eventually awoke, the sun was filtering through the shutters and people were clattering busily about the inn. For my part, I was feeling fighting fit again.

I was just wondering if I could escape from the Voyager before young Bertram came to find me, when he bounced into the ale room where I was eating my breakfast.

'There you are!' he exclaimed unnecessarily, before ordering a mazer of small beer.

'Not wanted by the Duke or Master Plummer today?' I asked hopefully.

He shook his head. 'I'm entirely at your disposal.' That's what I'd been afraid of. 'However, tomorrow I might be needed for other duties. If so, you'll have to manage without me.'

'Heaven forfend!' I exclaimed, but the sarcasm was lost on my companion. I swallowed the rest of my oatcake and honey.

While Bertram finished his beer, I debated whether or not to tell him of last night's incident. I didn't want to. It would admit my fallibility and make me seem a bit of a fool. In the end, I decided it would be unfair not to warn him to be on his guard, and to carry a knife or a cudgel at all times.

But the story seemed to excite rather than frighten him, nor did it move him to laughter at my expense.

'I wish I'd been there,' he said eagerly. 'I could probably have caught up with whoever it was. My legs are younger than yours.'

'Whoever it was wouldn't have risked attacking me if there'd been two of us,' I pointed out snappishly. 'And I'm not yet in my dotage. I'll thank you to remember that.'

He grinned and was about to make a further rejoinder

when I rose from the table and said it was time we were going. The ale room was filling up with my fellow guests, all looking for their breakfasts, and I was in no mood for idle conversation. I wanted to get this case over and done with so that I could be on my way back to Bristol. (Incidentally, I had no intention of riding or of being escorted home. Someone in Duke Richard's household could arrange for the horse to be returned to the Bell Lane livery stables. I urgently needed the freedom and solitude.)

'Where are we going?' Bertram asked as we left the Voyager.

'Where do you think? To visit Judith and Godfrey St Clair, of course. They are, after all, at the centre of this mystery. Then, if we're lucky, perhaps we can question their next-door neighbours, the Jolliffes, as well. And if we're *very* lucky, we might get a word with their other neighbour, Martin Threadgold, Mistress St Clair's former brother-in-law.'

The fitful May day had lost its early sunshine and turned cold and wet. As we crossed the River Fleet, a sudden squall of rain whipped spray from the water, and the houses on either side of the thoroughfare were shrouded in mist. This would undoubtedly clear as the day progressed, but for the moment, it made everything appear grey and insubstantial.

Secure in the knowledge that my arrival must be at least half-expected, I knocked boldly on the street door of Judith St Clair's house in the Strand and waited confidently to have my summons answered. I wasn't disappointed, and within a very few minutes the door was opened by the housekeeper, Paulina Graygoss.

She eyed me with a certain hostility. 'The mistress said as how you'd likely be paying us a visit,' she remarked acidly. 'But we weren't expecting you this early in the morning.' She jerked her head. 'Still, I suppose you'd better come in now you're here; but you'll have to wait. The master and mistress are still at breakfast.'

She left us to kick our heels in the main hall of the house while she disappeared through a door to the left of a fine, carved oaken fireplace. I looked around me. Everything – from the glazed windows opening on to the Strand, to the rich tapestries decorating the walls, to the corner cupboard with its sparkling display of silverware (interspersed with the occasional dull gleam of gold), to the Eastern rugs adorning the flagstones – spoke of money and plenty of it. Judith St Clair's wealth had not been exaggerated.

The housekeeper reappeared and, with a very bad grace, asked us to follow her, plainly disapproving of her mistress's decision to receive us without first finishing her meal. She led us through several more rooms, all as well furnished as the hall, to a small parlour at the back of the house, overlooking the garden and the river. The full force of a spring storm was suddenly upon us. Rain lashed down outside and candles had been lit, ribbing the room with shadows. The distant cries of boatmen echoed eerily through the horn-paned windows from the Thames.

I immediately recognized the couple seated at the table as the pair I had seen at Westminster the previous day. They were still in mourning, but the finery of the previous occasion had been replaced by more homely attire: a long, loose velvet robe, rubbed thin in patches, for him, and a plain woollen gown and linen hood for her. The man looked thinner than ever, hunched over his plate, his grey hair gilded by the candlelight. He didn't glance up as Bertram and I entered the room, focusing all his attention on the apple he was dissecting with a pearl-handled knife. Judith St Clair, however, raised her handsome head and gave me an appraising look.

'You must be this chapman Her Highness was telling me about.' Her eyes raked me from head to foot in a manner which, in someone else, could have been considered insulting, but which, in her, seemed merely curious. 'It appears that His Grace of Gloucester sets great store by your ability to solve mysteries. An odd occupation for a pedlar.'

'A gift from God, madam.'

At my slightly caustic tone, her gaze sharpened and she smiled grimly.

'Maybe . . . Well, no one will be happier than myself to see the villain of this particular crime laid by the heels.' I thought for a moment she was on the verge of tears, but

69

she straightened her back and gestured impatiently, as though ashamed to display any such weakness. 'So? What do you want from my husband and me?'

'Just to talk to you both; to ask you about Master Quantrell and to learn anything you can tell me about the night he was murdered. I'd also like to question Mistress Threadgold and your son, sir, if they've no objection.' I turned towards the silent figure at the other end of the table.

Godfrey St Clair did lift his eyes at that and sent me a long, penetrating stare. Then he nodded. 'Jocelyn has nothing to hide. I don't see why he should object.' He had a surprisingly strong, deep voice for someone who appeared so frail.

'When do you wish to begin this . . . this interrogation?' his wife asked with, I thought, a touch of resentment.

But before I could reply, the parlour door opened and a young girl entered the room. I judged her to be some eighteen or nineteen years of age, pretty in a plumpish way with large brown eyes and a mass of very dark hair which, at present, she wore loose about her shoulders. She had on a gown of soft grey wool with a low-cut neck and turned-back sleeves, both of which revealed her linen undershift.

'Who's this?' she asked of no one in particular, seating herself at the table.

Judith St Clair said, 'This is the chapman I told you of last night.' And to me, 'My stepdaughter, Alcina Threadgold.'

I had already guessed the young woman's identity, and gave her a polite bow. She returned the compliment by looking me over much as her stepmother had done, but with a greater degree of appreciation. Bertram received the same treatment, which made him blush uncomfortably and shuffle his feet. Alcina threw back her head and laughed.

'Be quiet!' Judith ordered. 'This is a house of mourning. Or had you forgotten?'

'I'm less likely to forget than any of you,' Alcina retorted. 'Fulk and I were betrothed to be married.'

'And that's a lie,' said a fourth voice.

A young man, a few years older than Alcina and not that much younger than myself, had joined the others at the breakfast table. This, surely, must be Jocelyn St Clair, although any likeness to his father was not marked. He had the same hawkish nose, it was true, but his eyes were blue rather than Godfrey's indeterminate grey, and his hair, worn fashionably cut and curled about his ears, was a lighter brown than I imagined the older man's had been in his youth.

Alcina was on her feet. 'What do you mean, a lie?' she demanded furiously. 'Fulk and I were going to be married. It was common knowledge!'

'He had no intention of marrying you,' Jocelyn threw back at her, equally furious. 'Lionel Broderer told me so. He told me all about that scene in the workshop the evening Fulk died. And Mistress Broderer confirmed it.'

'Liars, both of them!' Alcina was near to tears.

'No! There were other people present who'll confirm it. Stop deluding yourself, Cina! Face up to the facts! There are some who really love you.' Jocelyn hesitated, then finished lamely, 'Brandon Jolliffe, for one. And . . . And Lionel wouldn't say no if you looked in his direction.'

'That will do, both of you.' Judith rose from her place, magisterial in her anger. 'There are strangers in our midst and I will not tolerate this kind of behaviour in their presence. If you have differences, settle them in private.' She turned to me. 'Master Chapman, let us get this over and done with. If you'll follow me, we'll go to the winter parlour, which is always empty at this time of year. Although, goodness knows why. Today is more like winter than spring. Thank the saints the Duchess had a fine day yesterday.' She glanced at Bertram. 'Is he coming, too?'

Bertram drew himself up to his full height, such as it was. 'I am the representative of my master, the Duke of Gloucester,' he announced importantly. 'I am here to assist Master Chapman with his enquiries.'

I am a tolerant man as a rule, as all who know me will testify (well, most of them, anyway), but I was beginning to harbour unkind thoughts about young Master Serifaber. Visions of racks and thumbscrews and vats of boiling oil hovered tantalizingly at the back of my mind.

'Come with me, then.' Judith swept past us, out of the door, and we, perforce, had to follow.

We were led up a flight of stairs, along a narrow corridor, up another, shorter staircase and into a room not more than about seven feet square, again facing south on to the Thames to catch whatever there was of the westering afternoon sun. This morning, however, it was cold and dismal and no welcoming fire burned on the hearth.

'Wait,' Judith St Clair ordered peremptorily. 'I'll send for candles.'

She disappeared. I ignored Bertram and took stock of the room.

There were no expensive rugs as in the hall, but, like the parlour below, the floor was covered with fresh rushes mixed with scented herbs and dried flowers. (Some underling had been up and hard at work since the crack of dawn.) A broad window seat was strewn with cushions, two carved armchairs were drawn up, one on either side of the empty hearth, a harp and its stool stood in one corner, an oak chest, banded with iron, offered an extra, if uncomfortable, seat, while a couple of joint stools completed the furnishings.

Bertram had his own method of inspection. Not content with letting his eyes do the work, he wandered around the room, touching everything: prodding cushions, running his fingers across the harp strings, kicking up the rushes.

After a while, I could stand it no longer. 'For goodness' sake, lad, you're like a flea on a griddle. Stand still! You're making me nervous.'

Judith St Clair returned with a servant, a man in his mid-twenties, a surly expression marring features that might, in other circumstances, have been quite pleasant. He was carrying a flint and tinder-box and some candles which he was directed to light and set in holders about the room. Then he was ordered to kindle the pile of sticks and logs on the hearth, a feat he accomplished with a great deal of difficulty, for the room was damp. Finally, when this was done, he stumped off, grumbling under his breath. Judith St Clair heaved a sigh.

'You must forgive William,' she said. 'He's been in my employ since he was eight years old. His father was servant to my first husband, Edmund Broderer, and he regards himself as privileged. But he's very loyal.' She paused, plainly annoyed with herself for explaining and apologizing for something that was none of our business. We were uninvited and of lowly status, even if we did have the backing of a royal duke. She sat down in one of the armchairs. 'Well, what do you want to know?' She didn't ask us to sit.

I wasn't standing for that (literally). I drew forward one of the joint stools and motioned to Bertram to do the same with the other. Only when he was settled did I lean forward, elbows on knees, and request our reluctant hostess to tell us about her reunion with Fulk Quantrell.

'What can I say?' She was angry at what she considered my display of bad manners, but was powerless to dismiss me without indirectly offending the Dowager Duchess, who had given her blessing to our enquiries. 'He was my nephew, my sister Veronica's son. Her only child. My only living kinsman. Furthermore, he and his mother had lived with my first husband and myself from the time of his birth until he was six years old, when Veronica decided to go with the Lady Margaret to Burgundy.'

'You were expecting his arrival?'

'Yes, but not until yesterday. I knew that he would accompany the Dowager Duchess on this visit to London. He had written to tell me so at the beginning of December.'

'But he turned up much earlier?'

'At the beginning of March. He had come to tell me . . . tell me . . .' Judith's breath caught momentarily in her throat and she seemed to be in the grip of some powerful emotion. However, she took a deep breath and steadied herself. 'Fulk had come to tell me that my sister was dead. She had died shortly after Christmas. He had intended coming earlier, he said, but the Duchess had been too upset to spare him immediately. Except for those six years when she lived with me, Veronica had been with my lady ever since she was a child.'

73

I nodded, choosing my next words carefully. 'You . . . You became very fond of your nephew, I've been told.'

After a brief hesitation, Judith answered in a restricted voice, 'Very fond.'

It was my turn to hesitate. 'Perhaps unwisely fond?' I ventured at last.

Her chin went up defiantly. 'Some might think so. In fact,' she added candidly, 'nearly everyone thought so, and didn't refrain from making their opinions public. Roland and Lydia Jolliffe. Martha Broderer and her son, Lionel. My stepson, whom you met downstairs. Even my house-keeper had the gall to give me a piece of her mind.'

'And you?' I asked. 'What did you think of your conduct?'

The rain had ceased, as springtime showers do, as abruptly as it had started. I could hear the birds begin to sing again in the garden. The logs crackled on the hearth, but for a few protracted seconds there were no other sounds in the room. I wondered if I had been too impertinent. Even Bertram had stopped fidgeting on his stool.

Then Judith gave a sudden crack of laughter. 'If you knew me better, you wouldn't ask such a question. I never query my own actions. Only weak people do that. It's the sign of a vacillating mind.' She drummed her fingers against the arms of her chair. 'As soon as I saw Fulk again, I recognized him for what he was: the son I never had. Veronica was my twin. We were born within a few minutes of one another. There had always been a very close and very strong bond between us. As girls and as women, it had been an unwritten rule that we helped each other out of trouble. And although I hadn't seen her for nearly twelve years, that bond had never been broken. When Fulk told me the news of her death, it was like a blow to the heart; yet I wasn't altogether surprised. I had been feeling low in spirits and extremely melanchoy since Christmas without knowing why. Then, of course, I understood: somehow, the fact of her death had communicated itself to me. The thread of twinship that had joined us all our lives had at last been cut. I was alone.'

'Except for Fulk.'

74

She nodded eagerly. 'Yes, except for my nephew. He was the link that made her death bearable. He looked like her, too. Which meant he also looked like me. And now . . .' This time, Judith was unable to recover her poise so easily.

I finished for her. 'And now Fulk's dead, as well.'

'Yes.' The word was barely audible; a sigh of grief, a breath of air. She raised one hand to her mouth.

'Then we must find his killer,' I said gently. 'Don't you agree?'

She gave a little snort of laughter. 'Where will you start? Thanks to my folly – oh yes, I can admit now that it was folly, although I would probably do it all over again – you're not short of suspects.'

'That's true . . . Mistress St Clair, was it you or was it your nephew who made your intentions in regard to your new will general knowledge?'

'Those sorts of things can't be kept secret for long,' she answered evasively. I opened my mouth to argue the point, but she forestalled me. 'Very well! If you insist on the truth, I would have preferred that Fulk had kept quiet about it until I had had time to speak to the others most nearly affected. But Fulk was young, excited by his good fortune, anxious to let everyone know how high he stood in my affections. And he felt that he needed to learn about the embroidery business if he was one day to own the work-shop. It was only natural that he should call there from time to time in order to see for himself how things were done.'

'And natural, surely, that your cousin should resent it.'

'*Edmund*'s cousin,' she corrected me, as though anxious to distance herself from this man she had been planning to wrong. 'He's not my kinsman. Fulk was.' She was trying to justify the unjustifiable, as was only natural in someone with a conscience.

The door opened and the manservant, William, returned. 'You wantin' any more logs on that fire?' he asked.

I froze. I knew that voice. I recognized the Welsh accent. It belonged to my assailant of the night before.

Seven

'Who – who is that?' I croaked.

Judith St Clair, who had dismissed the man with a wave of her hand, turned to stare in surprise.

'I told you who he is just now. Don't you listen? He's William Morgan, who's been with me since he was a child. His father was servant to my first husband.'

'I . . . I didn't realize he was Welsh,' I said lamely.

The well-marked eyebrows shot up. 'Why should you? And what does it matter if he is? Have you anything against the Welsh race, Master Chapman?'

'N-No,' I stuttered. 'We do a great deal of trade with them in Bristol. All the same,' I added, recovering my equanimity, 'I should like to speak to this William Morgan later on, when I've spoken to the other members of your household.'

She inclined her head. Whatever else she might or might not have learned in the employ of Margaret of York, Judith had certainly learned how to behave regally. The Queen herself could not have been more condescending. But in spite of that, I found myself beginning to like her.

She started to rise. 'I must go. I have a house to see to and a workshop to visit. Yesterday having been a holiday, I must assure myself that everything is running smoothly once again.'

I stretched out a hand to detain her and she sank back in her seat, frowning with annoyance.

'What now?' she demanded.

'I must ask,' I said, 'about the night of the murder. 'Where were you? How did you hear about it?'

She bit her lip, and I thought for a moment that she would

refuse to answer. But Bertram, proving that he had more sense than I would have given him credit for, gave a little cough and shifted his stool forward until he was directly in Judith's line of vision. At the sight of his royal livery, she changed her mind.

'It was just over a fortnight ago,' she began, then stopped, kneading her hands together in her lap, trying desperately to control her emotions. At last she went on, but with a slight tremor in her voice, 'It was May Day, which, as it so happens, is also the Feast of Saint Sigismund of Burgundy. The young people – Alcina, Fulk, Jocelyn, Brandon Jolliffe – all went out maying before breakfast in the fields around Holborn, but when they returned, it was obvious that all wasn't well between them. For a start, Fulk and Brandon bore all the marks of having been in a fight; and although they both claimed it had been a fight with some other youths who had been out maying, I didn't believe them.'

'Why not?'

'Because of the way they looked and spoke – or, rather, didn't speak – to one another. Besides, I questioned my stepson later, and Jocelyn confirmed that Fulk and Brandon had come to blows.'

'What about? Did you enquire?'

Judith shook her head. 'I didn't need to. There had been bad blood not just between that pair, but between all three of them ever since Alcina fell in love with Fulk. I could hardly blame Brandon Jolliffe. There had been some talk of a betrothal with Alcina for months past. And as for Jocelyn, I've suspected for a while now that he was fond of her, and I knew my husband wouldn't have put any rub in his way if it had turned out that she favoured him.'

I interrupted yet again. 'Who would *you* have preferred your stepdaughter to marry?'

Judith shrugged. 'I had no preference. Alcina's happiness was, and still is, my only concern. But, of course, I wasn't in the least surprised when she fell for Fulk. Both Brandon and Jocelyn paled into insignificance beside my nephew. Neither could match him for looks or character. He was the handsomest young man I have ever seen, and, in addition, witty, clever, humorous, kind. So very kind. Moreover, he sang like an angel and played the lute like a troubadour. What more could any woman ask?'

'A veritable paragon,' I murmured, and she gave me a sharp look, searching my face for any sign of scepticism.

'You don't believe me?'

'Madam, unlike you, I didn't know the young man, so naturally I accept your word. But that morning, did you also get the impression that all was not well between Fulk and your stepdaughter?'

Judith hesitated, then inclined her head. 'I have to admit that I sensed some tension. I blame Alcina. She wanted to make sure of Fulk. I think that, because she was so much in love with him, she was pestering him for an acknowledgement that he felt the same way about her by agreeing to a date for their marriage.'

'Which he didn't. At least, not according to what Lionel Broderer and his mother told me. And they had obviously told others about that scene in the workshop, the night your nephew died. Your stepson, for example. Had you known about it, before Master St Clair mentioned it this morning?'

'I might have done. I really can't remember . . . Perhaps I dismissed it as spite on Martha Broderer's part. She was more outspoken than the rest about the making of my new will.'

'Maybe she felt that her son had more to lose than anyone else. If, that is, under the terms of your original will, he would have inherited the workshop when you and your husband died.'

Judith said nothing for a moment; then she nodded, accepting the truth of this statement.

'Well, Martha needn't worry any more,' she said in a low voice. 'The will has been altered for a second time and put back as it was. All the original bequests had been reinstated. So, is that all?' And she again made to rise from her chair.

And again I prevented her. 'You've told me about the morning of the day Fulk died,' I pointed out, 'but not about the evening of the murder.'

Judith sighed. 'There's little to tell. All three of the young people went out some time after supper. They didn't say where or why they were going, and I didn't ask. I think Fulk may first have gone to church, as it was Saint Sigismund's Day. My husband was in his chamber, reading. He is at present studying the Meditations of Marcus Aurelius. I had one of my bad headaches, which always lay me low, so I went to bed immediately after the meal finished. I took one of my draughts of lettuce and poppy juice and knew nothing more until I was awoken the following morning with the terrible news that Fulk's body had been found in Faitour Lane.' Her voice caught in her throat, but she went on bravely, 'He had received a mortal blow to the back of his head.'

A log flared suddenly on the hearth with a noise like tearing silk, and Bertram gave a little start. Judith, too, seemed to come out of a kind of daze, and fixed me with a haughty stare. 'Is there anything more you wish to know? If not, I really must insist on taking my leave.'

'I should like to speak to your husband, if he is willing and can spare me the time.' I was treading carefully. There was no point in putting up the backs of these people.

'I'll ask him to join you,' she said. 'Wait here.'

When she had gone, I looked at Bertram, but he was staring abstractedly at a posy of flowers which stood in a jar in a wall niche by the door: the purple glory of lady's smock and the damp, pale gold of wild iris.

'Do you think,' he asked in a dejected voice, 'that there can be many men as wonderful as this Fulk Quantrell seems to have been? My father's always telling me I could do better if I tried, but if I live to be a hundred, I don't believe—'

'Don't worry your head about it, lad,' I advised him heartily. 'The only advantage I can see that this Fulk had over the rest of us was that he was a damned good-looking fellow. All the rest of it you can take with a pinch of salt. A very large pinch. Women's gullibility when confronted by a pretty face never ceases to amaze me.'

On which lofty, masculine note, which would have infuriated Adela had she heard it and led to a right royal quarrel,

79

I got to my feet as the door opened to admit Godfrey St Clair.

'You didn't go out at all, sir, the evening of the murder? At least, so Mistress St Clair informs me.'

It had taken several frustrating minutes to get this far in my questioning of Godfrey. First, he had warmed his hands and backside at the fire; then he had walked over to the wall niche to straighten the jug of flowers before doing the same for the harp in the corner. Next, he had settled himself in the chair recently vacated by his wife, arranging his robe with all the fussiness of a pernickety child, rising to his feet more than once, pulling and tugging at the frayed material until at last he proclaimed himself comfortable. Then he had remarked on the chilliness of the day, discoursed on yesterday's pageant and his and Judith's subsequent visit to Baynard's Castle before, finally, announcing that he was ready to answer whatever I cared to ask him.

But before replying to my question, he produced a pair of spectacles from the pocket of his gown, perched them on the bridge of his nose and blinked at me through them as though I were some rare specimen of wildlife that he had just discovered taking up residence in his house.

'No. No, that's right,' he finally agreed. 'After supper, I went to my study and continued reading the Meditations of Marcus Aurelius Antoninus, emperor and philosopher. A truly remarkable man. Are you familiar with any of his dictums?'

'I – er – No, I can't call to mind anything of his just at the moment, can you, Master Serifaber?'

Thus appealed to, Bertram goggled at me like a stranded fish and mutely shook his head.

'Did you remain in your study, sir, until you went to bed?'

'What? Oh . . . yes. Until I went to bed.'

'And what hour would that have been? As near as you can tell.'

'Oh, I can tell you exactly,' Godfrey said triumphantly. 'I put my head out of my study window for a breath of fresh air and the watch were just crying midnight. I hadn't realized it was quite so late. Time flies when you're enjoying yourself.'

'Indeed it does.' Bertram gave a stifled giggle and I frowned him down. 'Was anyone else in the house still up at that hour, apart from yourself?'

Godfrey considered this. 'I . . . I'm not quite sure,' he said at last. 'I'd heard the young people return earlier in the evening from wherever they'd been, and presumed that they were all at home and asleep in their beds. However, I . . . I did think I heard a noise of some sort, but when I went to investigate, I couldn't find anything or anyone awake and stirring.'

'What sort of noise? Can you remember?'

Godfrey shook his head. 'At the time, I thought it was the door to the secret stairway opening and closing.'

'The secret stairway?' Bertram demanded excitedly. 'Whereabouts is that, sir?'

Having sat still for all of ten minutes, Godfrey began to fidget with his gown again, rearranging it beneath his thin buttocks, raising and lowering himself until he fancied he was comfortable once more. Only then did he turn his attention back to me.

'What were we talking about? Oh, yes! The secret stair. It isn't really secret, you understand. Apparently, that was the name Alcina gave it when she was a child, and it stuck. Of course, I didn't know her then. Didn't know my wife then. Wasn't even a widower probably . . .'

'This so-called secret stair, sir!' I had no compunction in cutting short the flow. He was one of those people who, if allowed to ramble into the byways of reminiscence, would be there all day. 'Where is it?'

'Oh, in Mistress St Clair's bedchamber – didn't I say? There's a second door in one corner of her room which opens on to a little landing at the top of a flight of stairs. They lead down into the passage running alongside the kitchen.'

'But doesn't Mistress St Clair bolt this door at night?'

'As a rule, yes, but she's sometimes forgetful. So when

81

I heard this noise and thought it was the door to the stair opening and shutting, I assumed that my wife, who had been suffering with one of her bad headaches, had gone to bed and forgotten to do so.'

'What's it used for, this "secret" stairway?' I wanted to know. 'What's the point of it? Why was it built?'

'Yes, yes! I understand what you're asking me.' There was a justifiable testiness in Godfrey's voice. 'No need to repeat the question three different ways. I'm not in my dotage yet, whatever you may think. I can't tell you what the original purpose of the stair was when the house was first constructed, but we use it as a shorter and quicker route for Mistress Graygoss, our housekeeper, to get up and down to the first floor to consult with my wife. If she uses the main staircase it takes her much longer.' He was getting restless again.

'So, sir,' I asked quickly before he could rise and amble off, 'why did you think that the noise you heard was made by the door to this particular staircase?'

'The damn door squeaks,' he answered irritably. 'Needs oiling. I keep telling William about it, but he doesn't take any notice of me. The only person he heeds is Judith, and then only if he feels like it or she gets angry with him. Old family servant,' he grumbled. 'Been in my wife's service since he was a lad. They're always the worst sort. Bloody useless. William isn't thirty yet – somewhere about your age, I should reckon – but behaves like he's an old man. Says he has a bad back.'

I suppressed a smile and let Godfrey have his moan. Then I asked, 'And what did you do next?'

He took off his spectacles, polished them on his sleeve and readjusted them on his nose before answering. 'What did I do next? What do you think I did next? What anyone would have done. I went into my wife's bedchamber to make sure she was all right.'

'And was she?'

'She was sleeping soundly. And before you ask me, yes, I'm sure. I bent over her, shielding the candle flame so as not to wake her. She was lying on her side and snoring, bedclothes drawn up to her chin. She'd taken one of her sleeping draughts. The empty cup was still on the bedside table and I could smell the dregs. So I closed the bed curtains again and checked the door to the stair. It was bolted all right, but I looked around just to make certain there was no one hiding in the shadows. There wasn't, so I came to the conclusion that I must have been mistaken. In fact, by that time, I couldn't have sworn that I'd heard anything at all. The noise had faded from my mind. So I went off to my own chamber, got myself undressed and into bed, and slept like a baby until morning. The next thing I knew someone was hammering on the street door. Member of the watch to tell us that Fulk had been found murdered in Fleet Street, on the corner by St Dunstan's Church.'

'Was anyone missing from the house when you got up? Your son, Mistress Alcina, the housekeeper, William Morgan? Any of the other servants, if there are any?'

'There are a couple of young girls who help Paulina – Mistress Graygoss – in the kitchen and generally make themselves useful about the house. Act as maids to my wife and Alcina. But that's all. They share a room in the attics. There used to be a young lad, brother of one of the girls, I believe, who assisted William in the garden, but he doesn't come any more. Don't know what happened to him. Nice, polite, well-behaved boy . . .' He was off again.

I sighed and repeated my question. 'Was anyone missing?'

'Well, Fulk obviously. No one else.'

I changed the subject. 'Why did you permit Mistress St Clair to alter her will in her nephew's favour? You must have known it would cause bad feeling. In the eyes of the law the money is yours.'

Godfrey gave vent to a sound that I presumed was a laugh, but came out as more of a derisive hoot. 'You don't know my wife very well, Master Chapman, I can tell. You're right, of course. Legally, anything she owns is mine. But I'm a man who values his peace and comfort and she can be a Fury when roused. I'd never cross Judith unless I absolutely had to. It wouldn't be worth it. And, to be fair, the money is hers, inherited from her first husband, as she doesn't scruple to remind me. So when she demanded that I alter our will in Fulk's favour, even though I could see it would lead to trouble, I did it.'

'Mistress St Clair was very fond of him.'

'Fond of him? She was besotted by him almost from the moment he arrived. To begin with, she was very upset about her sister's death and Fulk comforted her. They grieved together. That was the start of it. After that, he could do no wrong.'

'And what did you think of him?'

The abrupt question seemed to throw Godfrey. He looked startled and a little nonplussed, as if he had never really considered the matter before.

I tried again. 'Did you like him?'

There was a further bout of fidgeting. I let him get on with it. I had realized by now that settling his body seemed also to settle his mind.

'Did I like him?' he repeated slowly, rolling each word carefully around his tongue and savouring it as though it were something new and foreign. Then he leaned back in his chair and regarded me over the tips of his steepled fingers. 'Well, do you know, I really couldn't say for certain. Sometimes I did, sometimes I didn't. Fulk could be very charming, but . . .' Here he paused, deep in thought. Finally, he went on, 'But there was something sly about him. On several occasions, when he wasn't aware that anyone was watching him, I saw him looking at the others, even Judith, with a kind of mockery in his eyes. Oh . . . perhaps it was my imagination! One shouldn't speak ill of the dead. However, there's no doubt in my mind that he positively enjoyed stealing Alcina's affection from Brandon Jolliffe right under the poor boy's nose. Not, I have to say, that I ever thought Alcina's affection for Brandon went very deep. Indeed, if Jocelyn had continued to push himself forward more, as he was beginning to do just before Fulk's arrival, I believe he might have been the one to win her favour.'

'Would you have liked your son to marry Mistress Threadgold?' I asked, wanting confirmation of the suggestion that had already been made to me.

'Ah . . . Well now!' Godfrey was suddenly wary, like an animal scenting a baited trap. 'I'm not saying that. You modern young people nowadays, you won't be pushed. You like to make up your own minds. Different when I was a youth. We did as we were told.' He got to his feet. 'That's enough questions for the present, I think, don't you? I must be off, back to Marcus Aurelius. "Let your occupations be few," he writes, "if you would lead a tranquil life." Wise advice.'

I could tell that this time he was determined to leave and that nothing I could do, short of brute force, would detain him further. He had seen quicksands ahead of him and was anxious to avoid them if he could.

'You said you thought your son would be willing to speak to me, sir. If he's still in the parlour, would you ask him to come up?' I added in my most authoritative voice, 'Their Graces the Duke of Gloucester and the Dowager Duchess of Burgundy are hoping for a speedy resolution to this enquiry.'

'Yes . . . Yes, I see . . . All right! If he hasn't gone out, I'll send Jocelyn up to you.' And Godfrey, only pausing to give another twitch to the jar of flowers, whose position in the niche appeared to offend his ideas of symmetry, left the room.

I put another log on the fire. Outside, it was still overcast and raining.

'Well?' Bertram asked. 'What do you think?'

'What about?'

'Master St Clair. Could he have killed this Fulk Quantrell, do you think? He'd like his son to marry Mistress Threadgold, that's plain.'

I shrugged. 'He could have done. But in order to murder Fulk, he must have been following him. Now, Godfrey could have left the house and re-entered it without anyone seeing him, I grant you. But so could anyone in this house, thanks to this so-called secret stair. The murderer would only have had to ensure that the door in Mistress St Clair's bedchamber was unbolted on the inside – and that wouldn't have been difficult, seeing she was drugged with lettuce and poppy juice – and, similarly, have left an outside door in the kitchen passage unlocked – that's presuming, of course, that there is one – and there you are! But we've a long way to go yet, my lad, so don't go jumping to any conclusions.'

'I wasn't,' Bertram protested, offended. 'I was just trying to clear my head. I'm not that much of a fool.'

I grinned. 'Of course you're not. But the question bothering me at present is: was it William Morgan who attacked me last night? And if so, why? Two questions.'

Bertram gave a low whistle. 'Do you really think it might have been him?'

'He's Welsh. And although I couldn't swear to it, I thought I recognized his voice. Moreover, he's about the right height and size. But having said all that, I wouldn't be absolutely positive he was the man. Maybe when I speak to him, perhaps I shall be able to make up my mind.'

The door to the winter parlour opened again and Jocelyn St Clair appeared.

'My father says you want to see me, chapman. If so, make it brief. I've an appointment with a cordwainer in Watling Street about a new pair of riding boots, and I promised I'd be there before dinner time. What do you want to know?'

He threw himself into the armchair and looked at me down that hawk-like nose of his. The blue eyes were half-closed, indicating boredom, but I noticed a nervous tic at one corner of his long, thin mouth. He was not as indifferent to this interview as he wished to make out.

'Tell me about Fulk Quantrell,' I said.

Jocelyn gave a harsh laugh. 'He was arrogant, conceited and he got what was coming to him. But,' he added hastily, 'I didn't kill him. I wouldn't have soiled my hands.'

'You didn't like him?'

Jocelyn gave another laugh that grated on my ears as

much as the first. 'What an intellect! Does the Duke of Gloucester know what he's paying for?'

'His Grace doesn't pay me,' I answered quietly.

'Just as well for him, then,' retorted this objectionable youth. 'No, I didn't like Fulk Quantrell. And he didn't like me. Although that's not quite right. He was contemptuous of me, just as he was of Brandon. Just as he was of everybody! But, naturally, he didn't let everyone know it, only those who didn't matter to him. To my stepmother, to Alcina, to Lydia Jolliffe, he dissembled until he'd got what he wanted.'

'And that was?'

He gave another insolent smile. I noticed he had very small, even white teeth. 'Oh, come on! You can't be as stupid as you pretend to be!'

'Just answer me,' I said, keeping my temper in check.

'Well, what do you think he wanted? He wanted my stepmother's money: to be her heir. He wanted to get in between the sheets with Lydia Jolliffe. She's very attractive, if you have a fancy for the maturer woman, which I must admit I don't. I like 'em young.' Again he bared those small, predatory teeth and winked. 'More juice.'

I was beginning to dislike young Master St Clair very much indeed. 'And Alcina? What did he want from her? Not marriage, it would seem. At least, not according to Lionel and Mistress Broderer.'

'No. I never thought he did. He just wanted to take her away from Brandon. To prove his superiority. To prove his power over women. Once he'd done that, he had no more use for her. I tried to warn Cina, but she wouldn't listen. She was as besotted by him as my stepmother and that silly old fool of a housekeeper.'

'Mistress Graygoss liked him, too, did she?'

'All the women thought the sun shone out of his arse.'

'You speak with some bitterness. How had Master Quantrell offended *you*?'

After only a momentary pause, and somewhat to my surprise, Jocelyn made a direct and unflinching reply. 'He was trying to steal my inheritance, wasn't he? Mine and Alcina's and Lionel's, too. I knew what was in the will; my father had told me.' Probably had it bullied out of him, I thought. 'Lionel was to receive the workshop and sufficient money to continue running it for the remainder of his working life. Alcina and I were to share the rest of the fortune between us when both my stepmother and father were dead.' He expelled his breath on a great sigh of relief. 'Well, thank the saints that's all been put back as it should be. The will's been rewritten. Personally speaking, I hope Fulk's murderer is never caught. I owe him a great debt of gratitude.'

Eight

I let this go.

Jocelyn's frankness could be taken two ways: either as proof of his innocence, or as evidence of his cunning. He had made no attempt to hide or disclaim his hatred of Fulk Quantrell; on the contrary, he had paraded it in the hope, I presumed, that it would exonerate him in my eyes. But a guilty man, one with at least a modicum of intelligence, would surely think along the same lines. I continued to keep an open mind.

'Tell me about the evening of the murder,' I invited. 'Your stepmother says that you and Fulk and Mistress Threadgold all left the house after supper, but didn't mention where you were going. She didn't ask. Did you go together?'

'No. I called next door for Brandon Jolliffe and we went to the Bull in Fish Street, our usual haunt. We spent the evening there, drinking and slandering Fulk to the top of our bent. He and Brandon had come to blows that morning when we'd all been out maying. Brandon accused Fulk of stealing Alcina's affections. Foolishly, I thought, because it was obvious, to me at any rate, that she had done most of the pursuing and that Fulk was encouraging her in order to annoy poor old Brandon and prove himself superior. I tried to talk some sense into him – Brandon, that is – that evening in the Bull, but he couldn't or wouldn't see it. Eventually he stormed off in a temper and left me sitting there. Left me to settle our account, as well.' Jocelyn shrugged and gave a lop-sided grin. 'Not that I held it against him. He was upset.'

'Was this before or after curfew?' I asked.

'Lord, I don't know. After, probably. No one takes much

notice of curfew nowadays. And although all the gates are shut at sundown, there are a dozen or more ways of getting in and out of the city, if you know them. Half of London's walls are in a shocking state of disrepair.'

I nodded understandingly. It was the same in Bristol, as it was in other inland cities in the southern half of England. Lack of invasion and attack for so many years had made for complacency among the civic hierarchy, who were loth to spend good money – or throw it away, as they saw it – on mending city walls. No doubt the matter was regarded differently in the North, where the inhabitants were under constant threat of incursions from the Scots.

'Did you see Master Jolliffe again that evening?'

'No. I hadn't really expected to, but I waited awhile, then paid our shot and went home.'

'And during that journey, you saw nothing untoward on the corner of Fleet Street and Faitour Lane?'

Jocelyn laughed. 'If you mean did I see Fulk being done to death, I'm afraid you're out of luck. If I had, I'd prob-ably have given a helping hand.' Again, there came that disarming frankness. 'As it was, the usual congregation of beggars and layabouts were shouting and screaming, fighting, cursing, whoring. What you'd expect. But not a hint of murder.'

'At what time did you pass the corner of Faitour Lane, do you know?'

He shrugged again. 'Not late. I'd heard the watch calling the hour of ten as I left the Bull, so it was likely some twenty minutes after that. Maybe a little longer. I was forced to make a detour to find my exit from the city and then retrace my steps in order to cross the Fleet.'

'And when you left this house earlier, to call for Master Jolliffe, everyone else was still here?'

'Yes. My stepmother was suffering from one of her headaches and had gone to bed. I remember, at supper, she asked Paulina – that's the housekeeper – to make her up a draught of poppy and lettuce juice and leave it in her bedchamber. My father went off to his study to read. As for

Cina and Fulk, they were huddled together, whispering, in a corner of the parlour. I couldn't hear what was said, but it was obvious from their general demeanour that they were arguing.'

'Arguing or quarrelling?'

'Both, I should say.' Jocelyn paused, then went on, 'They'd been at odds all day, ever since they'd returned from the maying expedition that morning. My own opinion, for what it's worth, is that Cina was trying to persuade Fulk to announce their betrothal and name the wedding day. He was resisting because I'm pretty certain he had no intention of marrying her. Why should he leg-shackle himself when he could inherit all my stepmother's money and property for himself without the encumbrance of a wife?'

'According to Mistress Broderer, Fulk claimed to have a betrothed back in Burgundy.'

Jocelyn gave a shout of laughter. 'Moonshine! If he did say that, it was for Alcina's benefit, to dampen her ardour.'

'Are you sure?'

'As sure as I can be. He informed me once that he had no intention of ever getting married, and I believed him.' The small, childish teeth bared themselves in another grin. 'Oh, Fulk liked women all right. I told you, he was after seducing Lydia Jolliffe. But women were like feathers in his cap to Fulk. They were conquests. His real predilection was for men.'

I heard Bertram draw in his breath and saw his eyes widen in disgust. But he was young. He would learn that, whatever the teachings of the Church, it takes all sorts to populate the world.

'Did he make advances to *you*?' I asked.

Jocelyn shook his head. 'Too chancy. He couldn't risk my stepmother finding out. She's very strait-laced about such matters. But I know he'd made suggestions to Brandon, and been repulsed. Mind you, he was very discreet. I doubt if many people were aware that he favoured the vice of the ancient Greeks. Wouldn't have believed it of him, I daresay, even if they'd been told.'

This had been a most instructive and enlightening digression, but I forced the conversation back on to its original path. 'So you don't have any idea where Fulk or Mistress Threadgold may have gone, or what they did, before arriving at the Needlers Lane workshop? You've heard about the scene there, I daresay?'

'Oh yes! Martha Broderer made all of us and the Sheriff's men free of it after the murder. Her intention was, of course, to implicate Cina and minimise Lionel's motive for killing Fulk.'

'And did she succeed, do you think?'

Jocelyn laughed shortly. 'It doesn't matter if she did or she didn't, does it? Not now that the Duke of Gloucester, God save the mark, has taken the matter out of the Sheriff's hands and put it in yours.' He spoke with a sudden return to his earlier hostility.

'You don't think me capable of solving the murder?' I enquired mildly.

He hunched his shoulders, not bothering to reply. 'I must be off,' he said, rising. 'The cordwainer's waiting for me and I promised him I'd not be late. It's been interesting talking to you, Master Chapman.' He made no effort to keep the sneer from his voice.

I didn't try to detain him, and he had barely left the room when the housekeeper, Paulina Graygoss, appeared in the doorway.

'It's nearly dinner time,' she announced grudgingly, 'and the mistress says to ask you and your friend' – she nodded briefly at Bertram – 'if you'd care to eat with William and me in the kitchen.'

I did not hesitate to accept, although I could tell by my companion's face that the arrangement was not at all to his liking. But it was too good an opportunity to miss. I could study and talk to William Morgan at close quarters. Mistress Graygoss, also.

'Thank you,' I said, almost before she had finished speaking. 'If we may, we'll follow you down.'

The main staircase descended into the back half of the

great hall, whose inner door gave access to the stone-flagged passageway mentioned by Master St Clair.

As she turned into the kitchen, the housekeeper remarked tersely, 'Dinner isn't ready yet. Don't get under my feet.'

'I see a door along here,' I said, 'that looks as if it opens into the garden. So if you don't mind, Master Serifaber and I will take a walk outside to clear our heads and work up an appetite.'

Mistress Graygoss indicated with a dismissive gesture of her hand that we could do as we pleased – she wasn't responsible for us – and disappeared into the smoke and steam of the kitchen. I jerked my head at Bertram and we proceeded along the passage, heading for the door at the end. Halfway, I gave him a nudge.

'There,' I said. 'Look!'

An archway in the wall revealed the lower treads of a flight of stone steps rising into the gloom above.

'The "secret" stair, do you think?' asked Bertram.

'Undoubtedly, I should say.' I glanced back over my shoulder. I could hear voices – or, rather, one voice raised in annoyance – but could see no one. 'Shall we go up and make sure?'

'You wouldn't dare,' Bertram protested, horrified. 'Mistress St Clair might be in her room.'

He refused point-blank to accompany me; so, much against his will, I left him on guard with instructions to whistle if anyone emerged from the kitchen.

I judged there were no more than a dozen steps, although I didn't count them, ending in a small landing about three or four feet square. To my right was a door, partially open, and when I put my eye to the crack, I could see that the room beyond was indeed a bedchamber. The door was almost on a level with the head of the bed, but this was hidden from my view by richly embroidered curtains. The walls, too, as far as I could make out, were hung with those tapestry-like embroideries that I had seen being made in the Needlers Lane workshop. Such light as there was on this rainy May morning came through two windows whose shutters and horned panes had been opened to the elements. Mistress St Clair evidently liked fresh air.

I listened carefully for a few seconds, but the silence was absolute. Cautiously, I eased myself around the edge of the door and found that I was standing, not on rushes, but on a thickly embroidered carpet that covered most of the floor. (The mistress of the house was obviously a keen promoter of her own wares.) Two large chests, their lids carved with an elaborate pattern of grapes and vine leaves, stood against the far wall and were full to overflowing with clothes. Neither was properly shut, and several errant sleeves, part of a velvet skirt, a gauze scarf and one or two belts spilled over the sides.

The bed, whose hangings, as I could now see, depicted the story of Daphnis and Chloe, occupied most of the space and was set on a raised dais in the centre of the room. With even greater trepidation than before, I parted the curtains and peered through, wondering what possible excuse I could offer if I should come face to face with Mistress St Clair, resting there. But, fortunately for me, the bed was empty. Its coverlet was dazzling, so thickly embroidered with all the glories of an English summer garden, including birds, bees and dragonflies, that its basic material was invisible. A small, plain cupboard stood to one side of the pillows and supported a candlestick and candle.

I withdrew my head and examined the inside of the door through which I had entered. There *was* a bolt – quite a substantial one – near the top and, when tested, I found it ran easily and noiselessly in the wards. But whether or not Judith used it to secure her bedchamber as often as was prudent I had no means of knowing. A similar inspection of the bolt on the inside of the main door of the room showed this to be stiff with disuse. She plainly felt herself to be under no sort of threat from inside the house itself.

I gave a final glance around before deciding that I had tried my luck far enough for one day, and descended the stair to find a worried Bertram peering anxiously upward, praying for my speedy return.

'I thought someone was coming just now,' he chided me.

We completed the length of the passage and, before letting ourselves out into the garden, I also examined the inside of this door for locks and bolts. There were two of the latter, bigger than those in Mistress St Clair's bedchamber and both kept well oiled. The lock, too, was substantial, situated just beneath the latch, but the key, large and extremely visible, hung on a hook alongside the door where everyone could reach it without difficulty. Anyone leaving the house on the night of the murder had only to ensure that this door and the two in Judith St Clair's bedchamber were unlocked and unbolted to be able to go and come back at will.

The rain had stopped at last. The ground squelched under our feet as Bertram and I crossed the soaked and pallid grass. A wood pigeon rustled through the branches of a tree, and although it was only mid-morning, the light was poor, cloaking the garden in shadow. We walked down the gently sloping central path to the little landing stage on the Thames. Gulls, chasing the herring boats upstream to Westminster, wheeled and called overhead with their sharp, staccato cries, and a kingfisher, disturbed by their commotion, flew up from its nest in the bank, a flash of iridescent green and blue. Brown-fingered seaweed slapped the shore, and the river itself, London's great highway, gleamed like polished metal under a watery shaft of sunlight that suddenly pierced the overhanging clouds.

The garden itself was planted largely for pleasure. If there was a bed of herbs and simples for the cooking pot, or one for home-made physic and medicines, I did not notice it at the time. Nor were any vegetables grown that I could see. This was a household sufficiently well-to-do to buy the best and freshest produce from the local tradesmen who daily trundled into London from their smallholdings in the Paddington fields, watered as they were by their crystal-clear springs and running brooks. The grass on either side of the path was starred with periwinkles and daisies and dotted with rose bushes, some of which were already in flower; the red of the *Rosa gallica* and the white of the

Rosa alba, and the pink and white of the sweet-smelling Damascus rose. There were also lilies and gillyflowers, and, near the river's edge, a willow tree, stooping to trail its branches close to the water.

Bertram was unimpressed; he was not a natural admirer of God's creation, and a chill spring breeze, blowing in off the Thames, soon had him urging me back towards the house and the warmth of its kitchen. As we retraced our steps along the path, I glanced up at the windows of the next-door house, now to my left, just in time to glimpse a face hurriedly withdrawn into the shadows. I stopped, staring enquiringly, but it did not reappear. Its owner I guessed to be that Martin Threadgold mentioned to me yesterday by Mistress Graygoss; the older brother of Judith St Clair's second husband and Alcina's uncle. Unless, of course, it was one of his servants.

'He doesn't keep but the one servant,' the housekeeper snorted disgustedly when I mentioned the sighting to her. 'A maid-of-all-work you might call her, although, myself, I'd term her a lazy slattern. But fortunately most of the rooms are shut up, so she's not a lot to do. Martin Threadgold's generally held to be a miser. Now, do you and the lad come to table. And one of you' – she rounded on two young girls who were busily pulling pots and pans off the fire – 'go and call William in to his victuals.'

These were obviously the young maids referred to by Godfrey St Clair, one small and undernourished, the other a well set-up piece who looked as if she could eat a man a day for breakfast. But, as is so often the case, appearances were deceptive: she was the shy, retiring one who merely toyed with her food and left half of it on her plate, while the skinny girl had wolfed her way through two bowlfuls of an excellent mutton stew before William Morgan finally deigned to obey the housekeeper's summons. He slouched in some twenty minutes later, sat down, offering no explanation for his tardiness, and banged the table with his spoon until the bigger of the two maids had filled his bowl with stew.

I was at last able to take a good look at the Welshman,

and saw that he was indeed only about my own age, some-where in his late twenties. (I was still some four months short of my twenty-eighth birthday.) William's swarthy skin, blue eyes, dark hair and long, thin mouth were features which, as I remarked before, could have comprised a pleasant whole if it had not been for his sullen expression and seem-ingly perpetual scowl. He said nothing, but I could feel his hostility as he regarded me across the kitchen table. I pushed aside my own bowl, leaned forward and gave him back scowl for scowl. I was about to make his even fiercer.

'Was it you, Master Morgan, who attacked me in Needlers Lane last night and warned me to mind my own business?'

The housekeeper's head jerked up at that and she spilled some of her food as she looked from me to her fellow servant. I thought I heard her breathe, 'You fool!' but I couldn't be certain.

'Why would I want to attack *you*?' the Welshman growled; but he bent closer over his plate and refused to meet my eyes. 'I don't know you.'

'You must have heard of me, both from Dame Judith and from Mistress Graygoss here,' I said, glancing at the house-keeper as I did so. Her expression confirmed my guess.

William shrugged. 'Perhaps I did – what of it? It's no business of mine what arrangements Duke Richard wants to make to solve this murder. Besides, how did I know what you look like? This morning was the first time we'd met.'

'You may have been looking out of a window when I spoke with Mistress Graygoss yesterday. Or she may have given you a description of me.'

He shovelled another spoonful of mutton stew into his mouth, which he wiped on the back of his hand. 'I was home all yesterday evening,' he said thickly.

'You didn't go into the city to see the festivities in honour of the Duchess Margaret, then?'

He shook his head vigorously. 'Why should I? Seen enough of them during the day.'

'So my attacker wasn't you?'

'Told you, I was home.'

97

I didn't believe him, but there was no point in arguing about something I was unable to prove. I changed the subject. 'What was your opinion of Fulk Quantrell?'

Another spoonful of stew was shovelled out of sight and swallowed before he answered. 'Not my place, is it now, to form o-pin-i-ons' – he gave ironic weight to every syllable – 'about my betters?'

I turned to the housekeeper. 'Did you have an opinion, Mistress Graygoss?'

She was busy stacking dirty dishes into piles and did not look up from her task. 'Fulk was a nice enough young fellow,' she replied in a colourless tone.

'Oooh! He was lovely,' the smaller of the two girls protested. 'Ever so kind. Talked to me a lot, he did.'

'What about?'

'Oh . . . Just things. My family, where I lived.' She giggled and blushed. 'Once he kissed me.'

'Take no notice of Nell,' Mistress Graygoss advised me calmly. 'She's a daydreamer.'

'I am not!' Nell expostulated wrathfully. 'Master Fulk did kiss me. Ask Betsy if you don't believe me. She saw him do it.'

The bigger girl nodded. 'He did kiss her, it's true, but it was only a peck on the cheek.'

'And did he talk to you, as well?' I asked her.

'No. He could never be bothered with me.'

This surprised me. Of the two, she had by far the more attractive face and figure – something I should have expected to weigh heavily with any man. But then I recalled that Jocelyn St Clair had accused Fulk of really preferring men to women, which might explain the matter. I turned once again to William Morgan, who had finished his meal and was picking shreds of meat from between his teeth.

'What *did* you think of Master Quantrell?' I pressed him.

He spat into the rushes covering the kitchen floor. 'I've told you, haven't I? He was the mistress's nephew. If she was fond of him, that was good enough for me.' He tossed back some ale, got up and went out.

Paulina Graygoss said, 'You musn't mind him. William is devoted to Mistress St Clair. His father was servant to Edmund Broderer, her first husband, and his mother died, I fancy, when William was born. Owen Morgan seems to have been a harsh father and by all accounts beat him a lot. When Judith married Edmund, she put a stop to all that – said she wouldn't have an unhappy child under her roof and made herself responsible for the boy. William's never forgotten it.'

A thought occurred to me. 'Of course, William must have known Fulk as a child. Didn't Mistress Quantrell live with her sister and Edmund Broderer for some years after her husband was killed?'

Paulina Graygoss nodded, sitting down again in her chair at the head of the kitchen table. Betsy and Nell, who were waiting to wash the dishes, subsided gratefully on to their stools, glad of a further respite from their chores.

'Now that you put me in mind of it,' the housekeeper said, 'yes, he must have done. Funny, he's never mentioned it. There again, William doesn't say much about anything. He's a deep one. Welsh people are usually very voluble, but not him.'

'Have you been Mistress St Clair's housekeeper for long?' I asked. Bertram was ogling Betsy. I let him get on with it.

'Ten years. I came to her just after she married her second husband, Master Threadgold. Alcina would have been about eight at the time. A rather sad little soul I thought her. But not surprising, I suppose. Her mother had died when she was one and she'd been brought up in that house next door with just her father and that brother of his for company. But with Mistress St Clair to pet her and make a fuss of her, she soon blossomed.'

'Mistress St Clair seems very fond of children. A pity she's never had any of her own.'

'A great pity,' the housekeeper sighed. 'But that's so often the way of things, isn't it? God has his reasons, I suppose, and it's not for us to question them. All the same, one can't help wondering . . . Of course, she had Fulk for six years,

99

but as I'm sure you know by now, her sister went to Burgundy in the Lady Margaret's train, taking Fulk with her.'

Mistress Graygoss was growing loquacious and I was careful to keep refilling her cup from the jug of ale still standing on the table. 'Wasn't that also the year her first husband died?'

'Yes, I believe it was. He was drowned, poor soul, in the river. Mind you, he was a bit of a drunkard by all accounts. Spent a lot of his time in various city ale houses. Lost his way coming home one night and fell in the Thames. Not an uncommon history.'

'He left Mistress St Clair a very wealthy widow,' I remarked in what I hoped was a noncommittal tone; but the housekeeper eyed me sharply.

'That's as may be, but you needn't read anything into that. She was very fond of him, I fancy. I think, too, she must have missed him dreadfully after he died and her sister went to Burgundy, or she wouldn't have married Justin Threadgold.'

'You didn't like Master Threadgold?'

'No, I did not,' was the positive answer. 'A vicious man, who didn't hesitate to raise his hand to both the mistress and his daughter. I reckon Mistress St Clair knew she'd made a mistake in marrying him almost before the marriage was a few months old. Certainly by the time I came to her. I've seen bruises on her body that would make your hair stand on end, chapman. And I fancy she often protected Alcina from his anger and took the punishment herself. She must have been very lonely indeed even to have thought of wedding him in the first place. And he took his fists to all the servants – well, to those that stayed. In the end, it was just myself and William Morgan. Fortunately, after they'd been married four years, Master Threadgold caught a bad fever and died of it. No one mourned him, believe me. Then, two years ago, the mistress married the master and became stepmother to young Jocelyn. He and his father are a nice enough pair.' Mistress Graygoss sighed again. 'But I was quite happy as we were.' She suddenly seemed to recollect herself and jumped to her feet. 'Now, what in the Virgin's name am I doing sitting here gossiping to you?'

She emptied her half-full cup of ale into the rushes and ordered Nell to bring a bowl of water, together with a bundle of twigs and some sand with which to scour the dirty pots and pans, making it plain that our conversation was at an end. But I was quite satisfied with what I had learned. I gave Bertram a nudge and ruthlessly dragged him away from his flirtation with Betsy.

'Will the family have finished their dinner yet?' I asked the housekeeper. 'If so, I'd like to speak to Mistress Threadgold.'

Nine

I was informed that the family had been served before us, and that a plate of apple fritters had been left in a chafing-dish for consumption after the mutton stew. I at once felt hard done by. I could have fancied an apple fritter, had any been on offer, a sentiment echoed by Bertram in a disgruntled whisper as we again mounted the stairs to the same parlour where, only an hour or so before, the family had breakfasted. This brief interval between meals seemed not to have blunted the appetites of either Master or Mistress St Clair or of Alcina, judging by the scarcity of food remaining on the table. (There was no sign of Jocelyn; presumably our talk had delayed him and he had not yet returned from the cordwainer's in Watling Street.)

'What now?' demanded our reluctant hostess, glancing up and becoming aware of Bertram and myself hovering just inside the door. 'Has Paulina given you your dinner? And if so, why are you still here?'

'Mistress Graygoss has fed us and fed us handsomely,' I said, nobly suppressing a complaint about the lack of apple fritters and averting my envious gaze from the one that was left in the chafing-dish. 'But I need to speak to Mistress Threadgold. Then my henchman and I will be on our way.'

The henchman gave an indignant yelp at this description, but I took no notice.

Mistress St Clair looked enquiringly at her stepdaughter.

'Oh, very well,' Alcina conceded, glancing at my companion's royal livery. 'I suppose I must.' (Bertram continued to have his uses.)

Judith St Clair rose to her feet. 'You'd better stay here,

then. Nell and Betsy can clear the table later, when you've finished talking. Godfrey, I'm sure you're wanting to return to Marcus Aurelius.' There was a hint of long-suffering in her tone.

'Indeed, my love!' he readily agreed, clapping me on the shoulder as he shuffled in his down-at-heel slippers towards the door. '"Love the trade which you have learned and be content with it,"' he advised, obviously quoting his favourite author. I wasn't quite sure whether or not this was meant for me and had a double-edged meaning, so I made no answer, merely seating myself opposite Alcina in the chair vacated by her stepfather. I turned to bid Bertram take the stool next to mine just in time to see him wolfing down the lone fritter that I had had my eye on.

'It was going cold,' he mumbled defiantly, meeting my accusing gaze.

I maintained a reproachful silence and turned my attention back to Alcina. 'Mistress Threadgold,' I said, 'I know that on the night of Fulk's murder you followed him to the Broderer workshop in Needlers Lane. I also know from Lionel Broderer and his mother what transpired there. After Master Quantrell had spoken to you so unkindly and left, you ran out after him. What happened then? Did you catch him up?'

Alcina shook her head. 'There was no point. He was in one of his moods. He was punishing me because I had spoken up for Brandon when he and Fulk had come to blows that morning, during the maying. Fulk was very jealous of me,' she added, her eyes filling with tears. (She had obviously worked things out to her satisfaction. In her own mind, her lover's reputation had been salvaged.) 'I knew he'd be off drinking for the rest of the evening, but I guessed he wouldn't go to the Bull, as he usually did, in case he ran into Jocelyn and Brandon. So it was of no use looking for him there. He could have been in any of the inns or ale houses in the city.'

'So what *did* you do?'

'I came back to the Strand and went next door to see my

uncle. I hadn't visited him for quite some while.' She grimaced. 'We . . . We're not all that fond of one another's company.'

When I asked her why that was, she shook her head, but I suspected the reason to be that Martin Threadgold had made no push to protect her from her father when she was young.

'How long did you stay at your uncle's?'

'For the rest of the evening, until it was time for bed.'

'Even though you don't like him?' queried Bertram, spitting an apple pip into the rushes.

She flushed. 'I didn't say I don't like him. "Not fond of his company" was the expression I used. We get on well enough provided we don't see too much of one another.'

'What time was it when you returned home?' I asked.

'Not late.' Was the answer just a little too emphatic? 'It was dusk, but not perfectly dark.'

'Was anyone about?'

'Paulina was in the kitchen. I looked round the door and said goodnight to her.'

'Was she alone?'

'Yes. At least, I didn't notice anyone else. I expect Betsy and Nell had gone to bed. They knew my stepmother wouldn't be needing them again because she had one of her headaches and had taken a poppy-juice potion. I don't know where William was. Off in some alehouse, I expect. My stepfather was in his room, reading. I heard him coughing. I called out to him as I passed his door, but he didn't answer. Once he gets absorbed in one of his folios, he's oblivious to everything else.'

'How did you get into the house?'

Alcina looked surprised. 'From the street, of course. Paulina always waits up until the watch has cried twelve; then she goes round and bolts all the doors. It's one of my stepmother's few rules – but the one she's strictest about – that everyone shall be home and in bed by midnight.'

'And does Mistress Graygoss make sure that all of you are in before she locks up?'

104

Alcina looked startled. 'I shouldn't think so. She'd have to peep into all the bedchambers, wouldn't she? And I hope she wouldn't do that.'

'Has anyone ever been locked out?' I queried.

Alcina shook her head. 'Not that I know of. Certainly not Josh or me. I told you: we respect my stepmother's few rules because she's generally very tolerant of the liberties we take.'

'What about William Morgan?'

'Oh, him!' Alcina was dismissive. 'I wouldn't know. That man's a law unto himself. But if he ever *has* spent a night out of doors, it's never been mentioned.'

'There's the so-called secret stair,' I reminded her. 'The one that leads from Mistress St Clair's bedchamber to the passageway outside the kitchen. Where, of course, there's a door that opens into the garden.'

'But to use that, even if it was left unbolted, you'd either have to climb the wall from the lane that runs between this property and my uncle's . . . Mind you, it's not impossible,' she admitted after a moment's hesitation. There are plenty of footholds on both sides. I've climbed it myself when I was a child and didn't mind hoisting my skirt above my waist. But I wouldn't attempt it now.' She smiled primly and cast down her eyes. I had no faith in this sudden modesty.

'Or?' I prompted

'Or you'd have to take a boat to the landing stage and walk up through the garden.'

'No postern gate or door?'

'No, nothing. I've told you.'

I switched to more personal matters. 'You were in love with Fulk Quantrell. But – forgive me – before he arrived from Burgundy, I understand you were contemplating marriage with Brandon Jolliffe.'

'I'm fond of Brandon, yes,' she admitted. 'I always have been; but I've never loved him the way I loved Fulk. I knew the very first moment I saw Fulk that he was the man I had dreamed about since I was a girl. He was so handsome!'

'Looks aren't everything,' Bertram announced truculently,

evidently deciding that it was time to speak up for the plainer members of our sex.

Alcina regarded him with scorn. 'Fulk had a nature to match his looks,' she declared. 'He was kind, generous and loving. He fell in love with me, too, right from the start. He told me so.'

Until he realized he didn't need you, I thought to myself; *until he discovered he could wind his aunt around his little finger and make himself heir to her entire fortune without having to marry you to get your share. Then you became just another source of entertainment to him, my girl, if you did but know it; another proof of his ability to take a woman away from any man he chose . . .*

But I held my tongue. It was not my place to disabuse her mind or wreck her dreams; and anyway, I guessed that Alcina was unhappy enough already without being brought face to face with the truth.

'Was Brandon Jolliffe very jealous of Master Quantrell?'

'He was upset, naturally. But he had always been more in love with me than I was with him. There was a time when he was even jealous of Josh, because he thought I favoured my stepbrother.'

'And did you?'

The large brown eyes opened wide and she laughed. 'Not in the way you mean. I'm fond of Josh, but I regard him as a member of the family.'

I struggled to recall all the various bits of information I'd been given. Finally, I said, 'Yet surely I'm correct in thinking that he hasn't been a member of this family for very long?'

Alcina grimaced. 'No, he hasn't,' she agreed wryly. 'It's barely two years since my stepmother married Godfrey St Clair and he and Jocelyn came to live with us. But from the beginning I've thought of Josh as my brother. Oh, I'm perfectly well aware that my stepfather would like the pair of us to marry, and of course, looking at it from his point of view, I can see the reason why. It would keep most of the Broderer fortune intact, except for what would go to Lionel, and Josh and I wouldn't have to share it between

106

us when Judith and Godfrey are dead. But I'm not in love with Josh nor he with me. We're friends, that's all.'

I shifted my ground again. 'Are you fond of your step-mother?'

Alcina glanced at my face, then away again. 'I suspect that Paulina's been gossiping, so you already know the answer to that. I'm deeply in my stepmother's debt.' She drew a painful breath. 'My father, as you've no doubt been told, was a very violent man. I think . . . I'm almost sure that Judith only married him for my sake. She must have known what he was like, how he treated my mother, because she'd already been living in this house a year when I was born next door. And, of course, her first husband, Edmund Broderer, had lived here all his life.'

'You think she married your father to protect you from his violence? Couldn't your uncle have done that?'

'He was as afraid of my father's rages as I was or as my mother had been. Uncle Martin was useless. He would never cross his brother, even though he was the elder by seven years.'

I mulled this over. Bertram was shuffling his feet, growing bored. He had probably envisaged a more exciting life as my assistant: more action, less talk. He caught my eye and nodded his head towards the door, indicating that it was time to go.

But I was interested in Alcina's view of Judith St Clair. Would a woman marry a man she knew to be violent simply to protect a child who wasn't even hers? Perhaps; a lonely childless woman who had not only been widowed, but who had also, in the same year, been deprived of the company of a twin sister and six-year-old nephew of whom she had been deeply fond. The young Alcina had filled a void in her life, and for that comfort, Judith might have been prepared to pay a heavy price. If so, her altruism had been rewarded. After only four years of marriage, Justin Threadgold had died.

I got to my feet and bowed briefly. 'Thank you, Mistress Threadgold; you've been extremely patient. We'll take our leave.'

Bertram was already at the door, bumping into Jocelyn St Clair as the latter entered the parlour, looking for his dinner.

'That damn man still hasn't finished my boots,' he fumed, 'and, what's more, I'm starving. It's way past dinner time. You still here, chapman? This is all your fault, you know. You and your bloody questions.'

I didn't stop to argue the point, but left him to Alcina's more soothing ministrations.

'What now?' Bertram asked hopefully as we stood outside the St Clairs' house in the Strand.

It was well past noon and a bright spring day. Ribbons of sunlight were dispersing the clouds, shredding them with streamers of gold and pink. Birds sang in the trees and bushes that overhung the garden walls, and all the cobwebs trembled with a myriad diamond drops. Everything was sharply delineated, the sun swinging high in the heavens like a newly minted coin, the air clear and fresh. I took a deep, appreciative breath.

'What now, chapman?' Bertram repeated impatiently, fixing his eyes longingly on a seller of hot spiced wine.

'First,' I said, suppressing a grin, 'we're going to call on Martin Threadgold, and then we're going to see if any member of the Jolliffe family is at home.'

My companion emitted a heartfelt groan. 'Not more talking?' he begged despairingly.

I gave him an admonitory cuff around the ear. 'Talking, my lad, is the only way of trying to find out what people think. And what people think very often influences the way they act. And how people act can sometimes lead you to the truth.' With which sententious piece of advice, I raised my hand and banged Martin Threadgold's knocker.

I had almost given up hope of my summons being answered when there was the screech of rusty hinges and the door opened just enough to reveal a diminutive woman with a pale face and protuberant blue eyes. She wore a patched gown of grey homespun and an undyed linen hood that had seen better days. The hair, escaping from beneath this last article of clothing, was grey and wispy, yet her skin was as unwrinkled and unblemished as that of a (presumably) much younger woman. She looked us both over with a lack of curiosity that bordered on indifference.

'Yes?'

I considered it would be a waste of time to try to explain our mission, so I just asked baldly to speak to her master.

The woman didn't cavil, but merely jerked her head. 'I'll fetch him. You'd better come in.'

Bertram and I followed her into a commodious hall which was larger and had once been far more impressive than that of the neighbouring house, but which was now sadly neglected. Paint was peeling from the carved, spider-infested roof beams, the rushes on the floor smelled stale and were alive with fleas, a thick coating of dust lay like a pall over everything, and the furniture amounted to no more than a chair and table spotted with age and the grease of candle droppings. This was the home, I decided, of either a miser or a man who no longer had any interest in life.

Yet when Martin Threadgold joined us, after a prolonged delay, he gave the impression of being neither of these things, merely an incompetent, middle-aged man overwhelmed by the complexities of a bachelor existence. The furred velvet gown he wore had originally been of a better quality than that sported by Godfrey St Clair, and his shoes were of the softest Cordovan leather, which bulged with every corn and bunion on his malformed feet. He was almost totally bald except for a fringe of grey hair, which gave him a monkish appearance, while a smooth, round, cherubic face endorsed this impression. The blue eyes had the slightly bemused stare of a bewildered child, but they also had a disconcerting habit of suddenly sharpening their focus.

'Forgive my tardiness,' he said in a surprisingly mellifluous voice, extending a bony hand. 'When Elfrida came to tell me of your arrival, I was closeted in the privy.'

I didn't doubt this. The smell of urine and dried faeces hung redolently on the air. Still, it was no worse than the stink of the river and the city streets.

'Master Threadgold,' I began formally, 'I'm hoping you'll agree to have speech with me. I'm—'

'I know who you are,' he cut in, smiling slightly. 'Paulina Graygoss called on us earlier with the warning that you would probably be wishful of speaking to me. So how can I help you? I know nothing whatever about this murder. I was here, in this house, in bed when it happened.'

'Oh, I'm not accusing you of killing Fulk Quantrell,' I said quickly. 'I haven't any reason to suppose you guilty; nor can I see that you had anything to gain by his death. But I would like to ask you one or two questions.' I glanced suggestively at the lack of seating and added, 'Perhaps we could go elsewhere?'

He followed my gaze, then beckoned Bertram and me to follow him, not through the door that obviously led into the interior of the house, but to a narrow stair hidden in the inglenook of the empty fireplace. A dozen or so treads took us into a tiny parlour not more than about six feet square, which boasted a narrow window seat, an armchair and a reading stand that could be adjusted to form a table. A rusting brazier, for cold winter days, stood in one corner, but walls and floor were bare. Spartan comfort for a man no longer young.

Master Threadgold indicated that Bertram and I should perch on the window seat and dragged the armchair round to face it.

'Now,' he said, 'how can I help you, Master Chapman?'

But something was intriguing me and I had to know the answer. 'Why do this house and that of Mistress St Clair contain these odd little semi-secret staircases?' I enquired.

Our host readily explained. 'These three houses – this one, Mistress St Clair's and the one belonging to Roland Jolliffe – were once part of the great Savoy Palace, which, as you must know, was burned to the ground during the Great Revolt almost a hundred years ago. But because they were at some distance from the main buildings, they escaped the flames; and when the rest of the land was eventually built over, they remained as separate dwellings. My theory is that, originally, they were used as whorehouses. The "Winchester geese" were ferried across from Southwark to the landing stage, brought up through the gardens and lodged here. Gentlemen requiring their services, but who needed to be a little more discreet than their fellows, would use the "secret" stairs. Of course, such niceties didn't bother the last occupant of the Savoy, the great John of Gaunt. He kept his mistress, Lady Swynford, in regal state in the palace itself, until she had to flee before Wat Tyler's vengeful mob . . . There, does that answer your question?'

I nodded and thanked him.

'So,' he continued, settling back in his chair, 'what else do you wish to ask me?'

I leaned forward, my hands resting on my knees. 'Master Threadgold, on the night that Fulk Quantrell was killed, your niece claims to have spent the evening here, with you. An infrequent occurrence, I gather. Was she here?'

He replied without the smallest hesitation. 'Yes, she was here. My housekeeper will also vouch for Alcina's presence, if necessary. She let her in.' He paused, frowning. 'I thought she seemed upset about something – Alcina, that is – but I didn't enquire the reason. I didn't feel it to be my business. All the same, I suspected it might have had to do with young Master Quantrell.'

'You knew she was in love with him?'

'Oh, yes. I don't have a lot to do with her or with the St Clairs, but I get all the gossip from Felice, who keeps both ears closely to the ground. She and Goody Graygoss aren't exactly friends, but Paulina can't resist chattering about her employers' affairs every now and then.'

'What did you think of Fulk Quantrell?'

Bertram was beginning to wriggle, trying to get comfortable on the window seat. I administered a warning kick on his shins.

'I didn't think anything about him,' was the tart response. 'I didn't know him, except by report, and that might well have been biased in either direction.'

'And what did report say of him?' I wanted to know.

Martin Threadgold shrugged. 'This and that. This was good, that was bad. I had no way of sifting truth from falsehood.' But his gaze, until now clear and direct, suddenly avoided mine. 'So you see, I'm afraid I can't help you or the Duke of Gloucester's representative, here.'

Bertram stopped squirming long enough to smirk importantly, then resumed his search for a less uncomfortable position.

'Why do you think Mistress St Clair – Mistress Broderer as she then was – decided to marry your brother?' I asked, relying on my old tactic of an abrupt change of subject to disconcert my listener. 'He wasn't a very pleasant man from all I've heard.'

'He was a very unpleasant man,' Martin admitted candidly. 'Took after our father, I'm afraid: a violent man, easily moved to anger. I was more our mother's son.'

'Were you afraid of your brother?'

'Everyone was afraid of Justin when he was in one of his moods or in his cups. But he could also be extremely charming if he chose. Judith made the mistake that so many clever women make about violent men: she thought she could manage him, that he would be different with her. I'm sure he convinced her that she was special, more intelligent, more beautiful, more . . . more . . . oh, more everything than Alcina's mother had been. He would have represented himself as a man whose patience had been sorely tried by an inferior intellect; by a foolish, feckless wife . . . But, of course, people like him never change.'

That, I reflected, was very true. The faults of youth rarely lessen with age. More often than not, they become exaggerated.

'Did Mistress St Clair and your brother never get on together after they were married?' I asked.

Martin Threadgold considered this carefully, then shrugged. 'Not often. Although they must have had their better moments. Justin planted that willow for her down near the river bank – the one you can see from this window.'

Bertram and I obediently slewed round and stared down

across the walls, into the neighbouring garden, at the tree we had noted earlier.

'Judith's always been very fond of it,' our host continued. 'On hot summer days, she likes to sit in its shade and look at the water.'

'After the marriage, I assume that your brother and niece went to live next door,' I said. 'Was there never any suggestion that Mistress St Clair might move into *this* house?'

Our host gave a dry laugh. 'None. Once Justin had seen the luxury and comfort of the Broderer home, there was no chance of him staying here. As a family, we were not well off. We had little money and our parents had allowed the house to go to wrack and ruin before they died. My father hoped that either Justin or myself would marry money. In fact, he pressed it on us as a duty. But he died a disappointed man. I have never fancied the married state, and Justin's first wife, Alcina's mother, brought no dowry worth mentioning with her. That was hardly surprising: no woman of means would have looked at us.'

'Until Judith Broderer.'

'Until, as you say, Judith began casting lures in Justin's direction. Mind you, he wasn't a bad-looking man and loneliness can play terrible havoc with a person's judgement.'

'Your niece thinks her stepmother may have married her father in order to protect her from his violent ways.'

Martin Threadgold raised sceptical eyebrows and looked down his nose. 'A girl's romantic notion, surely! But there! Women are strange creatures and capable of things that we men find it difficult to understand. Especially when the flux is on them each month.'

'You're certain that Mistress Broderer, as she then was, was fully aware of your brother's violent nature?'

Martin blew his nose in his fingers, inspected them with interest, then wiped them on his sleeve.

'Bound to have been,' he said. 'Edmund Broderer and my brother were . . . well, not exactly friends – no, never that – but drinking cronies. There's an alehouse, the Fleur de Lys, where they both drank, and they would, on occasions, help each other home when they'd drunk too much.' Martin sighed. 'Justin always reproached himself that he hadn't accompanied Edmund the night that Master Broderer fell into the river and drowned.'

Bertram's discomfort was now impossible to ignore, so I got to my feet. He joined me with alacrity.

'Thank you for your time, Master Threadgold,' I said, holding out my hand.

He took it, saying, 'I hope I've satisfied you as to my niece's whereabouts on the evening of the unfortunate young man's murder?'

I nodded to set his mind at rest, although only too aware that there were still questions that remained unanswered. Then I clapped Bertram on the back.

'Right, my lad,' I said. 'Let's go and see if we can talk to the Jolliffes.'

Ten

Luck remained with us in so far as Lydia Jolliffe was at home. The little maid who answered my knock informed us that the young and old master were abroad, but that the mistress was in her parlour at the back of the house. And it was to this first-floor chamber that Bertram and I were conducted in due course.

It was a light, airy room facing both south and east, with windows looking out over the river at the back and the gardens and houses that clustered around the Fleet Bridge to one side. Shutters had been flung open to let in the brightness of a spring afternoon that completely belied the dismal, rain-sodden start to the day. The May sun shone proudly from a soft blue sky, and rooks, like a handful of winter-black leaves, wheeled and cawed beyond the casement.

The woman who rose to meet us was a handsome, statuesque creature with high cheekbones and almond-shaped eyes of a deep, lustrous brown that gave her an almost exotic, foreign appearance. Her skin, by contrast, was extremely pale, but so skilfully had the white lead been applied that it needed a second glance to realize that its colour was due to artifice and not to nature. She was plainly but expensively gowned in green silk cut high to the throat, a modest touch that might have been more convincing had it not served to emphasize her magnificent breasts. Her hennin, draped with a white gauze veil, was one of the shorter kind which, at that time, had just begun to replace the 'steeple'. She wore a dark-green leather girdle, tagged with silver and a jade cross on a silver chain, but no other ornament. The effect was striking and she knew it. It was easy to see why Fulk Quantrell could well have been attracted to this woman, in spite of his natural inclination towards men. (But even as the thought entered my head, I realized that, so far, I had no other proof of Jocelyn St Clair's allegation.)

'Mistress Jolliffe?' I queried with a polite bow. A silly question, as it was extremely unlikely she could be anyone else.

She didn't bother answering. Those remarkable eyes raked me from head to foot; then she let a long, lazy smile lift the corners of her delicately tinted lips.

'So you're the pedlar I've been hearing about from Judith St Clair.' Her voice was languid. 'Roger, isn't it?'

'I'm honoured, lady, that you've taken the trouble to remember my name.' I smiled in what I hoped was a seductive manner (I, too, could play that sort of game) and drew Bertram forward. 'This is Master Serifaber, the Duke of Gloucester's man.'

Bertram was growing used to this introduction and no longer tried to look worthy of it, but he was too young, and obviously too green, to hold Mistress Jolliffe's attention for long. She gave him a quick nod and then turned back to me, resuming her seat in the room's only armchair and picking up her embroidery frame as she did so. But if she had hoped to present a demure, wifely tableau (Penelope at her loom), she was wasting her time. She never could, and never would, look domesticated.

'Sit down,' she invited, but as there was only one stool, Bertram was forced to stand, supporting himself against the nearest wall. I removed a lute from the stool, which was far too small for my hefty frame, and perched awkwardly on its edge. Mistress Jolliffe smiled slightly at my discomfort, but made no comment. The fragrance of wild flowers rose from the rushes on the floor and, with my new-found knowledge, I recognized the rich wall hangings as being embroideries rather than tapestries. I wondered if they had been purchased from the Broderer workshop; or had they perhaps been a gift?

While I made an attempt to settle myself, I took covert stock of Lydia Jolliffe, trying to guess her age. If she had a son as old as, or older than, Alcina Threadgold, she was probably in her late thirties or, more likely, early forties; but she was one of those women whose years sit lightly on them. Nevertheless, self-confidence and the mature curves of her figure led me to believe she was older than she looked.

'I'm forty, Master Chapman,' she said with a rich, full-throated laugh that made me start violently and blush. 'Men are so transparent,' she added, selecting a long pale-green silk thread from a pile on a small table beside her, and once more plying her needle in and out of the white sarcenet stretched on the tambour frame. 'It's so easy to tell what you're thinking. Women are much better at concealing their thoughts. Now, I presume you wish to ask me about the murder of Fulk Quantrell. What is it you want to know?'

I rubbed my nose nervously. 'Well, to begin with, may I ask where you were on the night of May Day or the early hours of the following morning, when the young man was killed?'

'That's simple. I was home here, in bed with my husband. He'll vouch for the fact.'

Of course he would, just as she would vouch for him. A wasted question but, all the same, one that had had to be asked.

'Did you like Fulk?'

She shrugged. 'I neither liked nor disliked him. He was Judith's nephew. A pleasant enough lad, prettily behaved, respectful to his elders. He had more to do with my son than with me. You must ask Brandon about him. Fulk was young enough to have been my son.'

Her last remark was more revealing than she had intended, containing as it did an undertone of bitterness.

'Did he find you attractive?'

Lydia glanced up sharply, then laughed again, but this time it was a high-pitched, artificial tinkle.

'Dear saints, of course not! I told you: I was old enough to be his mother.'

There it was again – that insistence on the difference in their ages. I ignored it. 'Was your husband jealous?'

She tossed her embroidery frame angrily to one side, missing the table and letting it fall among the rushes. 'Don't you listen to anything I say? He was my *son*'s friend, not mine.'

'Even so,' I urged, 'you must have formed some opinion of his character other than that his manners and general address were good. What was he really like, underneath, do you think?'

I could see her struggling with herself for several seconds – women, whatever she maintained, are just as easy to read as men on occasions – but whatever it was she had in mind to tell me, prudence eventually won. She managed to smile.

'Fulk naturally had his own interests at heart; what young man of eighteen does not? One could hardly blame him for taking advantage of Judith's infatuation.'

'Did you and Master Jolliffe approve of Mistress St Clair's decision to make him her sole heir?'

Lydia picked up the discarded embroidery frame and continued with her stitching. 'Roland and I neither disapproved nor approved. It was not our business.'

Very commendable, but not what Judith St Clair had told me. I wondered what the Jolliffes had really said to one another in the privacy of the marital bed, and to their neighbours.

'But you must have had some feelings about Fulk's stealing Mistress Alcina's affection away from your son.'

Once again there was that hesitation while she decided what to say; and once again she decided to lie. 'Whatever you may have been told, Master Chapman, there was never anything settled in the way of a betrothal between Brandon and Alcina. If anything, he was less fond of her than she of him. They were friends. Something might have come of that friendship eventually, who can tell? But somehow, I doubt it. Brandon is a very good-looking boy. He can have his pick of any girl in London.'

I accepted this. Who was I to argue with a mother's fond delusion? Instead, I asked abruptly, 'Do you happen to know where your son was on the night Fulk Quantrell was murdered?'

She gave me a quelling stare. 'My son is twenty years old: I am not his keeper. However, I imagine he was drinking in some tavern or other, probably the Bull in Fish Street, which seemes to be his usual haunt. And most likely with Jocelyn St Clair. But you must ask him.'

'Can you or your husband confirm the time he came home?'

'No, of course not! Did your mother know what time you got in at night when you were that age?'

When I had been twenty, my mother had not been long dead, and I had just abandoned my novitiate at Glastonbury Abbey and was busy making my way in the world in my new trade of peddling. But I naturally did not burden Mistress Jolliffe with this personal history. Instead, I enquired, 'Did you know that Fulk Quantrell and your son had come to blows during the morning's maying expedition? According to young Master St Clair it was about Alcina. Master Jolliffe accused Fulk of stealing her away from him.'

I saw anger and something else – something akin to fear – flash in and out of Lydia's eyes. But she replied with creditable calm, 'That's the first I've heard of it. Mind you, you shouldn't believe everything Jocelyn tells you. He was hoping – maybe he still is now that Fulk is dead – to fix his interest with Alcina himself. It would certainly please his father if he did.'

'Mistress Threadgold insists that theirs is a purely brother-and-sister relationship.'

My hostess curled her lip (not an easy thing to do, but possible). 'Alcina might think that, but I doubt if Josh does. He may not be in love with her, but he's too canny to let the best part of half a fortune go begging for want of a wedding ring. And he wouldn't allow a little thing like marriage vows to prevent him from continuing in his normal hedonistic way.'

119

She didn't like Jocelyn St Clair, that was evident. But what had been her real feelings concerning Fulk Quantrell?

'Master St Clair – young Master St Clair – maintains that Fulk really preferred men to women. Do you think that's true?'

After a moment's incredulous silence, there was an explosion of laughter so hearty and so genuine that it was impossible to doubt its sincerity. 'You're making it up!' she accused me as soon as she could speak.

I shook my head and glanced at Bertram, who confirmed my statement.

'What a liar Josh is then!' she gasped, wiping her eyes. 'Of course he didn't!' But she sobered abruptly with the realization that her merriment and vigorous denial of Fulk's sexual predilections pointed to the fact that she had known him a great deal more intimately than she had claimed. 'Well, I shouldn't think so, at any rate,' she amended hurriedly, 'judging by the number of female hearts he enslaved.'

'Including yours, Mistress Jolliffe?' I suggested softly.

'How dare you!' she breathed, and this time there was no mistaking the combined anger and fear in both look and voice. 'I'm a true and loyal wife, faithful in thought and deed to the most loving, gentle and considerate husband a woman could ever wish for.'

She could try pulling my other leg, too, but I still wouldn't believe her. Once again, she had betrayed herself by overemphasis. I was certain that she had fallen for Fulk's charms quite as heavily as his aunt and Alcina Threadgold had done. Maybe, deep down, she hadn't liked him – I felt instinctively that she was too astute to be taken in simply by a handsome face – but had found him attractive enough to want to go to bed with him. But had she succeeded in seducing him, or in allowing herself to be seduced by him? And if so, had Roland Jolliffe discovered her infidelity and set out to remove his rival? (I recollected Martha Broderer's words: '. . . he's devoted to Lydia. And he's the sort who'd never blame her if she ever did play him false. In his eyes,

120

she'd have been . . . led astray by the man.') On the other hand, if Lydia had set her cap at Fulk and been rejected, could her pride have been sufficiently lacerated for her to have murdered him?

A moment's reflection convinced me that this latter notion was unlikely: most people are too used to rejection of one kind or another in their lives to retaliate by killing. But it was not impossible. And where the crime of murder is concerned, experience has taught me that all possibilities must be taken seriously until proved to be false.

I was saved from making a spurious apology for this slur on Lydia's virtue by the sudden opening of the door and the arrival of two men whom I presumed to be the Jolliffes, father and son. The elder again recalled to mind Martha Broderer's description of a 'big, quiet man who don't say much about anything', and his identity was immediately confirmed by his wife, who exclaimed in a relieved voice, 'Roland! I'm so glad you're here!'

He went at once to stand beside her, putting a protective arm about her shoulders.

'Who's this?' he grunted, his eyes, of a clear Saxon blue, regarding me with open hostility.

Mistress Jolliffe explained and also introduced Bertram, carefully drawing attention to his royal livery. 'Master Serifaber, the Duke of Gloucester's man.'

It was a warning, or maybe a reminder, to her husband of royalty's involvement in this affair. Not that Roland Jolliffe appeared to be the sort of person who would make a fuss or throw his weight about. He was a large, loose-limbed, shambling man quite obviously some years older than his wife. His sartorial preference, like that of Godfrey St Clair, was for comfortable, well-worn clothes in sober shades of grey or brown, with a pleated tunic unfashion-ably long and a surcoat trimmed with fur that might once have been sable but now looked more like moth-eaten budge.

Brandon Jolliffe, on the other hand, was the very height of elegance in an extremely short tunic of russet velvet which revealed a modish expanse of loin and buttock encased in black silk hose (at least he didn't favour the parti-coloured variety). A magnificent codpiece, made of the same material as his tunic, sported several black satin bows, a promise to any woman interested in the joys to be sampled underneath. He had his mother's striking brown eyes, but other than that seemed not to favour either parent, being shorter and stockier than both, with light-brown hair carefully curled and pomaded. Yet his dandified appearance was at odds with the impression of strength given by his compact frame and powerful muscles.

He was more aggressive than his father and less intimidated by Bertram's livery. 'What do you mean by coming here and annoying my mother?' he demanded, squaring his jaw and jutting his chin.

'That will do, Brandon,' Lydia admonished him sharply. 'Master Chapman is making enquiries about Fulk Quantrell's murder; and I understand from Mistress St Clair that not only Duke Richard but also the Dowager Duchess herself has asked him to do so. Just tell him where you were on the night of May Day. That's all he wants to know.' She looked up at her husband and squeezed the hand that was still lying protectively against her shoulder. 'I've already explained that we were at home in bed, my love. We saw and heard nothing that could have any bearing on Fulk's death.'

I saw Roland's grip tighten momentarily, and the fleeting sideways glance of those blue eyes; but then he relaxed and nodded.

'Quite right,' he muttered.

I waited a second or two, but when it became apparent that this was all he intended to say, I turned back to Brandon.

He responded to my raised eyebrows with a grunt very like his father's and seemed disinclined to answer my unspoken query. A nudge from his mother, however, changed his mind.

'Oh, all right! I suppose I might as well tell you. I've nothing to hide. I was drinking in the Bull in Fish Street all evening with Jocelyn St Clair. Then I came home and went to bed. There's really nothing else to say.'

'Did you and Master St Clair leave the Bull together?'

He hesitated, watching me with narrowed eyes, wondering how much I already knew. He decided not to take a chance and opted for the truth. 'I left before Josh. We fell out. I'm afraid I went off leaving him to pay our shot.' Brandon did his best to look contrite, but failed.

'What did you quarrel about?'

He grimaced. 'Lord! I can't remember. It's more than two weeks since it happened. We were both in our cups, and I daresay at the stage where you're ready to take umbrage at almost anything.'

'Jocelyn St Clair says it was about your fight with Fulk Quantrell that morning, during the maying. He says he was trying to talk some sense into you – trying to convince you that Mistress Threadgold was the one doing the pursuing; that he didn't think Master Quantrell was serious in wanting to marry her.'

While I was speaking, Brandon's face had grown slowly redder until even his ears seemed suffused with blood. 'It's a fucking lie!' he burst out as soon as I'd finished, oblivious to his mother's presence and her furious exclamation of 'Brandon!'

'Are you denying that you and Jocelyn St Clair talked about Fulk Quantrell?' I asked.

'We might have mentioned him. It's possible. Probable, even. But I've told you: it's over a fortnight ago. Anyway, there's no law against it, is there? Discussing a friend.'

'A friend?'

'A mutual acquaintance then! All right! We neither of us liked Fulk. I agree we might have uttered a few harsh words about him. Perhaps Josh and I did fall out over something that was said. I've told you, I don't remember. But that doesn't mean I went out and murdered Fulk. I didn't see him that evening. Our paths never crossed.'

'Besides,' Lydia cut in smoothly, although I could sense the suppressed unease informing her words, 'if you recall, Master Chapman, I, too, have told you that my son had no reason to hate Fulk. He wasn't interested in marrying Alcina.'

Both husband and son gave her a brief, involuntary glance of surprise before hastily schooling their features to express agreement. The young man who, according to his mother, could have his pick of any girl in London, went so far as to puff out his chest like a barnyard cockerel, but I just felt sorry for him. If the Burgundian had been one half as handsome as reputation painted him, Brandon would have stood little chance in competition.

It was apparent to me that there was nothing more to be got out of either man – at least, not for the present. I turned once more to Mistress Jolliffe.

'Have you known Mistress St Clair for long?'

'I've known her ever since she came here as Edmund Broderer's bride some nineteen years ago. I remember it clearly because it was the month King Edward was crowned.' Lydia's tone became confidential. 'It's my opinion that Edmund only married her because his widowed mother died very suddenly, and he wasn't the sort of man who could fend for himself. He was thirty-one by then and in a fair way of business with that workshop of his in Needlers Lane. A good catch for any woman. He was a skilled embroiderer.' Lydia swivelled round in her chair and indicated the wall hangings. 'He had those made for me and did one panel with his own hands.' She seemed to consider this a signal honour. 'Roses and lilies, as you see, the lily being the flower of virginity and purity, the personal emblem of the Madonna.'

It was also an ancient fertility symbol, but I didn't mention that. Instead I said, 'You must recall Fulk Quantrell when he was a little boy. He lived next door to you for six years. Did he and Master Brandon ever play together?'

Lydia shrugged and glanced at her son. 'I suppose you might have played together. I can't remember. It's a long time ago.'

'He broke my wooden horse,' Brandon reminded her sulkily. 'You wouldn't let me play with him again after that.'

'So he did. I'd quite forgotten. I went round and complained to his mother, but Veronica was a haughty, stuck-up piece, thinking herself better than anyone else because she'd been in the employ of the King's sister (although, at that time, some people might have considered poor old Henry as still the rightful king). Shortly after, she left and went off to Burgundy in Margaret's train. That wasn't very long after Edmund was drowned. It was weeks, you know, before they found his body, stripped completely naked. The river scavengers had discovered him first and taken all his clothes and personal belongings. Every last thing. Judith told me she was only able to identify him by various moles and the peculiar shape of his feet.'

'You also knew Mistress St Clair's second husband, then, Justin Threadgold?'

This was the sort of questioning that Lydia could understand and even appreciate. A good gossip about her neighbours was fun. She relaxed in her chair, while her son and husband joined Bertram in looking bored and resigned.

'Roland and I knew both him and his first wife, a poor little dab of a woman. Mind you, Justin was a bully and far too free with his fists; but timidity only encourages that sort of man. If he'd been *my* husband, he'd have had something more to contend with than the grovelling and terrified acceptance he was used to. His brother couldn't, or wouldn't, stand up to him, either – not even to protect his sister-in-law and niece.'

'Why do you suppose Mistress St Clair married him, then?' I interrupted. 'She was a closer neighbour even than you. She must have known what he was like.'

Lydia Jolliffe spread her hands, the left still holding her tambour frame. 'I've asked myself that question many times, Master Chapman, and never arrived at a satisfactory answer. Loneliness perhaps? Because he was there and available? Probably both of those things. In my experience propinquity and availability often have more to do with marriage than love and romantic passion. At least,' she added hastily, 'in older people. Second marriages. Of course, I was very young when I married my dear husband. Ours was a love match.'

Roland Jolliffe gazed fondly down at his wife and once more reached for her hand, pressing it affectionately. Lydia smiled up at him in a way that fairly turned my stomach. I was glad to note that Brandon was also looking queasy.

I decided it was time for Bertram and me to take our leave. I had discovered everything I was likely to find out here. The two elder Jolliffes would cover for one another whilst swearing that Brandon had no motive for killing Fulk Quantrell. Moreover, it was time that I – and, of course, my assistant – took stock of the information we had already gathered. I feared it would prove to be of no great use, but there might be among the dross a small nugget of gold that I had so far overlooked.

I rose from the stool, disentangling my long legs from one another, and again came under scrutiny from Lydia Jolliffe.

'If you need to call again, Master Chapman,' she said suavely, also rising and smoothing the green silk gown over her ample hips, 'please feel free. Something might occur to me that I've forgotten.'

I thanked her, managing to ignore the hand she extended for me to kiss, and beat a hasty retreat, aided and abetted by a more than willing Bertram. I did hear a phrase that could have been 'bad-mannered oaf' as I closed the parlour door behind me, but assured myself that it must have been intended for my companion.

'Can we go back to the Voyager now?' that young man pleaded as we once again found ourselves amid all the afternoon bustle of the Strand, now fairly overflowing with the two-way traffic of this busy thoroughfare linking Westminster to London. 'My legs are aching and I'm sick of the sound of people's voices.'

I laughed. 'Does this mean you wouldn't fancy a full-time position as my right-hand man?'

He shook his head vigorously. 'I'd rather go back to Yorkshire with the Duke.'

'I'm put down, indeed,' I said with a grin, and took him by the elbow. 'Come on. A beaker of Reynold Makepeace's best ale will make you feel better and restore your temper.'

126

We were almost at the Fleet Bridge when I felt a tap on my shoulder. Turning, I found myself looking down at Martin Threadgold's diminutive housekeeper.

'Mistress!' I said. 'What can I do for you?'

'If Master Threadgold wants us to return, I'm off to Baynard's Castle,' Bertram muttered mutinously.

Martin Threadgold *did* want us to return, but not, it appeared, until later.

'Master says will you come back this evening,' the woman said breathlessly. She must have been running to catch us up. 'After supper, he says. He has something he wants to tell you.'

'Can't he tell me now, while I'm here?'

'After supper is what he said and is what he meant. He's having a lie-down now. Sleeps in the afternoon, he does.' The woman turned away. 'He'll expect you after supper.' And, having delivered her message, she was gone, pushing between the crowds and quickly vanishing from sight. I swore softly. If the old fool had something to impart, why couldn't he tell me at once? I was wary of postponements. They could be dangerous.

Bertram grabbed my arm, afraid I might be tempted to return to the Threadgold house. 'Come along!'

Reluctantly I obeyed, but as I did so, I glanced back over my shoulder. Lydia Jolliffe was standing at the open side window of her parlour, staring in our direction, towards the Fleet Bridge.

Eleven

As I turned to follow Bertram, I collided heavily with a man coming in the opposite direction: William Morgan. His body was unexpectedly solid and well muscled, although why I should find this fact surprising I had no idea. I knew that the Welshman was only my own age in spite of the fact that, for some reason best known to himself, he took pleasure in acting older than he really was.

'Look where you're going, chapman,' he growled, surly as ever.

I apologized, wondering where he'd been. But it was no use enquiring – he would take a perverse delight in not telling me, and it was, in truth, none of my business – so I nodded a brief farewell and caught up with Bertram as he entered Fleet Street from the Strand.

'What do you think Master Makepeace will give us for supper?' he asked longingly, striding out in the direction of the bridge.

'Not so fast,' I said as we negotiated the slight dog-leg bend by the Church of St Dunstan-in-the-West. 'While we're here, I might as well question a few of the beggars. Someone could have seen something the night of Fulk's murder. Oh, admittedly it's probably a forlorn hope,' I added, forestalling Bertram's protest, 'but I'll have to do it sooner or later if I'm to satisfy myself and our royal patrons that I've left no stone unturned to find Fulk's murderer.'

'And under stones is where this lot belong,' my companion pronounced censoriously. He gave me a withering look. 'You don't really expect to get any information out of beggars, do you? Even if they did see something, they wouldn't tell *you*. But the chances are they didn't. They were all roaring drunk or off picking honest revellers' pockets or spending their ill-gotten gains in the local whorehouses. For goodness sake, Roger, you're wasting your time!'

I noted that I had become 'Roger' and not the more respectful 'Master Chapman' that he had accorded me earlier, a symptom of Bertram's increasing familiarity which, in its turn, was breeding contempt. Master Serifaber's cocksureness was growing too fast for my liking. I drew myself up to my considerable height.

'I think this is where we part company,' I told him firmly. 'You can return to Baynard's Castle and inform Master Plummer that I no longer have need of your services.' And without giving him a chance to reply, I strode off up Faitour Lane.

It was still only mid-afternoon, and many of the beggars had not yet returned from their daily stamping grounds, those jealously guarded patches of territory within the city walls where they sat all day rattling their cups and displaying the various disabilities that accompanied their hard-luck stories. But there were a few about, squatting in the doorways of houses and brothels, counting the contents of their begging bowls, removing their eye-patches and the filthy, blood-stained bandages that had bound their balled fists into pathetic 'stumps'. I even saw a man release one of his legs from a complicated sling that had held the lower half strapped to his buttocks, while on the ground beside him lay the crutch that had supported him throughout the morning. Don't misunderstand me: there were, and still are, many thousands of genuine beggars in every city in the kingdom; but hoaxing people with fake injuries is an easy way of earning a living that will always attract rogues and vagabonds. And why not? It's each man for himself in this dog-eat-dog, rich-and-poor world.

I made my enquiries, but for the most part I was met with blank-eyed stares or uncomprehending shakes of the head that might have been genuine or simply assumed – I had no way of telling. Even those who showed some intelligent interest

just laughed and pointed out that murders were an everyday
– or, rather, an every-night – occurrence in any big town and
its environs; certainly in London. Besides, it was difficult
enough, they said, to remember what had happened last night,
let alone more than two weeks ago. I began to realize that
Bertram had been right to accuse me of wasting my time.

But one should never give up too easily, so I hung around
for a while longer until I felt that I had outstayed my
welcome. Indeed, it became apparent from the mutterings
and squint-eyed looks I was getting that the faitours' tolerance was wearing thin. I decided the time had come to
concede defeat and retreat to the Voyager, where a cup of
Reynold Makepeace's ale would help to restore my good
humour. I thanked the last beggar I had spoken to – a poor
scrap of humanity with thinning hair and pock-marked skin
– and had already turned back towards Fleet Street when
someone laid a hand on my arm.

'You askin' about that fellow what 'ad his head bashed
in a fortnight or so ago?' a woman's voice enquired.

I stopped and glanced down into a delicate, flower-like
face framed in the striped hood of the London whore. She
must, I thought, be making a fortune for the pimp or brothel-
master who owned her, and reflected sadly that in five years
or less those pretty features would be coarsened and ravaged
by disease.

'Handsome fellow,' I said. 'Foreigner, name of Fulk
Quantrell.'

'That's him.' She nodded, smiling up at me with big,
sapphire-blue eyes.

'You knew him?'

''E paid fer my services a couple o' times, yes. 'E was
after the boys, too. The young ones.'

'He told you his name?'

'Why shouldn't he? I liked him. 'E liked me. Told me 'e
was going to be rich one day. Richer 'n 'e was already. Said
if I were patient, 'e'd rescue me from this hell-hole – me and
some young lad 'e'd got 'is eye on. Liked men and women
equally, he did, just so long as they were young and pretty.'

I reflected that Lydia Jolliffe hadn't known Fulk as well as she thought she did.

'Free with his money, was he?' I suggested.

The girl nodded. 'Mind you, didn't do me much good, did it? What I earn goes to Master Posset. 'E's my pimp. And it weren't no good giving me gifts.' She smiled sadly. 'Offered me 'is thumb ring, Fulk did. Lovely stone. All different colours and set in silver. But I told him he'd better keep it. It'd be stolen in a trice. The whorehouses ain't got no locks nor bolts on the doors. Can't hide nothing. But he *would*'ve give it me. And other things. Said 'e owned a 'broidery workshop where they kept a stock of jewels and such to sew on clothes.'

I grimaced. It would seem that Fulk Quantrell had not been above appropriating to himself an importance that he had neither deserved nor possessed.

'What about the night Fulk was murdered?' I asked. 'Do you know anything about that?'

'He'd been with me that night. Said 'e'd come straight from St Dunstan's. Some saint's day, he told me. Some saint of the place where he come from.'

'Saint Sigismund of Burgundy?' I suggested.

She pursed her soft, rosebud mouth. 'Mmm . . . could've been. Something like that.'

'What time did he leave you, do you know?'

'Late, I reckon. It was dark. Most of the wall cressets had been doused. I went with him to the door.' She broke off to indicate a mean-looking house a few yards distant, implying it was where she worked.

'Did you notice anyone follow him as he left?'

The girl wrinkled her brow. 'Strange . . . I'd forgotten, but now you mention it, I did fancy I saw someone walking behind 'im as he got further along towards Fleet Street. Didn't think nothing of it at the time. There's always folk moving about round 'ere at night.'

'What did this figure look like? Can you remember?'

'Long cloak, 'ood pulled right up,' she answered promptly. 'But then, there's nothing in that. It were a cold night. I

131

didn't hang around. Fulk was my last customer. All I wanted was my bed.'

'How did you learn of his death?'

'One o' the other girls told me next morning. She said, "You know that lad what comes here reg'lar an' always asks fer you? Well, he's been found battered to death down the lane." I went out at once, just in time to see Joe Earless and little Sam Red Eye moving the poor lad's body round the corner, into Fleet Street. "Why you doing that?" I asked 'em. "'E was right on our doorstep," little Sam said. "We don't want no Sheriff's men poking around our house." And I suppose,' the girl added fair-mindedly, 'they don't. The good Lord alone knows what they got salted away in that shack o' theirs.'

'Where do they live, this Joe Earless and little Sam Red Eye?' I asked.

She pointed at the other side of the road, to a noisome, lean-to hut which seemed to be made chiefly of bits of wood, branches of trees and ancient rags all held together by a thick coating of dried mud, erected against the outside wall of another older but equally dilapidated building. 'Over there. That's Joe Earless sitting on the ground outside, counting the day's takings.'

I thanked my beautiful little whore – who offered herself free of charge, 'for a nice big man like you', if ever I wished to avail myself of her services – and picked my way across the filthy lane to where a one-eared man was sitting in the dirt, dropping a succession of coins, one by one, into a canvas bag.

'Master Earless?'

The smell of him, like ancient, rotting fish, was over-powering even in Faitour Lane, not renowned for its perfumed zephyrs.

''Oo wants ter know?' He raised a belligerent, weather-beaten, pock-marked face, but seemed reassured by my shabby clothes and mud-spattered boots.

I explained my errand as briefly as I could, laying great emphasis on the fact that my enquiries were being made on behalf of the Dowager Duchess of Burgundy, who had been deeply attached to the young man in question. Even so, Joe Earless subjected me to a long and piercing scrutiny before grunting, 'You don't look like a Sheriff's man, I must say.'

'I'm not,' I said. 'I've been told you and your friend had nothing to do with the murder itself.' Not entirely true, of course, but I permitted myself the odd lie or two (or three or four or more, if necessary) in the cause of searching out justice. 'You and he merely moved the body round the corner into Fleet Street.'

'Tha's right.' He stood up, stretching and shaking out his flea-ridden rags – several of the little beasts hurled themselves straight at me – and the stench made me take a hasty step backwards. 'Right 'ere, 'e was. Right on our doorstep.' (Which was one way, I suppose, of describing the pile of rotting debris in front of the flap of material covering the hovel's entrance.) 'I said to Sam, "We've gotta move 'im," I said. "Look at them clothes," I said. "'E's someone, 'e is. Sheriff's men'll be makin' enquiries about 'im, swarmin' all over the place. You mark my words if they're not. We'd best move 'im," I said. Sam agreed, so we did. Round the corner into Fleet Street.'

"'Ere! 'Oo you talking to, you daft bugger?' demanded a small man of stunted growth, detaching himself from a party of returning faitours and addressing my companion. He regarded me with a pair of hostile eyes, the white of the left one being definitely tinged with red. The smell of him was even more pungent than that of his friend; and at some time or another his nose had been broken and mended at a very odd angle. He was completely bald, except for a few wisps of coarse hair adhering to the crown of his head. But what fascinated me about him most of all was a large agate-and-silver ring on the thumb of his right hand. I was filled with a sudden suspicion that amounted to total certainty.

I turned back to Joe Earless. 'When you found the body, nothing had been taken from it, had it? You two stripped it of any jewellery and money it possessed.'

'What you sayin'?' Joe demanded, his manner undergoing

a rapid transformation from friendly to hostile. 'You accusin' us of being thieves?' The righteous indignation he managed to drum up was wonderful to behold and made me want to laugh.

Little Sam, seeing which way the wind was blowing, didn't bother with words, but gave a piercing whistle. It was obviously a prearranged signal recognized by all the beggars in the street. They appeared suddenly from every direction and began to encircle me in an ugly, muttering crowd. Too late, I realized that once again I had failed to bring my cudgel with me, not wishing to appear intimidating when calling on respectable folks, but stupidly laying myself open to attack from any unfriendly quarter. I had my knife in my belt, it was true, but I had no desire to wound anyone unnecessarily. Besides, the sight of it might inflame the mob of faitours even further.

They were all around me and beginning to close in. I could feel their stinking breath on my face and on the back of my neck. My one advantage was that I was taller and stronger than any of them. I braced myself for the first assault . . .

'Hold! In the name of the King!' yelled a voice. And there was Bertram striding towards us, his Gloucester blue-and-murrey livery easily mistaken for King Edward's murrey and blue, the emblem of the white boar for that of the white lion. 'This man's my prisoner,' he continued, forcing his way through the beggars and laying a hand on my arm. 'Got you, my man! You're under arrest. Come quietly and you won't be harmed.' He was clearly enjoying himself at my expense, and who could blame him? I had been rude and he was taking his revenge.

I went docilely enough until we were clear of Faitour Lane and across the Fleet Bridge; then I clipped his ear. But he was laughing so much by this time that I don't think he felt it (although it may have stung him later).

'Well, aren't you going to thank me?' he gasped as soon as he could speak. 'And what a good job for you that I hadn't gone back to Baynard's Castle as you instructed.'

134

Ruefully I acknowledged the truth of this statement. 'But how did you know what was happening?'

Bertram grinned. 'I followed you. Kept my distance, of course. Watched you talking to that girl and then cross over to that one-eared fellow. Did you discover anything?'

'You mean apart from the fact that it's unsafe to go out without a cudgel anywhere in this city?' We passed under the Lud Gate and jostled with the lawyers around St Paul's, before proceeding along Watling Street to Budge Row.

'I'll tell you about it,' I promised, 'over supper.'

'You mean you're not dismissing me after all?'

I clapped him on the shoulder. 'How could I possibly dismiss you, when you've just saved my hide?'

Over a dish of beefsteaks cooked in red wine and dressed with an oyster-and-cinnamon sauce, I told Bertram everything I had learned in Faitour Lane. Mellowed by the food and ale, he conceded that I hadn't, after all, wasted my time and, with even greater magnanimity, that perhaps I knew more about investigating a case of murder than he did.

'So,' he said, as we started on a curd flan and our second jug of ale, 'you reckon it wasn't the murderer who stripped Fulk of all his valuables, but these two beggars who moved his body? Joe Earless and Sam Red Eye.'

'I'd stake my life on it. Sam Red Eye was wearing the thumb ring described to me by the little whore. Mind you, I only saw the one piece, but I'd bet my last groat there were other things belonging to Fulk hidden somewhere inside that hovel.'

'And what do you think that means?'

I sighed. 'Not a lot, except as confirmation of what we have rather taken for granted: that Fulk's murder was not a random killing by thieves, but by someone who wanted him dead for a specific reason – someone who didn't even stop to strip the body in order to make it look like a robbery.'

'Well, I suppose that's something,' Bertram said, a little dashed. He had obviously been hoping for some far greater revelation, some brilliant deduction and insight on my part that would instantly solve the whole case. 'So what about the others? Mistress St Clair and her family, the Jolliffes, Martin Threadgold. Did you learn anything from them?'

'They all said more or less what I would have expected them to say in the circumstances. There was a good deal of animosity towards Fulk, but then we knew that already.' I poured more ale into my beaker. 'One thing intrigues me, however, and that's the promptness with which the St Clairs' new will was rewritten in its original form. It's not much over two weeks since the murder, but both Judith and Godfrey said that the bequests had been restored as they were before Fulk arrived on the scene. I can only think that perhaps Judith had started to regret her impetuosity in leaving everything to her nephew, even before Fulk died.'

'Conscience, you mean?'

'Yes, probably . . . I wonder what it is Master Threadgold wants to tell me.' I shifted restlessly. 'Why couldn't the old fool say while I was there? I hate delays. They're dangerous.' I thought of Lydia Jolliffe standing at her window and watching Martin Threadgold's housekeeper running after me. An intelligent woman, it shouldn't have been too difficult for her to put the right interpretation on what she had witnessed. The thought forced me into making a decision. 'As soon as we've finished eating, I shall go back. I shan't wait until this evening.'

But my good intentions were destined to be no more than that. The sight of Reynold Makepeace anxiously pushing his way through the crowded ale room, and heading in my direction, filled me with foreboding. And I was right to be worried. A summons to Westminster Palace, where, it appeared, another great banquet was being held in honour of the Dowager Duchess – the poor woman would be as fat as a sow by the time she returned to Burgundy – had been brought by Timothy Plummer himself, no less, released temporarily from his relentless vigil against all those imaginary French spies and assassins in order to make sure that I obeyed. The invitation did not include Bertram.

'Is this really necessary?' I demanded peevishly as I mounted my horse, which, on Timothy's instructions, had already been led out of Reynold's stables and saddled and bridled. (I could tell that the beast was as annoyed about the disturbance as I was.) 'I saw Duke Richard only yesterday. He doesn't usually interfere like this. In fact, he promised to leave me alone.'

'Oh, stop grouching,' Timothy advised brusquely. He was no more pleased to be used as an errand boy than I was to see him. 'An important guest has particularly asked to meet you again.'

'Who? And what do you mean, again?'

'Wait! You'll find out,' he snapped, and I could coax nothing further out of him. Something had got under his skin.

As we jogged along the Strand, I cast a frustrated glance at Martin Threadgold's dwelling. I could see no sign of life except for William Morgan walking up the narrow lane between the two houses. Even as I looked, he scaled the St Clairs' garden wall with perfect ease, dropping down the other side and out of sight. What, I wondered, had he been up to? He was a man whose every action filled me with disquiet. I was still convinced he had been my attacker of the previous night.

Westminster Palace, when we finally reached it (not without difficulty, I might say, as so many people were making their way there) was a whirlpool of noise and lights – every cresset, every torch, every candle aflame – with servants scurrying all over the place, shouting, issuing instructions, countermanding instructions, falling over their own feet and everybody else's amidst an overpowering smell of roasting meat. God knows how many swans, peacocks, capons, cows, sheep, pigs had been slaughtered to make this feast. If the Burgundian ambassadors and courtiers failed to be impressed by such a display of grandeur, then they could never be impressed by anything.

Not that I was allowed to share in the occasion any more than I already had. Having seen my horse comfortably stabled, Timothy led me along a number of narrow corridors, up and down various flights of steps until he eventually, and thankfully, left me in a small, but richly furnished ante-room which, judging by the raised voice coming from behind the closed inner door, was part of a suite of rooms occupied by someone of great importance. (Well, judging by the way in which he was browbeating some unfortunate inferior, *he* thought he was of great importance, which is not, of course, always the same thing.) The voice was vaguely familiar, and yet I could not immediately recognize it. Nor was I able to understand exactly what was being said, although I caught a word here and there. But before memory had time to jog my elbow, the inner door was flung open by a page and a young man swept through, both hands outstretched.

'Master Chapman! Roger! Naturally you remember me!'

His confidence and vanity were, alas, not misplaced. Although I had last seen him when he was a bedraggled and penniless fugitive, escaping the clutches of his elder brother, King James III of Scotland, I knew him at once: Alexander Stewart, Duke of Albany.

'Your Highness.' I bowed, and he gave me his hand to kiss. 'I thought you were in France.'

'I was! I was!' he exclaimed exuberantly, moderating the thick Scots tongue for my West Country ears. 'And very civilly my dear Cousin Louis treated me – that goes without saying. But now, as you see, I'm enjoying the hospitality of my dear Cousin Edward.' He grinned broadly. 'There are reasons for this change of venue which I feel sure a clever fellow like yourself will be able to fathom.'

I made no reply except to bow and say, 'I'm honoured to see Your Grace once again, and in such good spirits, too.'

He punched me on the shoulder (I did wish people would stop doing that!) and said, 'Of course you are. Just as I'm delighted to be able to call you friend.' He paused, awaiting my reaction to this signal honour. When none came, he looked disappointed before producing the winning card from his sleeve. 'But think how far more honoured you will be when it's the *King* of Scotland who invites you to his court.'

I had, indeed, guessed which way the wind was blowing

as soon as I'd clapped eyes on him. He might have been well received at the French court, but Louis XI, that reportedly shrewd and wily monarch, would do nothing that might upset his Scottish ally, King James, who, with his constant harrying of the northern shires, was distracting English attention from its ties with Burgundy. It made sense, therefore, that there should be some devious scheme afoot, hatched by Albany and King Edward, to replace James III with his renegade brother.

I bowed. 'I wish Your Grace every success in your enterprise, whenever it may be.'

The Duke beamed, but the eyes above the smile were hard and calculating.

'A year perhaps,' he said. 'Maybe a little more, maybe less. 'But rest assured that I shall remember you, Master Chapman, when the time comes for me to ascend the Scottish throne, as I shall remember certain of your friends across the Irish Sea.'

I hurriedly disclaimed any such friends and silently suppressed a shudder: the Duke's promise sounded more like a threat to me, but naturally I couldn't expect him to see it that way. So like the craven that I was, I thanked him profusely for his interest and, sensing that the interview was at an end, backed out of the ante-chamber just as the trumpets began sounding for the start of the feast. In fact, I backed straight into the Earl of Lincoln, who had arrived to escort Albany to his place at the high table among the rest of the honoured guests.

'Roger!' Luckily, I divined the Earl's intention just in time and moved before he could slap me on the back. 'Have you discovered our murderer yet?'

'Not yet, Your Highness. But I'm getting closer,' I assured him, lying through my teeth.

'Good! Good! My uncle is relying on you. My Lord,' he went on, turning to the Duke, 'let me conduct you to your seat in the great hall.'

The two men swept past me, the candlelight gleaming on their satins and velvets, glinting on their jewelled buttons and rings. My moment of glory – if you care to call it that – was past. I was forgotten as easily as I had been recalled to mind. I had been the object of Albany's graciousness and gratitude just long enough to make him feel that he had repaid a debt (or so I devoutly hoped), and now I was free to go.

I rescued my horse from the royal stables and rode back along the Strand, my one object now to hear what Martin Threadgold had to say, and hoping against hope that he had not, in the meantime, changed his mind.

The late promise of the day had been fulfilled. The clouds were banked high in the evening sky and the dying sun made paths of ghostly radiance across the quiet gardens. It caught the tops of the shadowed trees, lighting them, like lamps from within.

As I reached the Fleet Street end of the Strand, I could see a cluster of anxious people outside the first of the last three houses, all trying to calm the figure in their midst. And that figure was a small woman in floods of noisy tears.

My heart and stomach both plummeted as I recognized Martin Threadgold's housekeeper.

Twelve

I hurriedly dismounted and, leading the horse, approached the group. Apart from Martin Threadgold's housekeeper, this turned out to consist of Lydia and Roland Jolliffe, the St Clairs, Paulina Graygoss and, somewhat surprisingly, Lionel Broderer. Of William Morgan and the younger members of both families there was no sign.

'What's happened?' I asked.

No one seemed to find my sudden appearance remarkable. (I think they had come to regard me rather like the Devil in a morality play, always popping up when least wanted or expected.) Judith St Clair gave me a resigned look and said, in an even more resigned voice, 'Master Threadgold is dead.' She finally managed to hush the little housekeeper's noisy sobbing with a curt word or two, which she palliated with an arm about the woman's shoulders. 'My dear Mistress Pettigrew, you have had a shock, but you must pull yourself together. Many people die in their sleep, you know. It's not uncommon, and your master was not a young man.'

Which was true, as far as it went, but there is old and then there is old; and if Martin Threadgold had been much past his middle fifties, I would have owned myself greatly mistaken. And he had died in his sleep, apparently. Now that really did surprise me; and when I had paid, and paid handsomely, two passing and fairly honest-looking youths to return my horse to Reynold Makepeace's stables, I followed Mistress Pettigrew and the rest of the party into Master Threadgold's house. I was not invited, but no one seemed to object to my presence.

Godfrey and Judith St Clair took charge, as, I supposed,

the representatives of the absent Alcina, the dead man's next of kin.

'Now, stop snivelling and let us see your master,' Judith instructed the housekeeper, quietly but firmly. She was not, I guessed, a woman who had much time for the self-indulgence of grief. Whatever life threw at her, she absorbed the shock and just got on with living, expecting others to do the same and ignoring the fact that not everyone is capable of such stoical behaviour.

Paulina Graygoss gave her fellow servant an encouraging pat on the back.

'Come now, Felice,' she urged gently, 'show us where Master Threadgold is.'

He was in the little room at the top of the 'secret' stair leading up from the inglenook of the empty fireplace, slumped in his armchair. A folio, bound in moth-eaten red velvet and with broken laces, had fallen from his hand to the bare flagstones, although, oddly enough, the reading-stand had been folded down on its rusty hinges to perform its other function as a table. A tattered brocade cushion was stuffed awkwardly behind his head.

It only took a swift glance to convince us that Martin Threadgold was indeed dead. The cold and pallid skin, the slack jaw, the thread of saliva glistening on his chin and, above all else, the stillness of the body twisted at an awkward angle, left no room for doubt; and at the sight of her master, Mistress Pettigrew renewed her lamentations.

'Paulina, take her downstairs and give her some wine if you can find any,' Judith St Clair recommended. There was an edge to her voice that suggested she might be more rattled by her neighbour's and former brother-in-law's death than she was prepared to admit. 'Now,' she continued when the two women had disappeared, 'Godfrey, you and Lionel, if he will be so kind, had better carry poor Martin to his bedchamber and lay him on his bed. There's nothing more we can do tonight. Tomorrow will be time enough for us – and, of course, Alcina – to make arrangements for his burial. I'll wait up for her tonight until she returns from wherever it is she's gone, and break the news. An unhappy occasion for her, but not, I fancy, one that she will find unduly distressing.'

'Did anyone visit Master Threadgold this evening?' I asked, butting my way into the conversation as I recalled the sight of William Morgan walking up the alleyway between the gardens.

They all turned to stare at me in faint surprise, as though I was something nasty that had just hopped out of the wood-work.

Again, it was Judith who answered. 'You'd have to put that question to Mistress Pettigrew, Master Chapman. Neither Godfrey nor I keep account of our neighbours' move-ments.'

And while I was prepared to accept that this was prob-ably true of herself and her husband, I was extremely scep-tical of the Jolliffes' exaggerated nods of agreement – well, of Lydia's, at any rate. I remembered her peering down from the side window of her house at me and Mistress Pettigrew.

But something else had attracted my attention: two small damp circles on the surface of the reading-stand table, as though a bottle and beaker had stood there at some time during the evening. But they weren't there now. I wondered what had happened to them.

Godfrey St Clair and Lionel Broderer were attempting to lift the body, but the former was struggling somewhat. Dead men weigh more heavily than you think, as the term 'dead weight' implies. I stepped forward and gently elbowed him out of the way, seizing Master Threadgold under the armpits and signalling to Lionel to take hold of his legs.

Judith St Clair gestured to us to wait, disappearing and returning after a minute or two accompanied by the house-keeper.

'Show these gentlemen to your master's bedchamber, Felice,' she instructed. 'Then you and Paulina can lay out the corpse.'

This procedure not only entailed the lighting of candles and wall torches, as it was by now growing dark, but also a good deal of swearing on my part as I backed down that narrow stair to the great hall, through the door leading into the bowels of the house and then up another flight of steps to a chamber at the front of the building, overlooking the Strand. This was as Spartan as everywhere else seemed to be, with nothing but a bed and a chest and a chamber-pot not yet emptied from the previous night.

The rich aroma appeared to offend Lionel Broderer's sensitive nose, for he grimaced, dropped his end of our burden and hastily departed. From beneath the bed, Mistress Pettigrew retrieved a stump of a candle in a candle holder, lit it from the one she held in her hand and placed it on a narrow ledge that ran around the bed head, to the imminent danger of bed curtains as thin as cobwebs. She started crying again and muttering about her 'poor, dear master', so I let her get on with it, bending forward to take a closer look at the dead man's face. Now that I had time to examine it more carefully, I noticed suffused patches of discolour-ation under the eyes and along the jawline. There were others, too, all suggesting to me that Martin Threadgold might have been suffocated. I remembered the cushion, pushed so awkwardly behind his head.

I repeated my earlier question to the housekeeper, who had not been present when I asked it before, but who was, of course, the one person who might know the answer.

'Did anyone visit Master Threadgold this evening?'

She shook her head in denial, but immediately added, 'Only Mistress Alcina.'

'When?' I demanded. 'When was this? And what did she want?'

Mistress Pettigrew looked surprised by the urgency of my tone, and I can't say that I blamed her. 'It was early, just after supper. She came to bring the master a flask of wine. Mistress St Clair had sent it.'

It was my turn to look surprised. 'Did Mistress St Clair often send your master gifts?'

'Occasionally. And why shouldn't she? She was once married to his brother.'

'Mmmm . . . Did Mistress Alcina speak to her uncle?'

'I told her where he was and she asked me to fetch a beaker. Then she took it and the flask up to him. At least, I suppose she did. I don't know for sure. I went back to the kitchen.'

'You didn't see her again?'

Felice Pettigrew shook her head. 'She isn't one as is over-friendly with servants.'

'Then what happened to the flask and beaker?' I asked. 'They're not in the room where you found your master. At least, I didn't see them.'

She looked at me, puzzled. 'I don't know. Maybe he got rid of them.'

'Where? Did he bring them down to the kitchen?'

She shook her head slowly. 'Not as I remember. But I did fall asleep for a while. I often do of an evening.'

'But surely you'd have noticed them when you woke up? On the kitchen table or somewhere.'

She shrugged, plainly beginning to lose interest. Her eyes had again filled with tears: the death of her employer outweighed any curiosity she might feel in what had become of a flask and beaker – a flask, moreover, that didn't even belong to the household. Why should she care?

'Did you see anything of William Morgan during this evening?' I persisted.

'No.'

That was brief and to the point. 'You're certain?'

She didn't even answer this time, but just nodded.

'Could he have entered the house without your knowledge? While you were asleep, for example?'

'Yes . . . Yes, I suppose so. The doors aren't bolted until after dark.' Her feelings were now threatening to overcome her, the tears spilling down her cheeks and her thin chest starting to heave. 'Why are you asking me all these questions? What does it matter? What does anything matter now that the master's gone?'

It occurred to me that I might be treading on delicate

ground, that her sentiments towards her late employer might be more than they should have been. In which case, I was sorry, but I had to know.

'What doors are those? The street door? The door into the garden?'

'Both of them.'

'You're saying that people can come and go at will? And if you were asleep, you wouldn't have any idea they'd been and gone?'

'Why would anyone want to come in here?' she asked in genuine bewilderment. 'There's nothing to steal. Everyone knows my master was a poor man.'

Glancing around me, I was inclined to agree with her. The house was a testament to poverty. On the other hand, there were more reasons than one for illegal entry. Looking again on that dead face with its patches of congested blood, the word 'murder' sprang forcibly to mind. And what of the missing bottle and beaker? Where were they? More importantly, *why* were they missing?

'Mistress Pettigrew,' I said earnestly, 'do you know the reason for Master Threadgold's wanting to speak to me this evening?'

She shook her head, as I had been afraid she would. 'He never told me anything.' She added resentfully, 'He was always a secretive sort of man.'

'But can you remember exactly what your master said when he asked you to run after me this afternoon?'

'He just said there was something he thought you ought to know and to tell you to come back after supper.'

'But why wouldn't he see me then?'

'I explained that.' The housekeeper was growing testy. 'He always sleeps in the afternoon. He's—' Her voice broke. 'He *was* a creature of habit. And he didn't like those habits interfered with.'

I sighed. In cases of murder, people who think they know something never seem to grasp the importance of sharing that knowledge as soon as possible with someone else. I had said to Bertram that delays were dangerous and I had been proved only too tragically right. Martin Threadgold's afternoon sleep had become all too permanent.

There was nothing more to be got out of Mistress Pettigrew, and the arrival of Paulina Graygoss, equipped with cloths and bandages and a ewer of water, put any further enquiries, however futile, out of the question. I left the two women to lay out the body and found my way downstairs.

The dilemma I faced was whether or not to mention my suspicion that Master Threadgold had been murdered to Judith and Godfrey St Clair. Or, indeed, to anyone. I had no proof except that of my own eyes. The discolouration of the dead man's face was not pronounced; he hadn't struggled; he had died easily. And there was only my word that I had seen William Morgan during my ride to Westminster. Moreover, if this death and that of Fulk Quantrell were connected, as I felt sure in my own mind they must be, then to voice doubts about Martin Threadgold's death might well impede the first enquiry. And that would suit neither of my royal patrons. I therefore decided to ignore my duty as a good citizen and hold my tongue – for the time being, at any rate. I salved my conscience by telling myself that the resolution of Fulk's death would probably solve this crime, also.

When I eventually found my way back to the great hall, I discovered that only Lionel Broderer had waited for me.

'The others have all gone home,' he said. 'I thought we might walk back together. And as curfew's sounded, the gates will be shut and you'll need someone to show you how to get into the city.'

We crossed the Fleet Bridge in silence. It was a clear night, the sky dusted with stars, promise of a fine day tomorrow. The distant trees had turned to a rusty black, the last shreds of daylight netted in their boughs. We turned northwards at the Bailey until we reached a sizeable hole in the city wall close to the Greyfriars' house, leading to the Shambles. From there, five minutes' brisk walk brought us into West Cheap and a straight run home to Bucklersbury and Needlers Lane.

'Have you discovered who murdered Fulk yet?' Lionel asked suddenly as we passed along Goldsmiths' Row.

'You're as impatient as everybody else,' I complained sourly. 'I've only been in London two and a half days.'

As I spoke, I glanced at one of the shops to my left, scene of an earlier triumph, just over two years earlier. I wondered if I would be so lucky this time. (I admitted to myself that I had made very little progress.) A lighted window showed at the top of the house. Master Babcary or one of his family was still about.

'What were you doing at Mistress St Clair's?' I asked Lionel, falling back on the maxim: 'When driven into a corner, attack.'

He looked mildly astonished. 'I was taking her the day's takings, of course. What did you think I was doing? As a matter of fact, I was just leaving when Mistress Pettigrew came banging on the door, shouting and crying. She wouldn't come in, so in the end we went out to her, Paulina and Judith and Godfrey and me. We barely had time to discover what the trouble was before the Jolliffes joined us. That woman, Lydia Jolliffe, doesn't miss anything that's going on.'

'Had you been at Mistress St Clair's long?'

'Not very. Judith is always civil, but she's never encouraged me to stay and talk. She doesn't treat either my mother or myself as members of the family. I've always had the impression that while she tolerates me – might even be quite fond of me in her own peculiar way – she doesn't like my mother.'

'Do you know why not?'

He shrugged. 'Who can ever tell why one woman doesn't like another? They're odd creatures. Irrational. The flux makes them that way.'

I said nothing. I thought of Adela and didn't dare.

Lionel accompanied me to the door of the Voyager, where he said goodnight, issued a pressing invitation for me to visit him and his mother at any time, then crossed the street and was immediately swallowed up in the darkness of Needlers Lane.

*　　*　　*

I didn't sleep well, a fact I attributed to a number of reasons.

To begin with, my conscience continued to trouble me that I hadn't voiced my suspicions concerning the death of Martin Threadgold; but I consoled myself with my previous reasoning that if the same person were responsible for both killings, I had no wish to alert him – or her – to the idea of further danger. A sense of having got away with murder under my very nose might make my killer overconfident, thinking me a fool, and therefore more likely to make a mistake.

Secondly, I was missing Adela and the children. But that, I recognized sadly, was the perverseness of my nature. I resented the claims of wife and family when I was with them, but thought of them longingly as soon as we were apart. My mother had always complained that I was like my father in ways, although not in looks, but he had died when I was too young to remember him, so I had no means of knowing if she was right.

But there was another reason for my disturbed night. The carousers in the Voyager's ale room had finally retired to their homes or beds at the inn, and the place had gradually sunk into silence. I must at last have fallen asleep some time after hearing the watch cry midnight. How long I slept before waking again, I had no idea, but I suddenly found myself sitting bolt upright in bed, convinced that someone was outside my window. I had closed the shutters against the night air, but there were chinks of light where the the wood had warped and weathered. Moreover, the shutters failed to meet properly in the middle, and as I looked, I could have sworn that a shadow passed momentarily across this gap at the same time as a board creaked, as if under someone's weight.

I think I have already mentioned that my room opened on to a gallery running around three sides of the Voyager's inner courtyard – a gallery that was easily accessible from the ground by a flight of steps. But entry into the courtyard could only be gained from inside the ale room, and the street door was locked and bolted by Reynold Makepeace as soon as the last customers had left. As far as I knew, none of the guests sleeping at the inn had any interest in me except as a fellow visitor to London. All the same, I slid silently out of bed and crossed the chamber on tiptoe, noiselessly slid back the bolt of the gallery door and eased it open.

There was no one there. Foolishly, still half asleep, I stepped outside. Immediately, the door was pushed violently shut, almost knocking me off my feet in the process, and the top half of my body was muffled in a musty-smelling cloak. By the time I had recovered from my initial shock, I found myself pinned against the gallery wall, being pummelled unmercifully by a pair of sizeable fists. On this occasion, my assailant worked in silence except for intermittent grunts of satisfaction; but after my first futile attempt to free my arms, I let my body go slack, then brought up my right knee with a well-aimed blow to the man's groin. He yelped with pain. I delivered a second kick and then a third with every ounce of strength at my command. This time he let me go, wrenched open the door to my room and pushed me through it with such violence that I landed sprawled on my back, my head cracking against the bedpost. Then he fled – or perhaps in the circumstances I should say hobbled – along the gallery and down the steps.

With some difficulty, I disentangled myself from the voluminous folds of the cloak and staggered to my feet, tenderly feeling those various parts of my anatomy which felt as if they had been trampled on by a herd of stampeding cows. When I eventually recovered sufficiently to go outside again and look over the gallery paling, it was to see a shadowy figure nimbly scaling the wall on the courtyard's fourth side and finally disappearing over the top. There was little doubt in my mind that my attacker was yet again William Morgan.

I half-expected that the disturbance would have roused the occupants of the rooms on either side of mine; but Reynold Makepeace's ale seemed to have acted as an effective soporific, for no one stirred. I returned to my chamber and lay down on the bed, letting my bruised body sink into the goose-feather mattress, which enveloped it with healing warmth.

While I waited for sleep to reclaim me, I thought about William Morgan and wondered why I was the target of his virulent dislike. There was, of course, an obvious answer, but somehow I was unable to connect the Welshman with Fulk Quantrell's murder. There seemed, on the face of it, to be no satisfactory link between them. Irrelevantly, it occurred to me to wonder why William spoke with such a strong Welsh lilt when, from what I now knew of him, he had never lived in Wales. From the age of eight he had been a part of Judith's household, and before that, he and his father had been members of Edmund Broderer's. He must have copied his parents' speech – and what perhaps more natural in a child? – but it also suggested to me a certain fierce loyalty to a country he had never seen. Perhaps, I thought drowsily, it was this same tenacious loyalty that lay at the core of his nature; loyalty to people, places and things . . .

When I opened my eyes again, daylight was piercing the chinks and cracks in the shutters. Somewhere a cock was crowing and I could hear the sleepy voices of the kitchen maids and ostlers as they crossed the courtyard to begin the day's work. Then the landlord's sharper tones chivvied them to get on with things. I turned over on my side, intending to go back to sleep for half an hour, but instead I suddenly threw back the bedclothes and swung my legs to the floor. I was a little unsteady on my feet and aching all over, but forced myself to get dressed before going down to the pump in the courtyard to wash and shave. Then I repaired to the ale room for breakfast.

'Something put the wind up your tail this morning?' Reynold asked as he served me with a beaker of his best home-brewed. 'Couldn't sleep?'

I toyed with the idea of telling him about my nocturnal intruder, but decided against it. If William Morgan wanted to pay me another visit the same way, I had no wish to discourage him. But next time he would find me and my cudgel ready and waiting. I certainly didn't want Reynold putting an all-night guard on the wall, or baiting the court-yard with a man-trap.

'I just need to get on with my enquiries,' I explained, 'if I'm to solve this mystery before the Dowager Duchess returns to Burgundy. If young Serifaber arrives after I've gone, would you be good enough to tell him he'll find me at the St Clairs' house in the Strand?'

One or two other early risers were drifting into the ale room by now and seating themselves at the long table in the centre. A dark-eyed man with a faintly foreign accent, whom I recognized as having one of the bedchambers next to mine, sat down beside me and enquired if I had heard anything untoward during the night; but upon my assuring him that I had slept like a log, he seemed more or less satisfied. 'Just thought I heard a noise, but obviously I must have been mistaken.'

'Do you always rise at this hour?' I asked in order to divert his attention.

Reynold returned with a plate of bacon collops in mustard sauce and a dish of hot oatcakes, both of which I attacked with gusto. I never allow bodily discomfort to stand between me and a good meal.

The man smiled. 'You have to be an early riser if you're in the employ of the Dowager Duchess of Burgundy.'

I nearly dropped my knife in surprise. 'You're employed by the Duchess Margaret?'

'I'm one of her grooms and she likes to go out riding before breakfast in good weather.' He glanced at me and smiled again. 'Did you think all her retinue was housed at Baynard's Castle? There wouldn't be room. There are over a thousand of us, and even so, My Lady thinks she's trav-elling light.' He swallowed his ale and helped himself to an oatcake and some bacon, but he ate quickly like a man in a hurry. 'I must get to the castle stables.'

'You speak excellent English,' I complimented him, and he laughed.

'I was born here, but after twelve years abroad, people say I sound like a foreigner.'

'Only a very little,' I assured him. 'Tell me, did you know a young man called Fulk Quantrell?'

'The Duchess's favourite? Oh, yes! Him and his mother. He returned to England just after Dame Quantrell died, after Christmas. Someone told me he'd since been killed.'

'He was murdered two weeks ago.'

My new friend shrugged, cramming the last of his bacon collop into his mouth and starting to get to his feet. 'That doesn't surprise me. Good riddance, I say.'

'You didn't like him. Why not?'

'No. As to why not, I just didn't, that's all. Like mother, like son. And now I have to go. The mare My Lady has chosen to ride this morning is in my charge. If she isn't saddled and ready when she's wanted, I shall be turned off and left to starve. The Duchess is a good enough mistress so long as her wishes are obeyed to the letter.'

'And if not?'

'Do you need to ask that? She's a Plantagenet!' With which succint remark, the groom wiped his mouth on his sleeve and fairly ran out of the ale room.

Thirteen

I sat there for perhaps another minute, enjoying the peace and tranquillity of the ale room in the early-morning sunshine – a peace shared by only one other customer – before suddenly leaping to my feet and rushing after the Duchess's groom. Of course, he had vanished, and I had no means of knowing which of the many routes to Baynard's Castle he had taken. I decided that I should therefore have to contain my soul in patience until the next time I saw him to ask what he had meant by 'like mother, like son'. As far as I knew – which, admittedly, was not as yet very much – no one had spoken the slightest ill of Veronica Quantrell. I went back into the inn and asked Reynold Makepeace for the man's name.

But the innkeeper didn't know and wasn't sure whom I meant and in any case had to go and oversee what was happening in the kitchens, having recently engaged a new cook whose methods and temperament were giving him some cause for concern. I reassured him that the inn's victuals were as good as ever, and begged him not to bother his head about it. Relieved, Reynold bustled away just as Bertram arrived, eager to know why I had been summoned to Westminster the previous evening. I had not, after all, managed to avoid him.

'Master Plummer says you can have me for two more days,' he announced, when I had finished a brief account of my meeting with the Duke of Albany, 'and then I must return to my normal duties. It would be nice,' he added wistfully, 'to be able to say that I'd helped to find the murderer. Do you think that might happen?'

I sighed deeply. 'Everyone, including you, is expecting me to perform miracles,' I reproached him.

But Bertram's attention had been distracted by the smell of bacon collops, and he was wrinkling his nose indignantly. 'It's Friday,' he said, pointing an accusing finger. 'All I had for breakfast was a dried herring.'

'Master Makepeace isn't as particular as he should be about Fridays,' I replied smugly. 'At least, not this early in the day. They were very good, too. The bacon collops, I mean. If you don't believe me, ask one of Duchess Margaret's grooms, who's lodging here. I don't suppose you've come across him by any chance?'

But it was too much to hope that, out of all the Duchess's vast Burgundian retinue, Bertram would have made the acquaintance of one particular groom, and, alas, my expectations were not disappointed. He shook his head and continued to moan about dried herrings and the Spartan regimen of Baynard's Castle until, in self-defence, I asked Reynold, on his next appearance, to bring the lad a plate of bacon and oatcakes. And while, sunny temper restored, Bertram munched his way through this welcome repast, I recounted all that had happened the previous night. The only thing I failed to mention was my suspicion – or, rather, my belief – that Martin Threadgold had been murdered.

Lacking this knowledge, Bertram's interest in the death of one whom he considered to be every bit as old as Methuselah – anyone over the age of twenty, including myself, being, to my companion, in his dotage – was transitory. He seemed to think it perfectly natural that Martin should have died in his sleep and did not even suggest the possibility of murder. All his attention was centred on the second attack on my person by William Morgan.

'You're certain it was him?' Bertram asked excitedly, actually forgetting to eat for at least twenty seconds and stabbing the air with his knife.

'Yes, I'm certain.' I pushed the hand holding the offending weapon aside and adjured him to take care what he was about. 'And I'm even more certain now that he was my assailant on the first occasion. But this time I have his cloak to prove it.'

'Are we going to arrest him?' Bertram demanded eagerly.

I shook my head. 'Not yet.'

'Why not?' My assistant was plainly disappointed. 'Why else would William Morgan try to kill you if he isn't the murderer?'

'But why would he have wanted to get rid of Fulk Quantrell? Ask yourself that. Fulk was no threat to him. William didn't stand to lose anything by Judith St Clair's new will. Furthermore, he hasn't attempted to kill me on either occasion; and surely he would have tried harder to dispose of me if that had been his object. Both attacks have been nothing more than warnings to me to leave well alone – to cease my enquiries into Fulk Quantrell's death.'

'Yet if you're right, and your enquiries pose no threat to William, what's the point of giving you a beating?' Bertram finished the last of the bacon and oatcakes and proceeded to drink what was left of my ale. Letting rip with a loud belch, he stretched his arms above his head until the bones cracked. By now the ale room was filling up, and several breakfasters glanced round to discover the source of the noise.

I said, 'I can only think that he's trying to protect somebody else, but I don't know who. When I do, I might be one step nearer to finding Fulk's murderer.'

'But you *are* going to confront him with the evidence?'

For answer, I bent down and pulled a rolled bundle from beneath my stool. It was the first time I had really examined the cloak since folding it up the previous night, and I was faintly surprised to note that, far from being made of that rough woollen cloth we used to call brocella, as I had supposed it would be, it was camlet, a much more expensive material of mixed camel-hair and wool.

'A decent cloak, that,' Bertram remarked, fingering it approvingly. 'So where are we going now? Mistress St Clair's?'

'All in good time. But first, on our way, we'll call at the Church of St-Dunstan-in-the-West. I think it might prove worthwhile to have a word with the priest there regarding Fulk's visit on the night that he was killed.'

Bertram was inclined to cavil at this, wanting action, but

he knew better by now than to obstruct me: a tacit accept-ance that I usually had good reasons for what I did. I just wished that I had the same confidence in myself as he did. I still felt as though I were groping my way in the dark.

The morning, unlike yesterday, was beautiful, a cornu-copia of sunshine and shade spilling its coloured profusion over the busy streets. The sky stretched richly blue above the jagged rooftops, with here and there a moth-wing cloud, pale and translucent in the soft spring air. It was the sort of day that made me glad to be alive, and I experienced that same chilling spurt of anger that I had felt so many times before at the act of murder. To kill, to deprive another human being of life, was the most dastardly of crimes.

Bertram and I passed through the Lud Gate, pushing our way against the general tide of people coming into the city from the fields around Paddington, where the purity of the rills and streams that watered the meadows produced lush harvests of lettuces, peas and beans, water parsnips and early strawberries. The beggars and lepers, already at their stations outside the gate, rattled their tins with a ferocity it was diffi-cult to disregard (although many hardened their hearts and managed it), and both my companion and I dropped a groat into the cup of the legless old man who propelled himself around at amazing speed on his little wheeled trolley.

We crossed the Fleet River, where small boats and barges floated like swans drowsing on the sparkling water in the early-morning warmth. Corn marigolds starred the banks with gold, and little clumps of scarlet pimpernel gleamed like blood among the grasses. All was bustle as maids appeared outdoors with their brooms to brush the doorsteps, raising clouds of choking dust over the muddy cobbles.

The Church of St-Dunstan-in-the-West was on the corner of Faitour Lane, tucked into that little dog-leg where Fleet Street starts to give way to the Strand. Dunstan has always been one of my favourite saints, being Somerset born and bred like myself, and having been Abbot of Glastonbury for many years before finally being raised to the see of Canterbury. A bit of a curmudgeon, judging by all I had ever read and heard tell of him; a man who had never hesitated to give the Saxon kings and thanes the rough edge of his tongue whenever he felt they deserved it; a man who had helped make Wessex the chief kingdom of the Saxon heptarchy and who had crowned Edgar the Peaceable first king of all England at Bath.

By sheer coincidence, the nineteenth of May was his feast day, and when Bertram and I entered the church, preparations were already under way for his patronal mass. A couple of stalwart youths were lifting down his statue from above the altar ready to be borne in procession around the church. Three women were seated on the dusty floor, busy making garlands of flowers and greenery, while the priest himself, a little man whose lack of inches told against him whenever he tried to assert his authority, was here, there and everywhere at once.

I caught his arm as he tried to push past me on his way to remonstrate with a pair of giggling altar boys.

'A word with you, Father, if you please.'

He stared up at me in indignation, as much, I think, at my height as at my presumption in accosting him. 'Who are you? Can't you see I'm busy?'

Once again, I found it convenient to indicate Bertram's livery. 'We're here on the Duke of Gloucester's business.'

This flurried him a little. 'The D-Duke of Gloucester?' he stammered, eyeing me uneasily.

I smiled to put him at his ease. 'Don't worry, Father, you've not incurred His Grace's displeasure. Could we talk somewhere? It won't take long.'

He took a hasty glance around him, trying, I could tell, to think up a way of refusing my request. Had I cited anyone but the King's brother, and had I not been accompanied by someone in the Gloucester livery, he would undoubtedly have sent me about my business. As it was, he complied, albeit with a very bad grace.

'Follow me,' he said.

He led us both outside, after ostentatiously issuing half a dozen orders to his acolytes (just to prove, I imagine, that he was not only in charge, but also a very important and busy man), and round the corner to a modest, two-storey house in the lee of the Chancellor's Lane side of the church.

'Well?' he demanded impatiently, having unlocked the street door and ushered us inside. 'What does the Duke of Gloucester want with me?'

There was nowhere to sit down in the stuffy parlour except for one stool stowed beneath a rickety table; and as the priest showed no inclination to draw this out, we all stood, half blinded by the motes and specks of dust that danced in the powerful beam of sunlight shining through the unshuttered window. A pewter plate and cup, the former displaying a few crumbs of bread, the latter some dregs of stale ale, bore testimony to our reluctant host's frugal breakfast.

I explained the nature of my enquiry and asked about Fulk's visit to St Dunstan's on the night that he had been killed; and I had the satisfaction of seeing the priest grow more mellow towards me. He was not, as he had feared, being called upon to account for any misdeed or misconduct, but rather to assist royalty in their quest for a murderer.

'The young man who was killed,' I finished, 'came here on the night of his death, May Day . . .'

'To celebrate the Feast of Saint Sigismund of Burgundy.' The priest nodded. 'Yes, I recollect his visit well. Mind you, I don't say I should have done, otherwise. Saint Sigismund is not, as a general rule, much remembered in this country. A violent man who had his own son strangled. He repented of it afterwards, of course – they always do when it's too late – and founded the Monastery of St Maurice at Agaunum, where, if memory serves me aright, the praises of God were sung day and night.' The priest added grudgingly, 'He was very good to the poor. But in spite of that, I've never thought Sigismund a suitable candidate for sainthood.' His face brightened a little. 'He got his comeuppance in the end, you know. He was defeated in battle by the three sons of Clovis and executed at Orleans. His body was thrown down a well.'

'Thank you, Father,' I said gravely, and frowned at Bertram, who had begun to fidget. 'It's always good to know

159

these things. But about the young man who came here that night—'

'Yes, yes, I'm coming to that. He was an admirer of Saint Sigismund and wanted me to offer up special prayers for the repose of the saint's soul on his festival day.'

'And did you?'

'Naturally. I'm a priest.'

I didn't ask if money had changed hands. It undoubtedly had, but there was no point in antagonizing my informant.

'What was your impression of the young man?' I asked. 'I mean, was he drunk? Frightened? Nervous?' I moved an inch or two around the table in an effort to avoid the sunbeam.

The priest pursed his mouth and contemplated the smoke-blackened ceiling. 'Now, it's odd that you should ask me that, because I did think him jumpy. A couple of times, he glanced over his shoulder as though to reassure himself that he hadn't been followed. But when I thought about it later, I decided I might have imagined his nervousness.'

'You know that he was the young man found dead in Fleet Sreet the following day?'

'Of course I know! The body was carried into the church while we awaited the arrival of the Sheriff's men. The back of his head may have been caved in, but his face was untouched.' The priest frowned and went on, 'I've wondered since if he might have come that evening to pray for Saint Sigismund's protection.'

'From whom? You didn't see anyone? No one came into the church while he was there?'

The priest thought long and hard for a moment, then shook his head.

'The church was empty that evening apart from you and Fulk Quantrell?' I pressed him.

'Was that his name? I don't believe I ever knew it. No, the church wasn't *completely* empty. A man had come in some half-hour beforehand and remained on his knees quietly praying throughout all the time this . . . this Fulk? – is that what you called him? – all the time this Fulk and I were talking.'

Bertram and I looked at one another.

'Did this man show any interest in Master Quantrell?' I asked eagerly.

'None whatsoever, nor the young man in him. In fact, now I come to consider the matter carefully, Master Quantrell, as you call him, might not even have noticed the stranger, who was kneeling in the shadow of the confessional, deeply absorbed in his own prayers.'

'Could this man have overheard what you and Fulk were talking about?'

'I should think it very unlikely. Our voices were low and, as you can see, the confessional is halfway along the nave. We were standing near the altar.'

'When Master Quantrell left the church, did this stranger follow him out, do you remember?'

The priest frowned, then shook his head. 'No, but nor do I recall seeing him still . . . Wait a minute! Something comes back to me! Another member of my flock entered the church to make a confession just as the young man left, and there was no one kneeling near the confessional then. The stranger must have got up and gone before this unfortunate Fulk Quantrell finished his prayers.'

'And you didn't think to mention any of this to the Sheriff's men when they came making their enquiries?'

The priest looked a little sheepish, but retorted sharply, 'I did not. I believe God will uncover the truth of any crime if He wishes it known without any help from me.'

'You mean, Father, that you believe in not getting involved in what doesn't directly concern you. Probably a wise philosophy in the troubled times of these past thirty years.'

He shot me a suspicious look from beneath his tufty eyebrows, but 'Quite so,' was his only answer.

The little parlour had grown even stuffier than when we entered it some minutes earlier. The weight of the cloak I was carrying was making my wrist ache and I shifted it to my other arm.

'We'll take our leave of you then, and thank you for all your help. His Grace shall hear of it.'

The priest, looking gratified if a little sceptical, nodded

towards the cloak. 'What are you doing with that? It's Master Threadgold's.'

I paused abruptly in the act of opening the door. 'I beg your pardon?'

'I asked what you're doing with Master Threadgold's cloak?'

'*Martin* Threadgold?'

'Who else? His brother's been dead these many years.'

'You recognize it?'

'Of course I recognize it. Martin's been wearing it, summer and winter, these decades past.' The priest leaned across and fingered the material. 'Camlet. Extremely hard-wearing.'

'But not that uncommon. How can you be sure that this is his?'

The priest poked the material with a stubby forefinger. 'There's a dark stain here, on the breast, just below the hood, and a rent just below that again. Then you'll notice that the drawstring at the neck is made of plaited yellow silk. Or it was yellow when the cloak was new, a long time ago.' He scraped at the cord with a blunt thumbnail, removing a coating of dirt. 'There you are! Yellow, as I told you. I suppose Martin's mislaid this somewhere and you're taking it back to him.'

'I had no idea it was his.' I protested. 'I thought it belonged to quite a different person . . . Father, has no one told you that Master Threadgold is dead?'

'Dead? When? How?'

'Yesterday, during his afternoon sleep.'

'Dear me! Dear me, no! No one has informed me.' I couldn't say that the priest seemed unduly upset by the news. 'Ah well! It comes to us all in the end. He has a niece, as you may know, but she's rather young. However, I feel sure Godfrey and Judith St Clair will do all that needs to be done on her behalf. Dead, you say? Well, well! Poor Martin!' He patted my arm. 'You'll find that cloak very useful in the winter, my boy.' And I realized that, in a change of opinion, he thought I'd been given the garment. Which, in a way, I suppose I had.

I didn't correct his assumption and thanked him for his time and help.

162

'Well, I hope what I've told you may prove to be of use. You . . . You'll be mentioning me to His Grace of Gloucester, I think you said? Ah, splendid!' He followed Bertram and me out of the priest house and disappeared once more into the church, still muttering to himself, 'Martin Threadgold. Dead. Dear me! Dear me!'

Bertram and I stood aside in order to allow a flock of sheep, on their way to market, to pass us by. The shepherd raised his crook in salutation. 'Thenk 'ee, masters.'

'Come on!' my companion urged, tugging at my sleeve. 'I want to hear what William Morgan has to say when you confront him with the cloak.'

I laid a restraining hand on his arm. 'No, that's no good, now, lad. I'll have to change my plans.'

'Why?' Bertram was indignant.

I sighed. 'Because he'll simply deny that it's his cloak. And it isn't. Which other people will confirm. It did cross my mind earlier to wonder why he was so willing to abandon it. Can't you see, it's no longer proof that he was my attacker?'

'You're certain it was him, though?' I nodded, and Bertram chewed his bottom lip sulkily, a disappointed man. 'What now, then?' he asked.

I hitched the cloak higher up my arm, took a firm grip on my cudgel and said, 'I must speak to Mistress Pettigrew.'

It was still early enough for there to be no obvious signs of life in any of the three houses at the Fleet Street end of the Strand, but I felt sure that the servants must be up and about. All the windows of Martin Threadgold's dwelling were decently closed and shuttered, as became a house of mourning, but so far no wreath of yew had been nailed to the door to indicate that an unburied body lay within.

I knocked as loudly as I dared two or three times, and was just praying that Mistress Pettigrew was not afflicted with deafness when the door opened a crack and the house-keeper's tremulous voice enquired, 'Who's there?'

'It's Roger Chapman,' I said. 'I must speak to you, mistress. May I come in?'

163

She inched the door open another fraction and peered out anxiously.

'My master's dead. But you know that. You were here yesterday with Master and Mistress St Clair. I can't let you in.'

'You must. I tell you I have to talk to you.' As a precaution against her closing the door, I put my foot between it and the jamb and held out the cloak with the stain and the tear uppermost. 'Do you recognize this? Does it – did it – belong to your master?'

I heard her give a little gasp and she put a hand through the crack as though she would snatch the garment from me.

'I've been searching for that,' she said. 'Where did you find it?'

I took a hurried step backwards before she could grab it. 'Admit me and Master Serifaber, and I'll tell you.'

There was a lapse of several seconds before the door creaked protestingly on its hinges as it opened a little wider. Bertram and I squeezed through the gap.

In spite of the warmth of the morning, the house felt icily cold as if, indeed, the Angel of Death had enfolded it in his wings. I was startled; I was not generally given to such flights of fancy, and I gave myself a mental shake. I was growing morbid with my advancing years, and that would never do.

Once again, Mistress Pettigrew made as though to snatch the cloak from me, but I prevented her. 'Where did you find it?' she whispered.

'More to the point,' I retorted, 'where did you last see it?'

She shivered. 'The master took it upstairs with him, yesterday, to put across his knees while he slept. But when I found him, it wasn't there. I didn't think about it at the time, I was too upset; but later, last night, I got to wondering where it had gone.'

'Something else that had vanished, like the flask and the beaker,' I suggested.

The housekeeper still evinced no overt interest in the two latter items, but I saw her eyes flicker. She repeated her question about the cloak. 'Where did you find it?'

'I can't tell you that just at the moment.' I clasped one of her small, cold hands in mine and said earnestly, 'It's very important that you say nothing to anyone else about this at present. Can you keep a secret?'

She stared up at me, her rheumy eyes suddenly wide with suspicion. 'Does the master's death have anything to do with the murder of that nephew of Mistress St Clair?'

'Why do you ask me that?'

'Because . . .' She hesitated, considering her words, then added in a rush, 'Because I wondered if the master's death was natural. There was something about his face, some discolouration, that didn't seem normal to me.'

'You mean, you think Master Threadgold was murdered, like Fulk Quantrell?' Bertram demanded, nudging me excitedly in the ribs.

'I . . . I don't know.' The housekeeper looked frightened, fearful that she was letting her tongue run away with her. 'It's just that . . . well, there was something else that occurred to me . . . during the night.'

'What was that?' I asked gently. She was plainly wishing she hadn't spoken, but, unlike me, felt impelled to voice her suspicions.

'Go on,' I urged. 'You can rely on Master Serifaber's and my discretion.' I looked sternly at Bertram as I spoke, and after a moment he gave a reluctant nod.

Mistress Pettigrew bit on her thumbnail with small, pointed teeth, rather like a rat's, but after a while she forced herself to continue.

'When I brought Mistress Alcina the beaker for the wine, she asked me if I'd like to have a cup before she took it upstairs to her uncle. She said the flask was overfull.'

'And did you?' I prompted.

She nodded. 'I thought . . . I thought it tasted a little odd. And then, very soon afterwards, I fell asleep. And I seem to have slept extremely soundly for quite a long time.'

165

Fourteen

'Are you saying you think the wine was drugged?' Bertram demanded eagerly, his brown eyes sparkling with the excitement of the chase.

The housekeeper eyed him with growing unease, obviously regretting her moment of indiscretion and wishing she hadn't confided in us. But of course, it was what she had meant, or at any rate meant to imply. She said nothing and looked anxiously at me.

'Hold hard a minute, Bertram,' I began, but my protest was ignored. The lad was pursuing his own train of thought.

'And if Master Threadgold had been drugged, it would have made it easy for someone to smother him. Roger!' He turned triumphantly to me. 'Didn't you mention a cushion stuffed behind the dead man's head? You know – when you were telling me about your viewing of the body?'

I cursed my too-ready tongue, which was prone to describe what I saw in detail. I was beginning to realize that Bertram was a sharp lad with a retentive memory and not the casual young layabout I had originally thought him.

'There was a cushion,' I admitted cautiously.

'There you are, then! So all we have to decide is who murdered Master Threadgold. It must have been his niece, Alcina. Don't you see?' He was well away by now. 'She must have murdered Fulk when she realized he wasn't going to marry her, and somehow her uncle found out the truth. So she had to get rid of him, as well. She brought him the drugged wine, waited until he fell asleep, then suffocated him with the cushion. The case is solved!'

He beamed at me with the ridiculous self-confidence of

the young. I could recognize myself nine years earlier, in those heady days when I was convinced that any man past the age of thirty must almost certainly be impotent, and that any person on the other side of forty was heading rapidly downhill towards senility and the grave. Ah, youth!

'If you imagine I haven't already thought of all this,' I admonished Bertram, belligerent at being made to feel old before my time, 'you're much mistaken. But unlike you, my lad, I intend to ask a few questions before leaping to conclusions.'

I again addressed the housekeeper. 'Mistress Pettigrew, are you certain that you didn't see or hear Mistress Alcina leave the house after visiting her uncle?'

She shook her head. 'No. I told you last night I didn't set eyes on her after giving her the beaker to take up to the master with the wine.'

'There you are!' Bertram exclaimed.

'I'm not anywhere,' I snapped. 'Mistress Pettigrew also told me last night that neither the street nor garden door was locked while she was asleep. Anyone could have entered the house during that time. And as yet we have no proof that the wine brought by Mistress Alcina *was* drugged. (It was, after all, a gift from Judith St Clair.) We only have Mistress Pettigrew's unconfirmed suspicion that it *might* have been.' Personally, I considered the housekeeper's suspicion tantamount to a certainty, but I wasn't prepared to say so at this juncture. 'Mistress Pettigrew,' I went on, 'what arrangements are being made for Master Threadgold's burial?'

She shrugged her thin shoulders. 'Not my affair. I'll be leaving here soon.' She dabbed her eyes with a corner of her none-too-clean apron. 'It's up to Mistress Alcina now. The master'd no other kith or kin that I know of. And she'll not want for guidance while she has Mistress St Clair to help her.' She jerked her head in the direction of the house next door. 'They'll be in directly, I reckon, after they've been to consult with the priest at St Dunstan's. And there'll be others poking their noses in, you can be sure of that.' The housekeeper sniffed disparagingly.

I glanced towards the windows. The clarity of light piercing the shutters and the muted noise reaching us from the Strand indicated that it was still comparatively early. With luck – and for the moment I had a feeling that the luck was running my way – it might be another hour, perhaps a little longer, before the efficient Judith St Clair arrived to take charge.

'Mistress Pettigrew,' I wheedled, 'will you give your permission for my assistant and myself to look around the house? Naturally, we shan't disturb your master's body.'

She hesitated for a moment before recollecting that she was no longer in a position to give or refuse permission. This was not her home any more. I suspected that Paulina Graygoss might have given her fellow servant a hint of what to expect last night, while they were laying out the corpse.

'If you want to,' she said indifferently and pattered away, presumably to the kitchen, leaving Bertram and me standing amid the dust and dead flies and mouse droppings of the musty-smelling great hall.

'I don't understand,' my companion protested. 'If we suspect Master Threadgold's death might have been murder, why are we pretending not to know? Why aren't we reporting it to the Sheriff's officers? Or to Master Plummer? Or to someone in authority?'

I didn't answer immediately, once again reviewing my reasons to see if they held water. At last, more or less satisfied, I explained, 'Because I believe the death of Martin Threadgold really is connected to that of Fulk Quantrell, and I don't want the murderer to be put on his or her guard. I want him – or her – to believe that he – she – has got away with this murder. When killers grow overconfident and think they're dealing with incompetent fools, they're liable to make mistakes. Don't worry! Martin Threadgold will be avenged when we eventually capture whoever killed the Burgundian.'

'You're sure about that?' Bertram sounded doubtful.

'As sure as I can be about anything. Of course, if you feel that you must speak up, I can't, and shan't, stop you. But if you do, I sincerely believe we shall find further evidence hard to come by. The murderer will take fright and go to ground.'

Bertram considered my words carefully before allowing himself to be persuaded. It was an unexpected sign of maturity in the lad: he was not as feckless as I had thought him. On the other hand, having to explain myself and get his agreement riled me. I had not wanted, nor asked, to be saddled with an assistant, and I silently cursed Timothy Plummer's interference in my affairs. I am much happier when working alone.

'Very well,' my companion finally conceded. 'So, why are we searching the house? What are we looking for?'

'For a start, a beaker and the flask Alcina brought the wine in. I'm not hopeful of finding either, I must admit, and in any case, they'd most likely prove nothing if we did. Both must have been rinsed clean by now: any tell-tale lees of wine are bound to have been removed. So . . . apart from those two items, nothing in particular, but everything in general. If I'm honest, I don't really know *what* we're looking for. We're just looking.'

I could tell by Bertram's expression that he found this an unsatisfactory quest, but he had the natural curiosity that is common to all human beings (men as well as women, however much they may deny it), and poking and prying among other people's possessions is one of the most intriguing occupations that I know.

By common, if unspoken, consent, we both made for the little room above the inglenook where Martin's body had been discovered. A keen scrutiny, however, revealed nothing more than we were already aware of; no missing beaker or flask came to light. The tattered cushion sat innocently on the abandoned chair and the cloak that had covered the dead man's knees was still rolled up under my arm. Someone had removed it from this room; either William Morgan or somebody who had later given it to him. My preference was for the Welshman himself, but whether that made him the murderer I was still uncertain. Martin Threadgold could have been dead when William entered the chamber.

169

That, of course, begged the question as to why William should have been there in the first place. Had he been sent by someone? And if so, for what reason? Or was he just a casual thief, entering a house he knew to be easy of access at certain times of the day when its two occupants were known to be resting, probably sleeping? Was he in the habit of doing this – of helping himself to money or small objects that he could sell for cash? Mistress Pettigrew had said there was nothing in the house worth stealing, but it was possible that there were things of whose value she was unaware, or just items that would raise a few coins to buy a thirsty man a drink. William Morgan had been in this room some time during the previous day, of that there could be no doubt. His possession of the cloak made it a certainty – if it was indeed the Welshman who had attacked me the preceding night. But *was* I sure of that? I had been until that moment, but now I was suddenly beset by misgivings.

'What are you looking at so intently?' Bertram's voice broke in on my thoughts and made me start.

'Looking at?'

'Yes. You're staring at those shutters like a man in a trance.'

I became aware that I was indeed standing by the window, my forehead almost pressed against the wooden slats through which the sun was filtering in a desperate attempt to lighten this dark and gloomy little room. On impulse, I threw open both the shutters and the casement, letting in the sweet scent of flowers combined with the stink of the river and the warm, balmy morning air. I put one knee on the window seat and took a deep breath, at the same time scanning the garden below.

It was plain to see that this had not been cultivated for some considerable time, probably years. Weeds ran riot, choking whatever flowers and herbs had originally been planted – all except the roses, which grew in profusion among the long seeding grasses and were slowly reverting to the pale hedge- and dog-roses from which they sprang. Part of the boundary wall had crumbled and the cracked grey stones thrust their way through the smothering ivy like bones through broken skin. A tangle of loosestrife showed purple amongst the green.

The contrast with the St Clairs' garden could not have been greater. There, all was order and neatness, culminating in the beauty of the willow tree, stooping to look, Narcissus-like, at its own reflection in the river, trailing its branches across the surface of the water. This was the tree that, according to Martin Threadgold, his brother had planted for the wife he had abused; a strangely tender gesture for such a brutish man. But then everyone, I supposed, had some saving grace, some moments when his better nature predominated . . .

I pulled myself up short. I was growing philosophical, God save the mark! A sure sign of advancing years! I should have to watch out for this deplorable tendency and nip it in the bud. I smiled at Bertram.

'There's nothing more to find here. Let's look at the rest of the house while we have it to ourselves.'

We descended the hidden staircase to the great hall and made our way through the door into the rabbit warren of rooms and passages beyond. But this inspection, alas, yielded little of any value to my pitifully slim store of knowledge. I was no nearer discovering my murderer than I had been three days earlier on first arriving in London. Bertram, of course, wavered between the almost total certainty of its being William Morgan and the conviction that our killer was Alcina Threadgold. Just at present, the former was favourite for immediate arrest. My demands for a motive, for a positive link between the two men, were either ignored or merely served to convince my companion – for the next five minutes at least – that Alcina was the culprit.

'Perhaps they're both in it together,' he suggested with a sudden burst of inspiration.

I couldn't deny that the lady had had a strong motive for disposing of Fulk Quantrell, and therefore, eventually, might also have had one for getting rid of her uncle, depending on what he knew. But I felt that she and the Welshman were unlikely allies; and for some reason that I couldn't quite explain, even to myself, I was reluctant to view Alcina as a suspect. Why this should be so, I had no idea, but I had an uneasy suspicion that I ought to know. In the end, I concluded that there must be something lodged in the deepest recesses of my memory, like a fishbone in the gullet, worrying and scratching at me; but for the moment I was unable to draw it out. It was a sensation I had often experienced in the past, but over the years I had learned to let these things go. My memory would regurgitate whatever it was in its own good time. For now, I would do well to follow my instinct to move slowly and cautiously towards the solution of this case.

I kept my promise to Mistress Pettigrew and left Martin Threadgold's body undisturbed, but this didn't prevent me from taking a good look around his bedchamber. (Promises, after all, depend on how you word them.) At first, I thought I was wasting my time; the room offered practically nothing in the way of furnishings, and what there were were either shabby and broken or torn. Moreover, Bertram was unhappy at his proximity to the corpse and anxious to get out of the room as quickly as possible. The sickly-sweet smell of corruption and decaying flesh, and the angry buzzing of several predatory flies were starting to make both of us feel ill. The bile was rising in my throat.

'There's nothing to be found here or anywhere else in the house,' I grunted, wondering why on earth I had ever thought there might be.

But leave no stone unturned has ever been my motto, particularly when it satisfies the nosy streak that my mother and, subsequently, scores of other people have accused me of possessing. And I have always prided myself on my strong stomach, which rarely turns queasy at the sights and smells other people find so distressing. So I was disgusted to feel a wave of dizziness and nausea as I followed Bertram to the door, and steadied myself by leaning heavily against the wall to the right of the bed head. To my horror, I seemed to become enveloped in the tapestries, which only released me from their dusty, tattered tentacles as I pitched through the wall into an empty space beyond.

Winded and more than a little shaken, I lay still for perhaps half a minute, then struggled painfully to my feet. In Stygian darkness, I cautiously felt all round me and judged I was in a chamber hardly bigger than an oubliette. The walls were rough stone and mortar except for a single wooden panel, presumably the entrance that had opened to let me in. I was forced to stoop to avoid hitting my head against the ceiling, but there were no other obstacles. The room – if one could dignify it by that name – was empty.

'Chapman, where are you?' I could hear Bertram's anxious voice on the other side of the wall.

For answer, I pushed against the wooden panel, expecting it to revolve as it must previously have done in order to let me in. Nothing happened. I pushed again with greater force, but to no avail. I began to panic, thumping the wood with both fists.

'Bertram! I'm here, behind the wall. I know it sounds silly, but—' The panel once more swung inwards and Bertram was standing beside me in the blackness.

'I've seen one of these things before,' he announced delightedly, pleased to be able to air his superior knowledge. 'It's called a fly trap. You can get in, but you can't get out without the proper key.'

'But we don't have the key,' I pointed out with enormous self-restraint. 'And now, thanks to your stupidity, we're both trapped inside and nobody knows where we are. I doubt if the air in here will last more than half an hour.'

'We'll have to shout, then.' Bertram didn't seem at all perturbed.

'I very much doubt,' I retorted with asperity, 'that we shall be heard. Mistress Pettigrew is most probably in the kitchen, and in addition, I suspect she's somewhat deaf.'

'In that case,' my young friend responded cheerfully, 'we'll just have to wait until Mistress St Clair arrives from next door.'

'We don't know when she'll be here. It could be hours yet before she comes.' My temper was getting shorter by the minute as I felt the sweat begin to trickle down my back. The air was already growing fetid and my heart had started to thump unpleasantly. I drew my knife from my belt and felt up and down both sides of the wooden panel. 'You say these "fly traps" have keys, therefore they must have locks. In which case, we'll just have to try picking this one.' And I made a desperate effort to remember all that Nicholas Fletcher, my fellow novice at Glastonbury, had taught me.

The first rule, of course, was to keep a steady eye and hand, two things in this hell-hole that were well nigh impossible. I couldn't even see the lock.

'Calm down, Master Chapman,' Bertram said with a chuckle. I could have sworn he was smirking. 'Give me the knife. The locks to these things are always in the middle of the door and have a double mechanism that it's almost impossible to undo without the key. Unless, of course, you have the knack.'

'And you do?'

'I was with my father when he installed one in a house at Holborn some years ago. Now, stand back and give me room.'

He ran his fingers lightly over the surface of the wooden panel, then nodded. 'Yes, here it is, just where I said it would be; plumb in the centre.' He took my knife, fiddled for a moment, twisted the blade first this way, then that, then back again, and finally gave a triumphant grunt as the door swung outwards. Seconds later, we were both safely back in Martin Threadgold's bedchamber.

I wiped the sweat from my face and tried to avoid looking at my companion's smug expression.

'What are these so-called "fly traps" used for?' I asked in a shaken voice.

'Well, the one whose lock and mechanism *we* installed at Holborn – we didn't build the trap itself, you understand. My father's a serifaber, not a builder – was for use as a safe. The owner of the house intended it as a store for his coin and plate.'

'But thieves can get in.'

'But they can't get out again, can they? Not without the key. Not unless they know the secret of the lock, like me. So if someone does try to rob you, you've caught the thief. That's why they're called "fly traps".'

'But supposing someone falls in accidentally, as I did?'

Bertram shrugged. 'You were just unlucky. You must have touched the hidden spring. It's not that easy to do unless you're trying to find the entrance.'

I glanced involuntarily at the dead man on the bed. Martin Threadgold had told me yesterday that these three dwellings had once been a part of the Savoy Palace: whorehouses, he had thought, standing at a distance from the principal building. But perhaps they had also been used as treasure stores. I wondered if the two neighbouring dwellings had 'fly traps' as well.

'Let's get out of here,' I urged. I was more upset by my recent ordeal than I cared to admit.

We made our way back through the shuttered gloom of the house to the great hall, only to discover Mistress Pettigrew in the act of opening the street door to Judith and Godfrey St Clair, who were closely followed not just by Alcina, but also by Paulina Graygoss and Jocelyn. Instinctively, realizing that our presence would be unwelcome, both Bertram and I shrank back into the shadows, but I held the door between the passageway and the hall ajar.

'William has gone for Father Arnold at St Dunstan's. They'll be here directly.' Judith's voice carried clearly across the intervening space. 'You can bring us some wine, Felice, here, in the hall, while we're waiting.'

The housekeeper muttered something under her breath, but obedience was natural to her, and she turned and shuffled across the hall. I gripped Bertram's arm, pulling him in the direction of a flight of steps to our right, which I guessed led down into the kitchens – a guess which proved correct. As in the St Clair house, there was also a stone-flagged passage with a door at one end that led into the garden. I ushered Bertram through and we found ourselves in the overgrown wilderness we had seen from the upstairs window.

In its ruined state the garden wall was easy enough to climb, and in a matter of minutes we had both dropped to our knees in the alleyway between Martin Threadgold's property and the St Clairs'. Brushing my hose clean of grit and dirt, I eyed the opposite wall meditatively.

'Everyone's out,' I said. 'Now's our chance to have another look around.'

Bertram shook his head decisively. 'Not in this livery, Chapman. I daren't. I can't afford to be caught trespassing in someone's house. Especially not someone like Mistress St Clair, who has influence with Duchess Margaret. I'll go back to the Voyager and wait for you there.'

And no doubt indulge in a beaker or two of Reynold Makepeace's best ale, I thought grimly, which you'll instruct him to add to my reckoning. Meanly, I nipped his little scheme in the bud.

'You'll stay outside,' I told him, 'and if anyone shows any sign of returning, you'll waylay them.'

Bertram looked sceptical, as well he might. He didn't even bother to enquire how he was to perform this feat. He knew my real motive for keeping him away from the Voyager as well as I did.

'Try not to be too long,' he said caustically. 'Here, you'd better give me that cloak. You must be tired of dragging it around with you, and it might prove a hindrance.'

Gratefully I surrendered the article in question, scaled the St Clairs' garden wall, not quite with the ease with which I had climbed its neighbour, and landed this time more heavily and with even less grace. For a moment, I was afraid I had wrenched one of my ankles, but after a few hesitant steps, all seemed to be well.

I had counted on the fact that the garden door would be unlocked, and I was not disappointed. It opened easily into the kitchen passage, and halfway along were the arch and the 'secret' stair. Luck was certainly with me this morning, for when I reached the top of the steps leading to Mistress St Clair's bedchamber, that door, too was unbolted.

I eased myself inside, where my feet gratefully encountered the softness of the embroidered carpet. Today, the two chests standing against the opposite wall, with their carvings of grapes and vine leaves, were properly closed. No belts or sleeves or scarves spilled over the sides. The bed under its dazzling counterpane was neatly made, the Daphnis and Chloe curtains pulled back and carefully wound around the bedposts beneath the canopy. A fresh candle – wax, of course, not tallow – had already been inserted into the candlestick ready for the coming night. This was a household where efficiency was highly prized.

I noticed also, which I had not done on my previous visit, that the walls were hung with the same beautifully crafted embroidered tapestries that I had seen both at the Needlers Lane workshop and in Lydia Jolliffe's parlour. They covered every inch of the grey stone walls except . . . except for one wooden panel near the bed head. My heart lurched excitedly. Was it possible that this house also boasted a 'fly trap'? And was this it?

These three houses were very similar in many respects, both outside and in. And why shouldn't they be? If they had indeed been a part of the Savoy Palace and built for the selfsame purpose, then it was more than likely that they contained many identical features. I already knew that this one and the late Martin Threadgold's had a 'secret' stair. Why not, then, a 'fly trap'? But this time I would not be caught. Forewarned was forearmed.

I walked round the bed and surveyed the wooden panel. Bertram had spoken of a hidden spring which I had accidentally triggered when I fell against it; so, now, I extended my arms to their full length and, with my hands, cautiously began pressing the surface.

Nothing happened for what seemed like an age, but was probably no more than ten or twelve seconds. Then I spotted a mark right in the centre of the wooden panel: a tiny circle with a thread-like circumference of silver, almost invisible until the light struck it at just the right angle. Hastily, I took off one of my boots and pressed the circle with the tip of my index finger. Immediately, the panel swung inwards, staying open just long enough, I judged, to allow someone to step inside. Then it began to close again. But this time it remained ajar, unable to move any further, jammed against the tough leather of my boot.

Fifteen

This left very little room for a man of my height and girth to get through, so I tried pushing the door further open, but it refused to budge. I then pressed the unlocking device again, but nothing happened. Obviously, this would only work if the door were closed. Exasperated and uneasily conscious that I was wasting time – time in which Mistress St Clair might return to the house – I removed my boot from the aperture, allowed the panel to swing shut, then took off both boots and, when I had once more unlocked the door, shoved them, side by side, into the vacant space. Now there was enough leeway for me to enter with ease.

This 'fly trap' was roughly the same size as the one in Martin Threadgold's bedchamber, being, I judged, no more than two to two and a half feet square – about as big as a large cupboard. The main difference was that the walls were panelled and a shelf, some five or six inches wide, ran along the back wall. A carved wooden box stood at one end of it and proved to be unlocked when I lifted the lid, but the contents were disappointing. Two gold chains, a necklet and matching bracelet of quite small emeralds set in silver – and, as even I could see, poorly set, at that – a gold-and-agate thumb ring, half a dozen pearl buttons and a jade cross on a silken string. Judith St Clair might be a wealthy woman, but one thing was certain: she didn't waste her money on the adornment of her person.

Beneath the shelf, on the floor, was a much larger box on which I had stubbed my stockinged toes as I stepped over my boots into the chamber. This, too, was unlocked – and indeed why shouldn't it have been, stored as it was in the 'fly trap'? – and held only a man's rolled hose, tunics, cloaks and bedgowns, all laid up in lavender in the vain hope of discouraging the moths. (Several overweight and overfed little monsters flew at me angrily as I raised the lid.) These, I presumed, were the clothes of either the late Edmund Broderer or Justin Threadgold or perhaps both; the sad remains of Judith's first two marriages.

There was nothing else except for an oddly shaped key hanging from a hook driven into the front of the shelf. I guessed that this must be the key which opened the 'fly trap' from inside, but I was not about to close the door in order to confirm this theory. I preferred to step back outside and pick up my boots, whereupon the panel completed its inter-rupted journey and closed with a quiet, but menacing thud.

I gave a hasty glance around the rest of the room, but nothing appeared to have been added or removed since my last visit; so, uneasily aware that time was passing, I slipped on my boots, opened the door once more and began to descend the 'secret stair'. I was about halfway down when someone below called, 'Who's there?'

I jumped and almost lost my footing, but my panic was momentary. I had recognized the voice as that of Betsy, the bigger of the two kitchen maids. Like a fool, I had forgotten the presence of the girls in the house, but I consoled myself with the thought that at least I would be able to allay their suspicions more easily than those of Paulina Graygoss or William Morgan. I took the remaining steps in a single leap (trying to show off and giving my spine a nasty jar in the process) and treated Betsy to my most charming smile.

It didn't work. 'What were you doing in the mistress's bedchamber?' she asked suspiciously. 'Does Mistress St Clair know that you're poking about among her things?'

'Er – no. And I'm hoping you won't tell her.' I tried again with the smile and this time was slightly more successful.

'Are you still looking for clues about Master Fulk's murder?'

'Yes.' Nothing but the truth could explain my presence in Judith St Clair's chamber.

'You don't suspect the mistress, do you?'

As questions went, that was a difficult one. I gave her my stock answer. 'I suspect everyone.'

'Even me and Nell?'

'Well . . .'

'Oh, we wouldn't mind if you did. It might be quite exciting.'

I had never considered that being a suspect in a murder enquiry was anything but nerve-wracking and something to be avoided at all costs. I laughed.

'I must go,' I said. 'I came in over the garden wall and through the back door, but do you think you could let me out at the front? – provided the coast is clear, that is.'

'I'll look out first and make certain,' she offered. (The smile must have worked even better than I'd hoped.)

Nell suddenly appeared from the kitchen and Betsy briefly explained my presence to her. With the morals of her kind, Nell seemed to find nothing reprehensible about my rummaging among Mistress St Clair's belongings, and I guessed that she had often done it herself when Judith was absent. It was one of the ways servants took revenge on their masters and mistresses for their long hours, poor wages and being constantly at everyone's beck and call.

Betsy led our little procession up the main staircase, towards the great hall. I followed. Nell brought up the rear.

'Do you really find out what's happened to people who've disappeared or got themselves killed?' the latter asked.

'Sometimes.' I decided I was being far too modest, so added firmly, 'More often than not.'

We had traversed another corridor and ascended a second, much shorter flight of stairs before she spoke again. As we at last entered the great hall and Betsy padded over to the street door, Nell said, almost offhandedly, 'P'raps you could find out what happened to my young brother then, when you've discovered who killed Master Quantrell.'

'Your brother?'

'Yes. He was called Roger, too. Used to work here, helping William Morgan in the garden; but about two years since, he just up and left. Vanished. Haven't seen him since.'

Memory stirred. I recalled Gordon St Clair mentioning the brother of one of the kitchen maids and seeming peeved that the lad no longer reported for work.

'How old was he?' I asked, and was told that Nell thought he might have been about ten when he disappeared. So he would be twelve or thereabouts now.

'Maybe he just ran away,' I suggested. 'Boys of that age do. They get all kinds of nonsensical notions into their heads. They think it could be fun to go for a soldier or stow away on a ship. It isn't, of course. Quite the opposite. But they don't know that until it's too late.'

'I don't think Roger was that sort,' Nell demurred. 'He liked gardening. He liked planting things and digging in the earth.' She shrugged her thin shoulders. 'I daresay he'll turn up again one day, like a bad penny.'

Betsy, who had been reconnoitring outside the street door, now turned and hissed at me, 'There's no sign of the master or mistress. They must still be next door. But I can see your friend. He's over on the other side of the road, buying a pie. Two pies,' she amended hungrily.

'That sounds like Bertram.' I slipped my arm about her waist and gave her a quick kiss on the cheek by way of thanks.

'What about me, then?' Nell demanded, coming alongside and proffering her lips.

I kissed the tip of her nose instead. I didn't believe in favouritism. Then I made my way across the Strand to Bertram's side and nipped one of the pies – fish, unfortunately: it was Friday – from his hand before he realized I was there. He protested, but faintly, too relieved to see me to make much fuss. And indeed, I was only just in time. As we stared across to the Threadgold house, Alcina, Judith and Godfrey St Clair emerged, followed by Jocelyn, the priest from St Dunstan's, Paulina Graygoss and William Morgan. I was amused to note that while I had been next door, they had also been joined by all three Jolliffes, who were having no compunction in adding their mite to the general discussion being carried on amongst the group. Only the housekeeper and the Welshman took no part.

Bertram and I were too far away to hear what was being said, but I could tell by Judith St Clair's stiff-necked attitude that she considered her neighbours' intrusion into her affairs unwelcome. I touched Bertram on the arm.

'Let's go back to the Voyager. It must be gone ten o'clock. This pie's rotten. The fish is all bones and no flesh.' I spat out the contents of my mouth on to the road. 'I fancy one of Reynold's good dinners.'

My companion flung an arm around my shoulder and, without saying a word, urged me forward.

We chose fish pies again, but these were vastly different affairs from those Bertram had purchased from the pieman in the Strand. A thick suet crust enclosed succulent pieces of eel, and the sauce oozed out all over the plate when they were cut – sauce which we mopped up later with chunks of good wheaten bread. Bertram, stuffing himself while he was able, to augment the meagre fare of Baynard's Castle, had a second helping.

While we ate, we assessed what we knew about the murder of Fulk Quantrell. And it wasn't much. In spite of my conviction that I had twice been attacked by William Morgan, I couldn't prove it. The cloak, which I had assumed to be his, had proved a false lead, belonging as it did to Martin Threadgold and having last been seen in his possesion by Felice Pettigrew. I was sure enough in my own mind that William had stolen it for his own use when he entered the Threadgold house and found Martin either asleep or dead. That, of course, raised the question: had he killed Martin? And if so, was he also the murderer of Fulk?

'Well, I'd say "yes" on both counts,' Bertram said thickly, raising his plate to his mouth and drinking the remaining sauce, afterwards licking his lips clean. He had evidently abandoned Alcina as the possible killer of her uncle.

'Why?' I asked, leaning forward and speaking quietly. We were in a secluded corner of the ale room and there was a good deal of noise and clatter going on all around;

but some people have very acute hearing, and I had no wish to make them free of our conversation.

'Why what?' Bertram swigged his ale.

I sighed. 'I've asked you this before. Why would William Morgan want to murder either Fulk Quantrell or Martin Threadgold? What grudge, what reward, links him to either man?'

Bertram squirmed a bit on his stool, but eventually announced defiantly, 'He didn't like them. They'd annoyed or injured him in some way, at some time or another.'

I considered this proposition, but found it dubious.

'You might kill one person for such a reason,' I agreed reluctantly, 'but not two.'

Bertram remained defiant. 'They say it's easier to do murder a second time, once you've committed the first.'

'Maybe . . .' Then I shook my head. 'I'm not saying William Morgan's innocent, but I'd want a better reason than sheer vindictiveness for him to be the guilty party.' I saw Bertram open his mouth to argue, but waved him to silence. 'Don't bother asking me why. It's just a feeling, but I've learned to trust my instincts. So! What else do we know?'

'We know Alcina took Martin the wine which was . . . which we believe to have been drugged.'

I smiled faintly. 'You're learning, lad. And we also know that some hours before Fulk was murdered, he had told Alcina bluntly that he had no intention of marrying her. He claimed to have a sweetheart in Burgundy. She was very upset and left the embroidery workshop in pursuit of him. She said she visited her uncle, a story Martin Threadgold confirmed. But . . .'

'But he's dead, as well,' Bertram finished slowly. 'Now there's a thought, chapman. Suppose Alcina's story wasn't true, and her uncle had threatened to expose it for a lie. Perhaps he was blackmailing her. Wouldn't that have been a motive for her to kill him?'

'Perhaps. But we must not let ourselves get carried away. Everything we've said so far is supposition. Maybe we're wrong and Martin wasn't drugged and murdered. We must concentrate our attention on Fulk.'

Bertram grimaced and finished his ale. 'That's opening the floodgates to a whole torrent of suspects: Jocelyn and Godfrey St Clair, all three of the Jolliffes, as well as Alcina herself.'

I nodded glumly. 'You've forgotten to mention Lionel Broderer and his mother. Not that I think Martha Broderer a likely suspect, but she might have killed on her son's behalf if she considered that Fulk was robbing Lionel of his just deserts.'

My companion chewed his bottom lip. 'What else do we know?'

'Fact or hearsay?'

'Both, I suppose. After all, if we rule out hearsay, there's not a lot left.'

I laughed and patted Bertram on the back. 'Timothy Plummer will live to be proud of you yet. Cynicism is of far greater value to an investigator than wide-eyed enthusiasm.'

Bertram looked pleased at this unexpected praise, and was about to say something when he paused, frowning, staring at a group of newcomers who had just entered the inn.

'Now what's he doing here? I didn't think the Voyager was one of his haunts. I thought he frequented the Bull, in Fish Street.'

'Who are you talking about?' I enquired, following his gaze.

'Brandon Jolliffe.'

A man was outlined against the bright sunshine blazing in through the open ale-room doorway, but with his back to the light, it was difficult to make out his features. He was certainly short and stocky. Then, suddenly, having spotted us, he changed direction and came towards us.

'It's not Brandon,' I said. 'It's Lionel Broderer.'

As the man approached and his face could be seen more clearly, it became obvious that he was a good deal older than Master Jolliffe.

Bertram smiled, a little sheepishly. 'They look similar at a distance,' he excused himself.

I had to admit that they did, at the same time experiencing an uneasy stirring at the back of my mind, as though some fact that I couldn't quite pin down was nudging me towards a connection that I was unable to make. I made a desperate effort, but it was already too late. Lionel had drawn up a stool to our table and was greeting me like a long-lost friend.

'Roger! We meet again. Do you have any idea of what's happening in the Strand? If I know Judith, she's taken charge. All the same, if you should happen to see Alcina, would you tell her that I was asking about her? I should be only too happy to render her any assistance in my power.'

'We've already visited the Threadgold house this morning.' I smiled sympathetically. 'And you've guessed aright, I'm afraid. Mistress St Clair has everything under control. I doubt there's anything left for you to do by this time.'

He looked so downcast that I whistled to a passing pot boy and ordered him a mazer of ale. He could buy his own fish pie: my generosity didn't extend that far.

'Strange, Martin going like that,' he remarked, after he had thanked me. 'He was only saying to me the other day that he felt better in health than he had done for a long time. He suffered from attacks of breathlessness, you know, but thought they had lessened since that stretch of the Thames had been cleared of some of the muck and sediment on the river bed. Farringdon Without has always been one of the more public spirited and progressive wards.'

The pot boy brought Lionel's ale, which he downed almost in one gulp, letting out a great 'Ahhh!' of satisfaction and wiping his mouth on his sleeve.

'You were thirsty.'

He nodded. 'The workshop gets very hot this time of day.'

'Tell me,' I said, 'do you recollect a young boy who used to work in Mistress St Clair's garden?' Even as I spoke, I wondered why I always referred to the house and garden as Judith's and never Godfrey's. Perhaps because it *was* her house, where she had lived ever since her marriage to Edmund Broderer. As Lionel looked puzzled, I went on, 'He'd have been about ten or so at the time. Nell's younger brother.'

'Nell?' His frown deepened.

'One of the kitchen maids.'

'Oh! Yes, I think I know who you mean: the little, thin one. That's right.' He broke off to shout for another mazer of ale before returning to his ruminations. 'Yes, I'd forgotten all about him. So he was Nell's brother, was he? I don't think I ever knew that. Nothing like her to look at. Square-set little fellow. Why do you ask?'

'Nell mentioned to me today that he'd disappeared. Vanished a couple of years ago without telling anyone where he was going.'

'Probably stowed away on one of the ships berthed along the wharves. Boys of that age want adventure.'

'That's what I said. But Nell seemed to think he wasn't that sort. Liked gardening. Not the adventurous kind, according to her.'

Lionel swallowed his second cup of ale with as much gusto as the first, then stared thoughtfully into the empty pot. 'Is this important?'

I pursed my lips. 'I don't know,' I answered frankly. 'Probably not. On the other hand, it might be. The truth is, any facts are better than no facts, and at the moment, I don't feel I'm any closer to solving the Burgundian's murder than I was three days ago.'

'I tell you what,' Lionel said, 'come back with me to the workshop. My mother's there today, helping out, as two of the girls are sick with the bellyache. She knows a great deal more about Judith and her household than I do. She gets all the gossip from Paulina Graygoss. You couldn't exactly call them friends, but Mother has a knack of wheedling information out of people.'

'Thank you. I'll do that if you think Mistress Broderer won't mind.'

Lionel roared with laughter. 'Mind! She'll welcome you with open arms. Apart from the fact that she's fond of a good-looking young man, she'll be delighted with any excuse to rest her eyes a while. She finds some of the close work more trying than she cares to let on.'

I glanced at Bertram. 'Do you want to come?'

But I wasn't surprised when he refused, giving as his reason that he ought to get back to Baynard's Castle and report to Timothy Plummer. Time spent in the company of someone old enough to be Lionel Broderer's mother lacked excitement. So I said goodbye to him, finished my ale and followed Lionel across the street to Needlers Lane.

Martha Broderer was as pleased to see me as her son had predicted, rising from her stool to embrace me warmly before planting a smacking kiss full on my lips.

'This is a pleasant surprise,' she said with a smile. 'I was only saying to Lal yesterday that I wished you would pay me a visit.'

'For any particular reason?' I asked.

She punched me playfully, and rather harder than I cared for, in the ribs. 'Are you fishing for compliments, my lad? If so, you won't get them from me.' But she winked broadly, nonetheless.

I blushed and denied the accusation, conscious of the giggling girls behind me. I had imagined – I don't know why – that Dame Broderer would be helping at the table where the purses and belts were decorated; but it became obvious that she was assisting, if not actually directing, two other women who were embroidering a magnificent cope.

'For the Bishop of Bath and Wells,' she told me, noticing my interest. And indeed I might have guessed, had I thought about it, by the border of white saltire crosses worked on a blue background: the cross of Saint Andrew. She eyed me curiously. 'Do you know Robert Stillington?'

I laughed. 'I've seen him, of course – I come from that part of the country – but only at a respectful distance. Do I look the sort of man who would be on speaking terms with a bishop?'

'False modesty doesn't become you.' Martha Broderer rapped me sharply across the knuckles with her spectacles (I had seen her whip them off her nose the moment I came in). 'You don't look the sort of man who's on speaking terms with a royal duke, but you are.' She went on, 'A strange man, the Bishop. I always think there's something a little shifty about him.'

'He was very friendly with the late George of Clarence,' I offered in support of her statement. 'I've always been convinced that there was some intrigue between them. Stillington was arrested round about the same time as the Duke, but later released.'

I watched idly as the other two women laid strand after strand of sapphire-blue silken thread side by side on the linen, then stitched them together to form a solid block of colour.

'That's called couching,' Dame Broderer explained. 'Now, isn't it time you told me why Lal's brought you to visit me? I'm sure there's a reason, and it isn't for the sake of my beautiful eyes.'

'I should just think not,' her son said jovially. On entering the workshop, Lionel had gone to have a word with the two men, Jeb Smith and Will Tuckett, who were setting up mesh on the wooden frames, preparatory, I guessed, to beginning a new wall hanging. But now he strolled across to join us. 'He wants to pick your memory, Mother. Do you remember the young boy who used to work in the garden for Cousin Judith?'

Surprisingly, Martha Broderer nodded. 'Yes. He was called Roger, the same as our friend here, and he was always referred to as Nell's brother although they had different fathers. Their mother, if I recollect correctly, was called Eleanor Jessop. A pretty girl, widow of a Thames boatman. Judith took her on to be her tiring woman. She died – Eleanor, that is – when Roger was born, and Judith had the boy raised to work in the household. When he was old enough, he started helping William Morgan in the garden and around the house.'

'You don't happen to know what became of him?' I asked, continuing to watch, fascinated now, as one of the women eased herself beneath the sewing frame and began stitching the blue threads from the cope's other side.

'Undercouching,' Dame Broderer informed me briefly before answering my question. 'He disappeared about two years ago. Just vanished overnight. No one knew why and nobody seemed to care. Certainly Judith made no move to find him.'

'Who was his father – do you have any idea?'

There was a short but quite audible silence. I was still watching the embroidress, but after a second or two, I turned my head to look enquiringly at Martha Broderer.

She gave me a limpid smile, but her eyes just failed to meet mine.

'Who can say? The boy might have been anyone's. Does it matter?'

I didn't answer directly. 'Your son remembers this young Roger as a heftier child than Nell. Is that your recollection, too?'

Again, there was a certain hesitation. Martha Broderer gave a little laugh. 'Almost everyone is heftier than Nell,' she prevaricated.

'Roger was a solid lad, Mother,' Lionel protested. 'You know he was. Now I come to think of it, he reminded me very much of what I was like as a child.'

Dame Broderer made no comment, but replaced her spectacles on the bridge of her nose and turned her attention back to the Bishop's cope. She took a huge medallion of azure velvet from a neighbouring table and placed it carefully in the centre of the garment.

'We'll embroider this with cloth of gold and silver thread,' she decided. 'It will be the centre-piece when His Grace turns his back to the congregation.'

The woman who had been undercouching heaved herself up from beneath the frame and gave it as her opinion that a smaller medallion of white velvet, sewn into the centre of the blue and embroidered, in its turn, with golden thread, would be even more eye-catching. Martha Broderer said tartly that she thought it might be overdoing things, but then, on reflection, and given the vanity of the Bishop, perhaps not.

The third woman, who had so far said nothing, suddenly addressed me. 'You were asking about the boy who used to work in Judith St Clair's garden. Nell Jessop's half-brother.' I nodded. 'Well, you know, I thought I saw him the other day when I was going to visit my sister, in Holborn. I was walking up Faitour Lane. I can't be certain, but it looked like him, only a little older.'

'Faitour Lane?' Dame Broderer asked sharply. 'What would he be doing there?'

The woman flushed uncomfortably, glancing askance at Lionel and me. 'He . . . He was coming out of one of the whorehouses,' she said.

Sixteen

'One of the whorehouses?' Lionel repeated, his tone a mixture of shock and envy. 'How old did you say this boy is now?'

'Twelve,' Dame Broderer answered, frowning. 'But I don't think Cicely meant what you're thinking, Lal. I think it was something far worse.' And she raised her eyebrows at the woman she had named.

Cicely made no answer, but pulled down the corners of her mouth. Her companion gave a little gasp, though she didn't falter in her couching. The lines of blue silk continued to grow into a soft, cushioned background for another white saltire cross.

There was an uncomfortable silence; then Lionel said, 'You're surely not implying . . . ?'

His mother nodded. 'That's right. I take Cicely to mean that young Roger is not availing himself of women's services, but is offering them, himself. The vice of the Greeks, Lal, is what we're talking about.'

'If the Church found out . . .'

Martha Broderer snorted with laughter and turned to me.

'Although, by my calculations,' she explained, 'Lionel is some thirty years old, you'll find him innocent for his age, as an unmarried man living at home with his mother naturally tends to be. My dear boy,' she went on, once more addressing her son, 'you can believe me when I tell you that brothels of both sexes are owned by some of the most eminent and outwardly respectable churchmen in the land. The great sin in their eyes is not sodomy, but being found out. Being caught in the act. Getting the whorehouse shut

191

down and losing them – the landlords – money. Then, of course, the poor souls so taken can expect no mercy from Mother Church.'

Lionel did redden slightly at his parent's derision, but seemed to bear her no ill will for it, merely grinning a little sheepishly and hunching his shoulders. She smiled back at him, her whole face alight with affection. I had been right in my estimation of these two: they understood one another.

I looked at the woman, Cicely. 'Can you remember,' I asked, 'whereabouts in Faitour Lane this particular brothel is located?'

She blinked reproachfully.

'No, no! Not for myself,' I added hastily. 'I need to speak to this boy, not make use of his services.' My manhood was insulted by even having to clarify this fact.

She blushed and muttered, 'Of course! Of course!' by way of an apology, before continuing, 'About halfway along on the left-hand side if you're walking north, towards Holborn.'

'You see, chapman,' Lionel said proudly, putting an arm around Dame Broderer's shoulders, 'my mother *has* been of use to you. I said she would be. She has a prodigious memory.'

'Nonsense! It's Cicely who's been of use,' his mother disclaimed, trying not to look too pleased at the compliment, and failing. 'Why do you want to speak to this child?' she enquired of me. 'What has he to do with Master Quantrell's murder?'

'I have information that Fulk visited a boy in Faitour Lane – whether to make use of his services or for some other reason, I don't really know – but I have a fancy that this young Roger may be the lad.'

'Why?' Lionel wanted to know.

'Because he has a link with the St Clair household, and Fulk's murderer could well be among their number.'

'That is, if it isn't Lal or me,' Martha Broderer pointed out with yet another laugh; but this time there was no mirth in it.

I gave her a brief bow and smile, but neither confirmed nor denied her statement. The truth was, I couldn't; but the first, inchoate seed of an idea, the first, small bud of a solution, was beginning to germinate in my mind. But the tender shoot was nothing like strong enough yet for me to give hope or despair to anyone.

'I must go,' I said.

But before I went, I was sufficiently interested to allow Mistress Broderer to conduct me around the workshop and explain all the different processes of embroidery, in order to demonstrate the skill of the men and women under Lionel's supervision, in which she seemed to take even more pride than he did. When she had finished, I thanked her and would have kissed her hand had she not seized me by the shoulders and kissed me on the mouth for a second time.

'There!' she said. 'I've been wanting to do that ever since we met.' She grinned at my discomfiture and slapped me hard across the backside with a stinging blow that was meant to hurt. 'Off you go!' She had an ambivalent attitude towards men. My guess was that she had been badly hurt by one of us at some time or another in her life.

I made my way back through the Lud Gate and across the Fleet River to Faitour Lane. It was fairly quiet at that hour of the morning, most of the beggars – those who were not sick or sleeping off the previous night's carousal – away at their various posts throughout the city or in Westminster. But the brothels were doing a roaring trade, men's carnal appetites seeming to know no limit when it came to time of day.

''Ullo! You come for that free ride I promised you?' enquired a voice; and there, standing in the doorway of a house to my left, was the prettiest whore in Christendom, her big, sapphire-blue eyes watching me appraisingly.

'Er, no,' I said, and was alarmed to detect a distinct note of regret in my tone. She certainly was beautiful.

'Pity!' She gave me a tantalizing smile, but I could tell that she was not as relaxed as she wished to appear. She was alert for any sound that would indicate the proximity of the madame.

'But perhaps you can help me in another matter,' I suggested, struck by a sudden thought. 'Do you remember when I talked to you yesterday, you told me that Fulk Quantrell – the young man who was murdered here two weeks ago – sometimes visited a lad he had his eye on?' She nodded. 'Well, did that lad work in Faitour Lane?'

The girl looked anxious. 'I shouldn't have told you that.'

'Where is this particular whorehouse?' I asked, hoping for confirmation of the woman Cicely's information.

I got it. The girl sighed, but capitulated. 'About fifty paces further up on this side of the lane. You . . . You ain't about to complain or snitch to the authorities, are you?'

'Certainly not!' I was deeply offended by this remark and let it show.

'Well, you might have to,' she pointed out, reasonably enough, 'if the lad you're on about's got anything to do with that there Fulk's death.'

This, of course, was true – she was no fool, this girl – but even so, live and let live has always been my motto. There are ways of doing, and not doing, things so that, wherever possible, they don't incriminate innocent people.

'What's the boy's name?' I asked, just to check that we were indeed taking about one and the same person. She was reluctant to tell me, so I asked, 'Is it Roger Jessop?'

'Yes.' Surprise jerked the answer from her. 'At least, he's called Roger. I don't know his other name. We leaves those behind us when we comes to Faitour Lane.'

'And how shall I recognize this whorehouse?'

'Told you. Fifty paces from 'ere, or thereabouts. You'll see a lad at the door, watching out for customers.'

She was right, and also surprisingly accurate in her measurements. I had barely counted out fifty paces when I saw a young boy, some thirteen or fourteen years of age, lounging in the shadowed doorway of a ramshackle house with a crooked chimney. This last was an unusual enough feature in Faitour Lane for it to be a mark of identification in itself, yet my little whore hadn't mentioned it. I wondered where she had come from and what was her history.

I approached the boy in the doorway.

He eyed me sharply. 'What d'you want?' he demanded.

'I'd like to speak to Roger. Roger Jessop. Is he here?'

The young fellow's face lost its suspicious look.

'Friend of Roger, are you? You better come in then. 'E's busy at the moment, but I shouldn't think 'e'd be long now.' The boy gave a raucous laugh. 'Shouldn't think 'is present customer's got a good shag in 'im.'

He moved his emaciated body to allow me access, and I stepped past him into a dark and dirty passageway. The smell of stale, unemptied chamber-pots and their contents made me gag, and I had to turn my head away so that the doorkeeper wouldn't see me. I had to look as if this sort of place was one of my usual haunts.

While I waited, various men went hurriedly in and out, shielding their faces with raised arms, as though to hide their identity even from one another. Doors opened and shut on glimpses of filthy rooms, and I found myself wondering why a lad who loved gardening would have exchanged it for this twilight existence. What had happened to Roger Jessop to bring him so low?

A door at the far end of the dingy passageway was flung wide, and a man pushed past me, showing the whites of his eyes. He threw a coin to the doorkeeper before dodging into the street, with an anxious glance in both directions.

'Roger! You got a customer,' the lookout yelled.

A stocky lad with a thatch of light-brown hair was strolling towards me, and once again something gave my memory a nudge, only to be lost a second later.

'Who are you?' he asked. 'Don't know your face. New to the game, are you? Someone tell you to ask for me?' He jerked his head. 'Better come in before you take fright and run.'

He pushed me into the room at the end of the passage and closed the door. It was tiny, with just about enough space for a bed, and stank of sour sweat and other, even

195

more unpleasant, bodily odours. A tattered mattress, the straw stuffing erupting through rents in the filthy ticking, had been pushed on to the floor, presumably during young Roger's last encounter, and I could see it was alive with fleas and bedbugs. The boy's arms and neck were covered with bites and sores.

'Right,' he said, loosening his points and starting to lower his breeches, 'What d'you want? Straight up or fancy?'

'No, no!' I said hurriedly. 'I haven't come for that. I just . . .'

'No need to be scared,' my namesake assured me. 'You needn't be afraid anyone here'll tell on you. Matter of fact, it's the Bishop of London what owns us.'

'No, no! You misunderstand.' I held out my hand to ward him off. 'I just want to ask you a question or two about Fulk Quantrell.'

'Who?'

'Fulk Quantrell – the Burgundian who was murdered in Faitour Lane two weeks past.'

'Oh, 'im!' The boy adjusted his clothing and scowled. 'Friend of 'is, are you? He was another one that just wanted to ask me questions. Paid, mind! Same as if he'd buggered me.'

I nodded and jingled the purse at my belt. 'I'm perfectly willing to do the same.'

'Oh . . . All right, then,' was the grudging response. 'As long as you understand and plays fair by me.' He held out a grime-encrusted hand. 'Come to think on it, I'll take the money first. Just in case you tries to cheat.'

I passed over the necessary coins and looked around for somewhere to sit, but there was nowhere except the floor, and I didn't fancy that. I propped my back against the wall.

'Go on, then,' he said. 'I'm waiting for the questions.'

'Well, to begin with, why in heaven's sweet name did you leave Mistress St Clair's house for' – I made a sweeping gesture of distaste – 'for this!'

He shrugged, but his eyes were shifty. 'It's not a bad life, once you get used to it. I got a roof over me head, food in

196

me belly. Food of a sort,' he added honestly. 'Better 'n begging on the streets, at any rate.'

'Is it?' I sneered. 'I'm willing to wager you get as much, if not more, abuse than a beggar, and a lot less money. And what little you do earn is taken off you to be shared amongst your pimp and your landlord, His Grace the noble Bishop of London.'

I thought for a moment the lad was going to burst into tears. He did indeed sniff and wipe his nose in his fingers, but continued to stare at me more defiantly than ever.

'So?' I prompted. 'You could still be helping William Morgan in the garden, living with your sister.'

'Half-sister,' he corrected.

'All right,' I agreed. 'Nell's your half-sister. But it doesn't alter anything. It still doesn't explain why you're here.'

An expression of fear flitted momentarily across his face. 'You ain't told Nell where t' find me, 'ave you? Tell me you ain't! 'Ow *did* you find me, by the way?'

'I haven't seen Nell since discovering your whereabouts,' I assured him. 'And as to how I found you, one of the women at the Needlers Lane workshop thought she recognized you when she was walking to Holborn through Faitour Lane.'

His fear turned to puzzlement. 'Why would you be talking about me to one of Master Broderer's workers? And what's it all got to do with Fulk?'

So I took a deep breath and started at the beginning, working my way through what had happened so far until today, when Nell had mentioned his disappearance. There were, of course, things that I didn't tell him. I also had to cope with a certain amount of initial – and natural – scepticism on his part concerning my past and present involvement with the King's younger brother; but I managed to convince him in the end. Unfortunately, I didn't foresee, although I should have done, that this would make him even more wary of me.

He clammed up, refusing to offer any reason for his change of living beyond saying that he had grown tired of gardening for a pittance, and being bullied by William Morgan. A boy he met had told him there was good money to be made as a whore, and had offered to find him a place in this brothel, where he had been ever since.

'You came here,' I hazarded, 'because it's close to the St Clair house in the Strand.' I saw his sudden flush of colour and knew I had guessed aright. 'Do you ever go back there in the dead of night to climb the wall to sit in the garden?'

'No I fuckin' don't!' he exploded with such venom that I jumped in surprise. 'I came 'ere for safety. Someone in that house was tryin' to kill me! Safety! Same as I told that there Fulk, or whatever he was called. They look after me 'ere.'

I was beginning to feel like Theseus in the labyrinth, but without his ball of thread.

'Master Quantrell asked you the same question? How did *he* know where to find you? Nell doesn't know where you are.'

Young Roger shrugged. 'Just chance. 'E came 'ere looking for pleasure and, when we finished, we got talking. 'E found out I was Nell's half-brother. Then 'e come back once or twice more. 'E wasn't really a sodomite. Just did it now and then, I reckon, for the thrill of it. Doin' something 'e shouldn't. 'E was that sort. But 'e did like asking questions.'

'What about?'

'Well . . . 'Bout the garden, mainly. What sort o' things we planted. Did Mistress St Clair and the rest take much interest in it.' He shrugged. 'Nothin' more.'

'Is that all?'

'More or less. I did ask 'im once why 'e wanted to know about the garden. I said I thought he must've heard the story 'bout the old Savoy Palace that used t' be in the Strand.'

'What story is that?' I queried. I found I wasn't sweating as much as when I had first entered the room. I was growing accustomed to the stench and finding it less offensive than before.

Young Roger, too, grew easier in his manner as he became

used to my presence, and convinced that I posed no threat.

'You ain't a Londoner,' he said, nodding sagely. 'Though I s'pose I'd guessed that already by the funny way you talk.' I raised my eyebrows, but otherwise ignored this slur on my West Country burr. 'Everyone in London,' he went on, 'knows the story that there's treasure buried somewhere in the Strand.'

'Treasure? What sort of treasure?' I was intrigued.

'Usual kind. Money, jewels, gold.'

'Why? How is it supposed to have got there? And whereabouts?'

My final question made him laugh, showing stumps of blackened teeth. 'If anyone knew *whereabouts*,' he answered, carefully mimicking my tone, 'some greedy sod would've found it by now, wouldn't 'e? As to 'ow it got there, well! When that Wat Tyler 'n' John Ball 'n' Jack Straw 'n' their howling mob sacked London and burned down the Savoy Palace all them years ago, Wat Tyler 'n' John Ball gave orders that no one was to loot the place on pain o' being strung up from the nearest tree. What they was doin', they said, was for the King and liberty and so on, and not for making themselves rich.' The boy curled his lip. 'Well, I mean to say! Askin' a bit too much of any man, ain't it? John o' Gaunt was the richest man in the country after the King. The Savoy was stuffed with treasures. Bound to 'ave been! More 'n flesh 'n' blood could resist. The story reckons there was looting, and plenty of it, and a good few managed to get away with it. But a group of men got caught, an' one o' Wat Tyler's captains ordered 'em to be hanged there and then, without trial nor nothin', an' the very people who'd been lootin' themselves performed the deed.

'But there'd been a fourth man in the group who managed to slip away unnoticed to where they'd piled up their loot. An' while the others were hangin' his three comrades, he buried it all, meaning to come back for it later. But later was no good. 'E was recognized and fingered as being one o' the group and strung up, as well. The treasure 'e'd buried was never found, and still 'asn't been found to this day.

They reckon it's still there, somewhere. Probably in some-body's garden.' He grinned. 'Or maybe under one of the 'ouses. More 'n one owner's had his cellar floor dug up, so they say.'

I thought this over. 'But those three houses at the end of the Strand,' I pointed out, 'are considered to have been a part of the original palace; therefore, if this tale were true, the treasure – if it exists at all – is unlikely to be buried *underneath* them . . . Do you believe this story?' I asked the boy.

My namesake grimaced. 'Naw! There are tales like this un by the dozen about almost every part o' London. The streets are paved with gold, we tell strangers. Just dig a bit an' you'll find it. Meantime, buy my nice new shiny spade. Or, better still, this old un that's cost me nothing, 'cause it belonged to my great-great-grandfather.'

A cynic at twelve years old! My heart warmed to him in spite of his unprepossessing appearance and smell.

'And what did Fulk Quantrell say when you asked him if *he* believed this story?'

'Said 'e hadn't 'eard it. What was it about? So I told 'im, like I've just told you.'

'Did *you* believe *him*?'

Young Roger, who, until now, had been perched on the empty frame of the bed, shifted and slid down the curve of the mattress to sit cross-legged on the floor.

'Well . . . that's the funny thing. When 'e said 'e'd never 'eard the tale, yes, I did believe 'im. But later that visit, just as 'e was going, 'e laughed and said something like, "There's plenty of treasure buried in the Strand if you know where to look for it. I've been hopin' you'd tell me where it can be found. But seems like you don't know." Then 'e laughed again and added, "But I don't really need it. I can make my fortune without." 'E went away and that was the last time I saw 'im. Next thing I 'eard, he was dead. Been found murdered in Faitour Lane.' After a pause, Roger asked eagerly, 'Anythin' else you want t' know?' He glanced at the coins in his hand and jingled them suggestively.

'I'm not a rich man,' I protested. Nevertheless, I dipped into my purse and doled out a couple more groats. 'You haven't yet explained exactly why you ran away from Mistress St Clair's. What made you think someone was trying to kill you? And who do you think it was?'

'I don't know who it was,' was the disappointing response. 'But I do know that I had some very peculiar accidents in that house.'

'Such as?'

'Well, once, I was by myself at the bottom of the garden, plantin' some cress seeds along the water's edge, like Paulina Graygoss told me. I 'ad me back to the 'ouse and wasn't thinkin' about nothing but what I was doing, when suddenly, I toppled into the river. I swear to you, chapman, that someone pushed me, but when I came to the surface, there was no one in sight. Everyone swore they was somewhere else at the time and said I must've slipped. But I didn't. I know I didn't. Somebody pushed me in. Luckily, I can swim like a fish. Then, another time, I'd to go down the cellar to bring up some o' the master's favourite wine. I'd a candle, o' course, but I still didn't see the wooden ball on the third or fourth step from the top. I went crashing to the bottom and was lucky not t' break me fuckin' neck. As it was, I was laid up the best part of a month.'

'What sort of a ball?' I queried.

'A child's ball. A painted thing Mistress Alcina used to play with when she was a child, or so Paulina Graygoss said. Said, too, she thought it was put away with all the other old toys in a chest in Alcina's bedchamber, but that someone must've got it out, though goodness knows why. That's what Paulina said. And there was the time I was terrible sick after eating me dinner. It was mutton stew, and no one else was ill. I reckon somethin' 'ad been added to me bowl when I wasn't lookin'.'

'Whom did you suspect? Mistress Graygoss?'

'Any of the women. Not Nell, but everyone else. They were all in and out the kitchen that day, I remember. The master and mistress were 'avin' Master and Mistress Jolliffe and Master Brandon to supper, 's I recall, and were out to impress. Mistress Alcina was quite sweet on Brandon Jolliffe in them days, though I 'ear she ain't so much now. Wanted Master Quantrell. We 'ad a laugh about that, we did. But, as I say, all the women were in 'n' out o' the kitchen at some time or another that morning. And William Morgan. Any of 'em could've put somethin' in me stew without me seeing.'

I was a little doubtful about this last instance; and in the first, whatever Roger thought, he *could* have slipped. But the incident with the child's ball certainly appeared more sinister.

'Did anything else happen after that?' I asked.

He gave a scornful snort. 'I didn't wait t' find out. I ran away and came 'ere, where I've been ever since. What's more, I'm goin' to stay 'ere. Now, mind! Don't you go tellin' anyone in that house you've seen me. Not even Nell.'

'She's worried about you. She'd like to know that you're alive and well.'

'Daresay,' he replied unfeelingly, 'but she ain't one for holding her tongue. Never could keep a secret, couldn't Nell.'

'Very well,' I agreed. 'I promise to say nothing. But I can't answer for Lionel Broderer and his mother. Or for the other women. They must all have heard what was said.' I didn't add that once I had established my interest in young Roger Jessop, he had at once become a more interesting subject for discussion, and, doubtless, was even now a general topic of conversation in the embroidery workshop.

Roger was dismissive. 'None of 'em knows me well enough t' care what I'm up to. They got other things to talk about.'

I didn't like to disillusion him, and, after all, he might be right. It did cross my mind that I ought to use any means in my power to wean him away from his present existence, and that to frighten him into running again might not be such a bad idea. But I didn't. The smell and the close confines of the room were beginning to make me feel queasy once again, and my one thought was rapidly becoming of escape.

I tossed the lad two more coins, mumbled my farewells and left, stumbling along the fetid passageway and staggering thankfully into the less noisome air of Faitour Lane. I walked back to the Strand and down the alleyway between the St Clairs' and Martin Threadgold's houses to the river's edge, where I paused for a moment, breathing in the cleaner river smells and staring out across the Thames, a streak of silver studded with the russet and blue, crimson and emerald of hundreds of barges.

'Ah! Master Chapman!' said a voice. 'Do you have any news for me yet concerning the death of my nephew?'

I jumped guiltily and turned to find myself looking over the wall, into the stern, questioning features of Judith St Clair.

Seventeen

'N-No,' I stammered nervously. 'At least . . . er . . . no, not yet.'

'Not yet?' The well-marked eyebrows were raised and the blue eyes surveyed me with a faint hauteur. 'What precisely does that mean? Do you have any idea as to the murderer's identity or do you not? If not, why don't you just admit defeat and return to Bristol, or wherever it is you come from? I thought from the start that it was a mistake allowing a pedlar to usurp the office of sergeant-at-law. But of course, it's not my place to question the decision of Duchess Margaret or My Lord of Gloucester.'

I felt my hackles begin to rise, but schooled my expression to one of civility – servility, even.

'I still have some further investigations to pursue, mistress, but I hope to be able to satisfy both you and your royal patrons in the very near future.'

She darted a suspicious glance at me, as though convinced that I was bluffing; but she permitted herself to be mollified a trifle.

'Come and look round my garden,' she invited most unexpectedly. 'You can easily scale the wall.' She raised herself on tiptoe, so that her shoulders as well as her head came into view, and by dint of resting her arms along the top of the wall, she was able to peer over to the other side. 'Look! You see those protruding stones? There, there and there. Simple, particularly for someone of your height. Those long legs of yours should make light work of such a climb.'

I could hardly refuse such a pressing invitation, even had I wished to, and within a matter of moments found myself standing beside Judith St Clair on one of the numerous paths that intersected the beds of flowers.

'A beautiful garden, mistress,' I said admiringly, staring about me as if seeing it for the first time. She smiled proudly, but there was a hint of something else in her expression that I could not quite define.

'I like it. I love flowers,' she answered simply. 'And my favourite place is under the willow tree, looking out across the water. In spite of the river traffic, which has greatly increased in recent years, I find it very peaceful. Come and stand there with me for a minute or two and you'll see what I mean.'

I followed her to the main path and walked to the little landing stage on the river bank, where we stopped beneath the willow tree's trailing branches. On the opposite bank, shimmering in a faint heat haze, I could see the landscape of Southwark set out before me. Nearer at hand, pale spears of yellow iris glimmered among the reeds at the river's edge, and marigolds peered at their ghostly reflections in the water. A reed warbler swooped towards its nest among the grasses.

'A truly lovely spot,' I said, glancing sideways at my companion and surprising a look of amusement on her face.

'It is, isn't it?' she answered. 'You appreciate beauty in nature, Master Chapman?'

'I'm a countryman at heart,' I explained. 'Bristol may now be my home, but I was born in Wells.' Judith inclined her head, but made no comment, so I continued, fearful of an uncomfortable hiatus in the conversation, 'I was told that these three houses' – I jerked my chin over my shoulder – 'once stood in the grounds of the Savoy.'

She laughed. 'Oh, yes! I've heard that story, too. Whorehouses – isn't that the theory? But I very much doubt it. In my opinion, they're built too far eastwards. You must have seen what remains of the old palace during your to-ing and fro-ing along the Strand. I admit it was reputed to be a vast enclave in its day, but even so, I don't believe it stretched this far towards the Fleet.' She shrugged. 'Of course, I could be wrong. Perhaps I just don't like the idea of living in what was once a brothel.'

Her last word jogged my memory. I said, with what to her must have seemed like total irrelevance, 'Your kitchen maid, Nell, said that her young brother once worked here, helping William Morgan in your garden, but that the boy disappeared some two years ago. William must miss him. There's a lot of work just for one man.'

Judith St Clair looked faintly surprised, as well she might, by this sudden change of subject, then puckered her forehead in perplexity. 'Nell's brother . . . ? Ah! Now you mention it, yes, I do have a vague recollection of him. More of a hindrance than a help, according to William, if I remember rightly. William and he nearly came to blows on more than one occasion. I'd forgotten him.'

A vague recollection? She had to be lying, of course. Martha Broderer had told me that young Roger had been brought up in Judith's household and that his and Nell's mother, until her untimely death, had been Judith's tiring-woman. My companion obviously had no idea of the extent of my knowledge, but I wondered why she had bothered to lie at all. In fact, I wondered about this whole episode: why she had invited me into the garden; why she seemed to derive a certain satisfaction from showing me the view.

Footsteps sounded on the path behind us, and we turned to see William Morgan trudging towards us, looking as surly as ever; an expression that became even more sullen the moment he saw me.

'Ah! William!' Judith remarked coolly. 'Master Chapman and I were just talking about Nell's brother, who used to assist you in the garden.'

'Stupid little varmint,' he grumbled. 'That boy would never do as he was told, would he? Always planting things where he shouldn't and trying to dig up things that I'd just planted. Couldn't tell a weed from a flower. I remember, down here, when he tried—'

'Thank you, William.' Judith, losing patience, interrupted the reminiscence politely, but firmly. 'Did you want me for something?'

'Paulina asked me to tell you that her next door has called

to see you – Mistress Jolliffe. I was coming down the garden anyway, so I said I'd save her legs by giving you the message myself.' He glowered vindictively at me. 'Do you want me to show the pedlar out?'

'There's no need,' Judith answered coolly, not best pleased, I could tell, by his familiar tone in front of an outsider. But the Welshman seemed to hold a privileged position in his mistress's esteem, and she offered no reprimand. She turned instead to me. 'I feel sure, Master Chapman, you can leave by the same way that you entered. There's no need for you to go through the house. You'll see that the wall is as easy to scale from this side as from the other. I'll show you where you climbed over. Thank you for your company. I've enjoyed it.' She laughed softly, as if at some private joke.

I should have liked to stay and have a few words with William Morgan concerning his murderous nocturnal activities, but with Mistress St Clair's eyes fixed upon me I had no choice but to climb the wall again and make my way up the alleyway into the Strand. I realized that our conversation had omitted any mention of Martin Threadgold's sudden death and, on reflection, found it a strange oversight, considering it should have been a topic uppermost in both our minds, but particularly in that of Judith St Clair.

The thoroughfare was as busy as ever and, above the never-ending clamour of the bells, vendors of hot pies, cold ale, sweetmeats, ribbons, laces, silks, or anything else you fancied could be heard screaming, 'Buy! Buy! Buy! What do you lack? What'll you buy?' It made my head begin to ache just listening to them.

While I hesitated, unsure what to do next, I saw, coming out of the Jolliffes' street door, Brandon and his father, the former stocky, thickset and brown-eyed, the latter large and shambling and with eyes the same Saxon blue as my own. I hailed them, but my voice got lost in the general hubbub. I was convinced that Brandon had glimpsed me out of the corner of one eye, but he gave no sign of having done so except to hurry Roland forward at a quickened pace. I let them go. I knew where to find them if ever I needed to speak to either of them in the future.

Once again, however, the sight of Brandon Jolliffe touched that elusive chord of memory within my brain. What was it I was trying to remember? Or perhaps remember was not quite the right word. Maybe I was trying to make a connection with some other fact lying dormant somewhere in the farthest recesses of my mind. I struggled to find the missing link, unaware that I was standing stock-still in the roadway until I found myself being jostled and pushed aside by various irate passers-by, who made uncomplimentary comments on the irritating habits of country bumpkins not used to the capital's busy ways. As I had been priding myself on how well I blended into the London scene, I found this particularly galling, and I was willing to bandy words with anyone spoiling for a fight. But Londoners appeared to have no time even for a quarrel, so I gave up and went back to the Voyager, where I went to my room and stretched out on the bed, promising myself an hour of quiet reflection. But no sooner had I started to review all that had happened in the four days since my arrival in London than, lulled by the warmth of the sun coming in at the open shutters and the comfort of the goose-feather mattress, I inevitably fell deeply and dreamlessly asleep.

It was nearly dusk when I finally awoke. The May twilight glimmered fitfully before the approaching dark. Beyond the window the sky was rinsed to a thin, fragile blue above the last flushed clouds of the sunset. Shadows muffled the outline of roofs on the opposite side of the Voyager's court-yard and, in the heavens, a single star shone, dimly as yet, the colour of unpolished steel.

My first thought was that I was famished: I had missed my supper. The second was that there was someone banging at my chamber door. The third was that the someone had to be Bertram. No one else would hammer and kick at the wood with such abandoned familiarity, and, a moment later, my suspicions were confirmed when his by now instantly recognizable voice called impatiently, 'Roger! Master Chapman! Let me in!'

With a groan, I slid off the bed and drew back the bolt near the top of the door. Bertram tripped over his own feet as he literally tumbled inside.

'What on earth's the matter?' I demanded crossly, my hunger making me irritable. 'What's so urgent that you must make all this racket? Don't tell me!' I added waspishly. 'You've discovered who killed Fulk Quantrell?'

'No.' He smirked. 'But I fancy it's a question the Dowager Duchess wants to put to you. I've been sent to bring you to Baynard's Castle.'

I ground my teeth in fury (not something that's easy to do, let me tell you).

'What does the bloody woman want now?' I fairly shouted. 'What does she expect? Miracles?'

Bertram giggled in exactly the same way as my children did when I lost my temper. Why was it, I wondered resentfully, that I was unable to terrify the younger generation with a display of righteous wrath?

'I think,' he offered, 'that His Grace of Gloucester so sang your praises to the Duchess and My Lord of Lincoln that they expected you to arrive at an immediate conclusion once you'd heard the story.'

I sighed. Duke Richard's touching faith in my powers of deduction could sometimes have disastrous consequences. I asked, 'Is there any way in which I can avoid this meeting?'

Bertram shook his head. 'I've been instructed to bring you back with me to Baynard's Castle *immediately*.'

'You could tell Her Grace you couldn't find me.'

He shook his head. 'She's not the woman to take no for an answer, chapman. I'd only be sent out to scour the city for you until I did. And I don't fancy spending half the night on the streets, pretending to search for someone who's really asleep, in bed.'

'We could find a cosy nook in the ale room,' I tempted him, but he regretfully declined this offer.

209

'I've two of Her Grace's gentlemen-at-arms waiting for us downstairs.'

I cursed long and fluently, to Bertram's unstinted admiration. It was obvious that some of the phrases and expressions were new to him, and I could see him storing them away in his memory for future use, in order to impress his friends.

There was no help for it, then. When royalty requests one's presence, there's no option but to obey. I didn't even dare to stop to eat.

The two Burgundian gentlemen awaiting us in the ale room were looking around them with a superior air, palpably disgusted at the antics of the swinish English. (All foreigners know, of course, that we are the spawn of the Devil, with tails concealed in our breeches.) They barely glanced our way as Bertram reappeared with me trailing reluctantly in his wake, but nodded curtly to Reynold Makepeace, ignored the goggling (and, if they'd only known, sniggering) drinkers at the scattered tables, and preceded us out of the inn, magnificent in their black-and-gold livery.

Our progress through the streets to Baynard's Castle was punctuated by the catcalls and rude remarks of passers-by, my fellow countrymen being, as always, deeply resentful of foreigners, whom they have always regarded with the greatest suspicion and derision – fair game for any insult they can lay their tongues to. Fortunately, our Burgundian friends seemed ignorant of most of the expressions hurled at their heads, for which I was truly thankful. They looked a couple of tall, stout lads who wouldn't hesitate to crack a few skulls together in defence of their own and their duchy's honour.

We finally reached the castle to find it in the grip of its usual hustle and bustle, but magnified several times over. There were torches and flambeaux everywhere; men-at-arms polishing their daggers and halberds until they positively shone; the kitchen quarters in a ferment, with scullions and pot boys and cooks frantically dashing in and out of doors, rushing from bakery to butchery to buttery and back again;

groups of jongleurs and acrobats and minstrels all practising their various arts in different corners of the courtyard, and setting up such a cacophony that even the palace rats ran squeaking in agony back to their holes.

My tentative enquiries elicited the fact that the King and Queen were riding over from Westminster to dine at Baynard's Castle that night, and were expected in about an hour, so Bertram and I were hurried in through a side door to a small and very chilly ante-room and told to wait. Our fine Burgundian friends then disappeared while we kicked our heels and tried to keep warm – exactly the sort of treatment I had grown to expect from my 'betters'.

'"When Adam delved and Eve span, / Who was then the gentleman?"' I muttered darkly to Bertram; but he obviously had never heard that seditious rhyme and looked at me as though I had taken leave of my senses.

After what seemed like an eternity, but was probably no more than a lapse of ten minutes or so, a gentleman-usher made his appearance to inform us that Her Grace the Dowager Duchess was not yet ready to receive us, but that My Lord of Lincoln would be grateful for a word – 'grateful for a word' being, of course, just another euphemism for, 'John de la Pole has spoken. Come at once!'

Needless to say, we didn't keep him waiting, but meekly followed the gentleman-usher into the royal presence. This proved to be in Lincoln's bedchamber, where he was wallowing in the scented water of a sponge-lined bath. As we were announced, he heaved himself into a sitting position and gave me his friendly smile, at the same time waving a well-manicured hand in the direction of an exotic-looking personage to whom he had been talking as we entered.

'Are you acquainted with Captain Brampton, chapman?' he asked in the free and easy way that assumed I would be on speaking terms with anyone and everyone at court.

As it happened, I *did* know who this tough, swarthy, swashbuckling gentleman was, having come across him five years earlier during my attempts to foil a plot on the Duke of Gloucester's life, and having learned his history then.

Edward Brampton was a Jew, a rarity in England since the expulsion of his race by the first Edward almost three centuries earlier. Duarte Brandeo (his original Portuguese name) had, however, embraced Christianity and lived in the House of the Convertites in the Strand. At his baptism, the King himself had stood as godfather, and Brampton had taken his sovereign's Christian name along with his new surname. (I mention him here, not because he played any significant role in this particular story, but because, in a few years' time, he and I would find ourselves unexpected allies against the usurper Henry Tudor. But that is to anticipate . . .)

I murmured that I had indeed once had the honour of the Captain's acquaintance, but as he obviously had no recollection of me, I said no more, waiting silently to know why the Earl had summoned me. Captain Brampton kissed Lincoln's hand and took himself off in a flurry of good wishes and gusts of jovial laughter that made everyone in the room grin in sympathy – even the Earl's Master of the Bath, an ascetic, stern-looking gentleman who kept a beady eye on the three young pages whose job it was to keep the tub topped up from the large pan of water heating over the bedchamber fire.

I eyed the Earl a little warily, wondering if, this evening, he was his mother's or his father's son – Plantagenet or de la Pole; the descendant of Alfred and Charlemagne, or Geoffrey Chaucer's great-great-grandson. I was relieved to find it was the latter and that My Lord was all smiling condescension and affability.

'Pull up a stool, Roger,' he invited, waving an arm from which water dripped in a sparkling arc. He indicated in an equally moist fashion that Bertram could make himself scarce, much to that young gentleman's ill-concealed chagrin. (He felt himself to be quite as much a part of this investigation as I was, and resented his exclusion.)

When Bertram had duly bowed and departed to kick his heels outside the bedchamber door, Lincoln leaned his head back against a cushion, which had been thoughtfully placed on the edge of the tub by one of the pages, and regarded me with his frank, wide-mouthed grin.

'I understand my aunt, Her Grace the Dowager Duchess, has sent for you?' I nodded, and he laughed outright. 'Don't let her fluster you, Roger. She's an impatient woman who thinks that everyone should dance to the pace of her own tune. All the same' – his eyes narrowed – '*have* you discovered anything yet? Anything at all? If so, you can tell me. I can keep a secret.'

I shook my head. 'I prefer to have the whole story, Your Highness, before giving away any part of it.'

The Earl made a moue of disappointment. 'Poor stuff,' he complained. 'Haven't you any idea at all who might have killed the Burgundian?'

'There are one or two clues that point in a certain direction,' I admitted, 'but they're not of sufficient strength to justify my making my suspicions public just yet.'

'I've told you. I wouldn't say a word to anyone,' he wheedled. 'On my word of honour.'

It was my turn to laugh aloud. 'Your Highness, you are *surrounded* by people, all of whom have ears. If I said anything to you now, it would be all over the castle by nightfall. Don't you agree?'

I gestured at the Master of the Bath and the three pages, and towards a fourth servant with a large sheet draped across one arm, standing ready to towel his royal master dry the instant Lincoln should step from the tub. As I did so, it occurred to me how alike two of the pages were to one another: blue-eyed and fair-haired, tall and well built. I glanced from one to the other with interest.

The Earl, following my eyes and at once understanding what had attracted my attention, let out a roar of raucous laughter that brought a reproving frown to the face of his Master of the Bath.

'You're looking at Edmund and John and thinking how alike they are – isn't that so?' I agreed with an inclination of my head. Lincoln grinned. 'You'll see that particular cast of countenance frequently in the royal palaces of my uncle, the King.' I must still have looked nonplussed, for he gave another shout of laughter and said, 'Think, man, think! His Highness has never been renowned for living like a monk. If, that is, monks ever do live like monks!' (He was convulsed with merriment at his own wit: he was still quite young – only eighteen.)

I realized belatedly what the Earl was trying to tell me: that the two boys were bastard sons of the King. Not the sons of high-born ladies, of course, but offspring of some of the chambermaids and kitchen maids His Highness had seduced. For Edward Plantagenet, fourth of his name, was known to have an almost insatiable sexual appetite that no one woman – and probably not even two or three – could satisfy.

Lincoln signalled to the man holding the towel that he was about to get out of the bath just as a knock fell on his chamber door and Bertram reappeared, to announce that the Dowager Duchess was now ready to receive me. The Earl held out his wet right hand.

'Then I won't keep you, Roger. As I told you, my aunt of Burgundy is not a woman who can brook delay. But I'm very glad to have seen and spoken with you again, even though I can't be said to have gained much by it. You're as close as an oyster. But I have good memories of our journey together from Bristol to London, and those convivial evenings we spent on the road. I trust we shall meet again soon.'

I kissed the hand he had extended and smiled. 'Your Highness is very gracious. And you need not feel too downcast. If it's of any comfort to you, you have just given me a valuable clue – the key to something that has been puzzling me for the past two days.'

'And can you now divulge the name of the murderer?' he asked eagerly, his boyish face agog with excitement.

I shook my head. 'Let us simply say, My Lord, that you have provided another stepping-stone to help me on my way.'

'But you do *have* a name in your head?'

'I do, Your Highness. But it may not be the right one.'

Lincoln gave a crow of laughter. 'You're a cautious one, chapman, and no mistake. I'd never hesitate to entrust a secret to you. And now, you mustn't keep my aunt waiting any longer.' And as I was going out of the door, he called mischievously, 'Good luck!'

The Dowager Duchess was ready for the evening's festivities, resplendent in a gown of cloth-of-silver tissue, the Order of the Golden Fleece in brilliant enamels hung about her neck. Diamonds, emeralds and rubies sparkled in riotous profusion over every inch of her royal person, and a magnificent gold crown, set with enormous pearls, rested on her once famous golden hair. This was now demurely hidden beneath a veil of white silk, and I wondered, meanly, if there were any grey in it that the Duchess was happy to conceal.

'Well?' she asked abruptly, as I was ushered into her presence, and ignoring Bertram who, this time, had insisted on sticking close to me. 'What have you to tell me, Master Chapman.'

I bowed low. (It seemed like a good idea.) 'At present, Your Grace, I cannot give you a name, but in a day or so, I believe it might be possible.'

'Why can't you tell me your suspicions now?' she demanded imperiously. 'If, that is, you really have any.'

'Suspicions are not proof, madame. I have no desire to blacken anyone's name without good cause.'

She made no answer for several seconds while she considered this, then nodded, as though satisfied. 'Very well. But I return to Burgundy soon. I should like to know the truth before I leave.'

I regarded her straitly. 'Madame . . . Your Highness, the truth is not always what we want to hear.'

She raised her eyebrows. 'Is that a warning?'

'A caution, perhaps. No more than that at present.'

The Duchess bit her lip, then, as trumpets blared throughout the castle, nodded a curt dismissal, rising swiftly to her feet and summoning her ladies about her.

The King and Queen had arrived.

Eighteen

I was consumed by a sense of irritation. Was this what I had been summoned to Baynard's Castle for? Was this what I had forgone my rest and supper for? A delay while My Lady the Duchess finished an elaborate toilet, half a minute of questioning and then dismissal? Was that really it? My Lady had asked nothing, and I had told her nothing, that could not have been settled by sending one of her servants to the Voyager. My annoyance, however, might have been much greater had it not been for my interview with the Earl of Lincoln, and the sudden revelation that had been vouchsafed me while I was there. My visit had not, after all, proved to be a complete waste of time.

It was, in fact, to prove even more rewarding.

As the Duchess sailed regally from the bedchamber, surrounded by a bevy of pretty and not-so-pretty young women, all chattering animatedly in French, a language in which, alas, I am not at all proficient, Bertram gripped my elbow and indicated that we should leave.

'We'll go down by the eastern turret stairs,' he whispered, 'and out past the stables. That way, we'll miss all the fuss of the King and Queen's arrival.'

'And the arrival of all their hundreds of retainers, and the bowing and scraping and speechifying,' I added nastily. I was still smarting under a sense of outrage and the confirmation of my belief that those set in authority over us are often arrogant and thoughtless, with no consideration for mortals less fortunate and important than themselves.

'Well, yes, there's that as well,' Bertram agreed, eyeing me curiously. 'Has something happened to upset you, Roger?'

'Master Chapman to you, my lad,' I snapped, refraining from boxing his ears, but only because I was following him down a very narrow and ill-lit staircase.

'My, my! You are annoyed,' Bertram replied, turning his head to grin cheekily at me over one shoulder. 'Mind you, I understand. The Dowager Duchess can have that effect on some people.'

Our descent ended in a corner of the castle's brilliantly lit and frantically busy outer courtyard, where the royal party's horses were being rubbed down, watered, fed and stabled while their owners sat through several hours of banqueting and festivities in the great hall. There was still some activity with late arrivals. Rich satins and furs gleamed dully in the flickering light of dozens of torches, and a thousand rainbows glimmered among the flash and sparkle of gems.

'I'll take you to the gate,' Bertram offered, before adding pompously, 'After that, I must leave you. I expect I'll be needed.'

I was just about to ask in my most scathing tone, 'What for?' when all other thoughts were driven from my head by a brief glimpse of the Duchess's groom who had been breakfasting in the Voyager that morning.

'Don't bother! I'll find my own way out,' I flung at Bertram, before plunging into the crowd of ostlers stable boys and grooms, shouldering and elbowing them aside and keeping a sharp lookout for my elusive quarry. Finally, I saw him, leading a handsome bay mare into an empty stall. He kicked the lower half of the door shut behind him.

By the time I was near enough to lean my arms along the top of the half-door and peer inside, my friend was rubbing the bay down with a handful of straw.

'You are the Dowager Duchess's groom who's putting up at the Voyager in Bucklersbury, aren't you?' I enquired, more to attract his attention than because I had any doubts on the matter.

The man jumped and turned, straightening his back and advancing into the patch of torchlight near the door in order to see me better. He considered my face thoughtfully for a minute or two, then nodded. 'I remember you. We were talking at breakfast. But I can't stop now. You can see I'm busy. It's like a madhouse here tonight.'

I grinned, but made no attempt to move away. 'A banquet, or so I've been given to understand. All fish dishes, I suppose as it's Friday?'

The groom snorted derisively and paused in his work. 'What do you think?'

'A special dispensation to eat meat – that's what I think. Plenty of roasted venison, beef, pork, mutton, swan, pheasant, fowl . . .'

'Peacock, suckling pig,' he added, entering into the spirit of the the thing.

We both laughed, and he stood upright again, patting the mare's rump. 'Maybe I could do with a rest,' he conceded. 'A couple of minutes.' He forked fresh hay into the manger.

'We were talking this morning,' I said quickly, before he had time to embark on any topic of his own, 'about Fulk Quantrell, who was murdered here in London just over two weeks ago. You said you knew but didn't like him. When I asked why not, you muttered something about "like mother, like son". What did you mean by that?'

He shrugged. 'Nothing personal. A lot of people didn't like Dame Quantrell. Not that they voiced their opinion too loudly, you understand. She could do no wrong in the Duchess's eyes. She was her devoted childhood friend and servant, come with her from England to make her exile bearable. Mind you, she was always civil enough whenever she visited the stables. Please and thank you, as pretty as you like.' The groom was now getting into his stride, his arms folded, like mine, on the top of the half-door as he leaned forward confidentially. 'The boy, though, was a different matter. Arrogant, overbearing and thinking he was God's gift to an expectant world. Had to be mounted on the best horses, and ran with his complaints to the Duchess if he didn't get his way. And Her Highness encouraged him with her orders that he was to ride any horse that he chose – just so long as it wasn't one of hers, of course. But Fulk knew better than to push his luck too far. His demands were always within reason. But he was a sneak and a troublemaker when he was young, and he didn't improve as he got older.'

'You still haven't told me why Mistress Quantrell was disliked,' I pointed out. 'If she wasn't arrogant or rude, and didn't carry tales to the Duchess, what exactly was it about her that people objected to?'

The groom bit a callused thumb. Behind him, the mare shifted her hindquarters restlessly. He gave her another absent-minded pat.

'We-ell, I heard – not that I know this for certain; I never experienced it myself – but I did hear that Dame Quantrell had a habit of prying and poking into other people's business and then threatening to use the information she'd gathered against them.'

'Blackmail, do you mean?'

The groom sucked his teeth and pulled down the corners of his mouth. He seemed reluctant to commit himself.

'Ye-es,' he admitted at last. 'I suppose that's what I do mean. As I say, I never had any experience of it, myself. But then, I've no secrets to hide.' He grinned and winked. 'I lead a blameless life.'

I returned a perfunctory smile, too busy turning over in my mind the information he had just given me.

'What about Fulk?' I asked. 'Was he up to the same tricks as his mother?'

The groom shook his head. 'I never heard so, but it wouldn't be surprising, I suppose, considering how close the two of them were reported to be. And now it seems that he's been murdered. It makes you wonder. It makes me wonder, at any rate.' The mare turned her head and nudged him in the back. Her water trough was empty. The groom made a clucking sound under his breath and said, 'I mustn't stay gossiping like this or I shall be boiled alive in oil. This beauty belongs to one of Queen Elizabeth's sisters. I'll bid you goodnight.' And, grabbing a black leather bucket, he ran towards the well in the middle of the stable yard.

I called an answering 'Goodnight!' but it was doubtful if

he heard me. He was too busy winching up the bucket. There was no sign of Bertram. He was probably nursing a sense of grievance at my abrupt departure and had abandoned me to my fate. Not that I needed him. I found the outer gate quite easily and, after a short but acrimonious colloquy with the gatekeeper as to who I was and what had been my business in the castle (I was *leaving*, I pointed out, not trying to get in!), I finally made my exit. Five minutes later I was in Thames Street, then heading north towards Knightrider Street, making my way back to the Voyager.

I had heard the watch cry midnight before I eventually closed my eyes. I had been staring for more than an hour into the blackness and an impression of the room remained, like reflections in a river, distorted and dark.

I had realized, long before reaching Bucklersbury, that I could no longer resent my summons to Baynard's Castle that evening, however abortive my interview with the Dowager Duchess Margaret might have been. The inspiration and information I had received while there had been invaluable. Things were finally beginning to fall into place. A pattern was emerging that inexorably led me forward to one conclusion, and one only. In the morning, I would pay another call on the Jolliffes. Meanwhile, sleep was claiming me at last . . .

I was back in the Earl of Lincoln's bedchamber, watching from the shadows where no one could see me. But the man in the sponge-lined tub wasn't the King's young nephew: he was a man I had never seen before, and standing, waiting to attend him, were his three pages, Lionel Broderer, Brandon Jolliffe and Roger Jessop.

Suddenly, the man in the bath tub began to laugh, throwing out his arms and saying, 'Think, man, think! I've never been renowned for living like a monk!' and then laughing so hard that his whole body shook – and continued to shake until he slowly sank beneath the water and disappeared. The other three men stood like statues and made not the slightest effort to save him. I tried to go to his aid, but my limbs were like lead and I was unable move.

'He's drowning!' I yelled, but my voice made no sound. Then, just as I managed to reach out a hand to the edge of the tub, the stranger bobbed to the surface of the water again, like a cork, and laughing harder than ever.

'Nonsense!' he shouted. 'I haven't drowned!' And he heaved himself out of the tub, only to collapse in a pitiful heap on the floor. This time, I was in no doubt at all that he was dead . . .

I woke up, sweating profusely and with a terrible thirst, astonished to see that it was already morning. Sunlight was pouring through the cracks in the shutters, and I could hear the maids and tapsters and stable boys calling to one another as they set about their tasks for the new day. Reynold Makepeace, too, was calling a brisk greeting to his workers as he crossed the inner courtyard from his private quarters on the opposite side.

I dressed swiftly and went outside to hold my head and hands under the pump, before dragging one of my best bone combs, taken from my pack, through my tangled mop of hair. A quick rub of my teeth with the willow bark I always carried, and I was off to the taproom to bespeak breakfast, and in the hope that I might meet my friend the groom once again. But my luck was out: there was no sign of him and, upon enquiry, I was told that he had left the inn over half an hour ago. The morning was more advanced than I had thought.

I ordered a meal of pickled herring, porridge and a bacon collop, and while I was eating it, I thought back over my dream. It was no ordinary dream – not one of those jumbles of ridiculous events and even weirder facts that plague one's nights with their nonsense. This had been one of those visions that have haunted me from childhood, and that are a pale version of my mother's ability to 'see'. She had always denied having second sight, but there was no doubt that she had had sufficient accuracy in foretelling the future to make people a little afraid of her. In a larger community than Wells, where the town huddled around the cathedral like chicks around their mother hen, she might well have been denounced as a witch. But our neighbours knew and trusted

221

Mistress Stonecarver (my father's profession) and even came to her for advice.

As I say, I had inherited a fraction of her power in the form of these dreams, and last night's – or, rather, this morning's – needed very little interpretation in the light of what I now thought I knew.

I was just congratulating myself that I was at last free of Bertram's company (although, admittedly, I had grown fond of the lad) when he walked into the ale room, grinning all over his face.

'I've persuaded Master Plummer to give me one more day's grace,' he announced, beaming with self-congratulation. He sat down on the bench beside me. 'You have the benefit of my company and advice for one last time. By the way,' he added in a more aggrieved accent, 'where did you get to last night when you suddenly disappeared like that?'

'I saw someone I knew,' I answered shortly, rising from the table. His face fell. 'If you want to buy yourself a stoup of ale and some breakfast, by all means do so,' I encouraged him. 'I highly recommend the pickled herring and bacon collops. You can catch me up later.'

But he wasn't so stupid. 'I see!' he mocked. 'I can catch you up although you're not going to tell me where you're going! No, I thank you. I'm coming with you.'

I sighed. 'I'm paying a visit to the Jolliffes. You can find me there.'

He eyed me suspiciously. 'And that's the truth you're telling me?'

'I swear it.' I didn't say where I might be going afterwards. I didn't see any need.

His natural caution put up a short, sharp struggle against the near-starvation rations of Baynard's Castle servants, but his hunger won.

'I'll see you at the Jolliffes', then,' he grinned, as a pot boy came to take his order.

I had no doubt he would add the meal to my bill, but felt it was worth it not to have him constantly at my elbow.

It was another fine day and the Saturday traders were out

in force. The usual vociferous crowds thronged the streets and flooded in and out of the Lud Gate, where there was even more delay because of decorations being erected over the arch. Evidently, the Dowager Duchess and her train were due to pass that way some time today.

By paying an early-morning visit, I had counted on finding all three of the Jolliffes at home, and I was not disappointed. They were still at breakfast when my arrival was announced.

Lydia Jolliffe, whom I had particularly requested to see, received me – somewhat ungraciously, I thought – in the upstairs parlour where we had previously met.

'Well? What now, Master Chapman?' she demanded.

Today, she was dressed in yellow silk: a fortuitous choice, yellow being the colour of hostility. This gown was cut lower over the breasts than the green one she had worn previously, decorated with amber beads and clasped around the hips by a chestnut-brown leather girdle. She looked magnificent, and knew it. I glanced at the wall hangings behind her. They, too, were magnificent in their way.

Lydia seated herself in the armchair, but today made no suggestion that I should pull up the stool, leaving me to stand.

'Well?' she repeated. 'You've interrupted my breakfast. I beg that you'll say what you have to say and go.'

I was silent for a moment, staring thoughtfully at her, which, I could see, she found unnerving. Then I said abruptly, 'Your son, Brandon – he's not much like your husband, is he?'

She flushed angrily. 'He takes after me.'

'A little,' I conceded. 'But the person he most resembles is Lionel Broderer. In fact, my assistant mistook him for Lionel only yesterday. He also resembles a young lad, Roger Jessop, who used to work for Mistress St Clair in her garden.'

The flush became a deep, angry red. 'What are you suggesting, chapman?'

'I'm suggesting,' I answered steadily, 'that these three young men had one and the same father: Edmund Broderer. And there may be others, for all I know. I think Edmund Broderer was fond of women. And women were fond of him.'

I held my breath. If Lydia chose to deny my allegation, I

was unable prove it, and she could, and probably would, have me thrown into the street. I'd still believe it to be the truth, but I would have preferred confirmation of my suspicions.

Slowly the angry tide of red receded from her cheeks, to be replaced by an appreciative smile. 'Very astute of you, Roger,' she said at last. 'I hope you're not intending to blackmail me by threatening to tell my husband, because it wouldn't do you a bit of good. He already knows. In fact, he encouraged my affair with Edmund. Roland's impotent, you see, and he wanted a son. He's perfectly happy to acknowledge Brandon as his.' She turned to glance at the embroidered wall hangings. 'He bought me these as a gift after Brandon's birth. From Edmund's workshop. Appropriate, if somewhat ironic, don't you think?'

I smiled. 'Very appropriate,' I agreed. 'But I don't suppose all the husbands were as complaisant as yours, Mistress Jolliffe. Martha Broderer's, for instance.'

Lydia Jolliffe shrugged. 'But he wasn't likely to find out, now, was he? He was Edmund's cousin, so a family likeness was unremarkable. As for the boy who used to work next door, his mother was a widow.'

'But I don't imagine these three are the only bastards of Edmund Broderer, are they?'

The word 'bastard' brought the blood back to her face for a moment, but then she shrugged and laughed.

'You believe in calling a spade a spade, my friend. No, I don't suppose they were Edmund's only by-blows. He was a very virile man. He enjoyed . . . copulation.' Lydia looked me up and down provocatively. 'Where is all this leading, chapman? I can't believe you're intending to tell my son. You're not that sort.'

'Certainly not,' I assured her.

'So?'

'Was Judith St Clair – Judith Broderer, as she must have been then – aware of her husband's – er – activities?'

This time Lydia threw back her head and laughed out loud, all her previous animosity forgotten.

'"Activities", is it? What a splendidly prudish word . . .

I don't think she could help but know. There were too many children around these parts who all had the same set of features.'

Like the royal palaces, I thought to myself.

I asked, 'Didn't this distress Mistress St Clair? Especially as she seems unable to bear children herself?'

Lydia pulled down one corner of her mouth. 'I should think it probably did – it would distress any woman – but you'd never have got Judith to own as much. She was, and still is, very proud. Even today, she would most likely scorn such a notion as Edmund's infidelity, if you put it to her.'

'In spite of the evidence of her own eyes?'

'I've told you: she's extraordinarily high in the instep. She could never admit that Edmund was unfaithful to her. She's a person who cannot tolerate disloyalty. One of the reasons she puts up with that oaf William Morgan, and allows him such licence, is because he is fanatical in his obedience to her wishes. She can do no wrong in his estimation, and I truly believe he would condone any action of hers, however bad. I believe he would kill for her, if necessary.'

I felt sure she was right, but did not say so.

'The lad who used to work in the garden, Roger Jessop,' I said, 'told me that he ran away because he thought someone in the St Clair household was trying to murder him. What do you think of that?'

I should have foreseen that I would have to spend the next few minutes fending off Lydia's queries as to how and when I had managed to speak to Roger, by what means I had traced his whereabouts; but finally, reluctantly accepting that I had no intention of betraying the boy's confidence, she consented to answer my question.

'I think it's nonsense,' she answered roundly. 'Who would want to get rid of him? He'd grown up under Judith's protection and he was a good worker. In fact, he was a better worker, probably, than he was allowed to be. I've heard him arguing with William Morgan on more than one occasion that he could be trusted to do more on his own. But William, typically, treated him like an idiot and followed the lad around the garden, supervising everything he did. It was always my opinion, for what it was worth, that Roger knew more about gardening than William. However, that might have been the trouble. William resented a child of that age being better at his job than he was.'

'You don't think, then, that the Welshman could have tried to get rid of the boy for that very reason?'

My companion shook her head decisively. 'No. William Morgan relied on young Roger's knowledge – goodness knows where the lad got it from: I suppose it was just a gift from God – to keep the garden looking as Judith wanted it, and to earn her praises. For there's no doubt that William took all the credit. Judith was forever lauding his ability as a gardener.'

'So, would there have been anyone else in the household who might have wanted Roger Jessop out of the way?'

'No, of course not! Why should they? Godfrey and Jocelyn and Alcina could have had nothing against him. They may not even have been aware of his existence.'

'Master St Clair was,' I corrected her. 'He mentioned the lad to me; mentioned, also, that he didn't come to work in the garden any more.'

Lydia shrugged, and there was silence between us for several seconds. Eventually, she asked, 'What has all this to do with the murder of Fulk Quantrell?'

I gave her my most winning smile. 'I'm afraid I can't divulge that just yet . . . Tell me, did Edmund Broderer possess a gold-and-agate thumb ring?'

Lydia looked startled and, suddenly, a little wary.

'Did he?' I pressed.

'As a matter of fact, he did. It was something he acquired in the final month of his life. I remember remarking on it and asking him where he'd bought it. But he wouldn't say. Just told me it was a gift and extremely precious to him. He made the remark very pointedly, in front of Judith. I've never forgotten because of the look on her face – a look that made me quite sure a woman was involved. But I really don't see how you could know about the ring,' she went on. 'Edmund was wearing it the night he was robbed and thrown in the river, and his body was mother-naked when it was finally found. Not a jewel nor a scrap of clothing on him.' She eyed me uneasily. 'You don't practise the dark arts, do you?'

I ignored this last question, but asked one of my own instead. 'Are you certain that Master Broderer was wearing the ring the night he disappeared?'

'Quite certain. Edmund called here immediately after leaving home and before he went off to the inn for an evening's drinking – if that was, indeed, where he was going. He brought Brandon some new arrows for his bow from the fletcher's in Turnbaston Lane. He was very fond of the boy.' Lydia took a deep breath before adding, 'Brandon was, after all, his son . . . So, I repeat, how did you know . . . ?'

I interrupted her ruthlessly. 'You said "if that was indeed where he was going". What exactly did you mean by that?'

'I – I don't know. For heaven's sake! It's twelve years ago! How can I be expected to remember? Oh, very well! I just had this feeling – intuition, if you like – that he was going to see a woman. There was an air of . . . of suppressed excitement about him, and he was all spruced up in his best hose and his new red velvet tunic. Now, will you please tell me . . . ?'

This time I was saved from answering by the opening of the door, and by Roland Jolliffe entering the room in his slow, shambling way, but with a martial light in his kindly blue eyes.

'Why are you keeping my wife so long, Master Chapman?' he demanded belligerently. 'I won't have her worried by all your questions. She's not strong.' (I'd have bet money on Lydia outlasting everyone around her.) 'Come, my love.' He offered her his arm, which she rose and took with the greatest reluctance. 'I'll bid you a very good morning, pedlar. I don't look to see you bothering my wife again.'

227

Nineteen

I had intended to go next door, to the St Clairs' house, as soon as I quit the Jolliffes'; but instead I returned the way I had come and struggled through the crowds, which had now become clogged with sightseers waiting to cheer the Duchess, to Needlers Lane, where I went straight to visit Martha Broderer, relying on the fact that Lionel would be across the street, at the workshop. I looked for Bertram as I went, but he had either not yet finished a protracted breakfast or we missed one another in the throng.

Martha Broderer was still at home and still at table. A dirty bowl and beaker opposite her place suggested that my hopes had been realized and that Lionel had at least left the room, if not the house.

'If you're looking for Lal, he's already gone,' his mother confirmed. 'But stay and have a cup of ale with me, chapman, before you seek him out.'

'It's you I want to see, not your son,' I said, pulling up a stool and accepting her offer of ale. When she raised her eyebrows, I went on, 'I've just come from talking to Lydia Jolliffe.' I added significantly, 'About Brandon.'

Martha, filling a clean beaker from a jug of small beer, shot me a suddenly apprehensive glance from beneath frowning brows. 'What about Brandon?'

I took the beaker and swallowed several mouthfuls before replying. But at last, I said, 'Mistress Jolliffe has admitted to me that Edmund Broderer was Brandon's father. And Brandon looks extraordinarily like Lionel. My guess is that your son, too, was fathered by Edmund.'

Martha looked at me, her lips compressed, her hands

228

gripped together in front of her, on the table. I was afraid she was about to order me from the house, but, finally, she heaved a great sigh, almost of relief.

'Edmund and I were once very much in love. He was nineteen, I was fifteen – old enough to know better, perhaps, but not old enough to be wise. At least, I wasn't. I was already betrothed to Edmund's cousin, you see. And when I discovered I was pregnant with Edmund's child, I was too frightened to admit the truth – frightened of the shame and the recriminations. In spite of Edmund's pleas, I went ahead and married my husband and passed Lionel off as his.

'Edmund found it hard to forgive me, and who can blame him? But he stayed single for the next eleven years. I don't mean there weren't women; there were – a number of them. He was a very virile man. And I must admit that I have often wondered about Brandon Jolliffe's paternity. The boy bears little resemblance to either of his parents, and the likeness to Lal that you've mentioned is really quite marked . . . Then, quite suddenly, at the age of thirty, Edmund met and married Judith Fennyman, a seamstress in Margaret of York's household. It must have been the same year as the battles of Mortimer's Cross and St Alban's. The same year that King Henry was deposed and the present king crowned. Margaret of York was suddenly of great importance, a member of the reigning dynasty. Edmund told me later that he was never in love with Judith: his mother had died and he didn't care for the idea of living alone, and Judith had a certain attraction for him, being as she was in the employ of the new princess. Besides, he wanted a child whom he could acknowledge openly as his own.'

'He was disappointed, then,' I put in as Martha paused to draw breath.

She nodded. 'Yes. Judith proved to be barren. But more than that, the year after Edmund and Judith's marriage, her brother-in-law, James Quantrell, was killed when he was thrown from his horse, and Veronica and Fulk, who was just a baby, went to live at the house in the Strand. Edmund and his sister-in-law didn't get on. The two women were as thick as thieves, and Edmund felt himself to be an outsider in his own home.

'This went on for six years and, more and more, he began to turn to me for comfort – I was a widow by this time – and, gradually, all our old love was rekindled. He gave me a gold ring as token of his love, and I gave him a gold-and-agate thumb ring, which he told me he would wear until he died. He promised to tell Judith that he was leaving her for me. He could obtain a divorce, he said, on the grounds of her inability to have children . . .'

Martha broke off, her voice suspended by tears, so I finished for her. 'But before that could happen, Edmund Broderer disappeared and no one knew what had happened to him until some time later, when his body was fished out of the Thames, almost unrecognizable.' I paused, then asked, 'Didn't it ever occur to you, Mistress Broderer, how very convenient for Judith his death was?'

Martha gave me another sharp look. 'Yes, of course it did. But not only Veronica Quantrell, but William Morgan also, swore they were all at home together and didn't leave the house the night he vanished.'

I made no comment, but finished my beer. 'Were you surprised,' I then asked, 'when Judith married a violent man like Justin Threadgold?'

'Yes, I must admit I was. But she's always had this passion for children and young people. I thought she must have married him for Alcina's sake.'

'And her passion for Fulk Quantrell?'

Martha laughed, gesturing with one hand. 'Oh, that's easy enough to explain! A nephew, her twin sister's son, whom she hadn't clapped eyes on for the past twelve years! Handsome and with a tongue dripping with honey! Poor Judith stood no chance. She was lost from the first moment of setting eyes on him.'

'Yes . . . I rather fancy that she was,' I answered slowly. I got to my feet. 'Well, thank you, Mistress Broderer. I won't take up any more of your time. You've told me what I wanted to know.'

'Where are you going now?' she enquired curiously. 'Do you know yet who killed Fulk Quantrell?'

'Yes, I think so,' I said. 'It's just a question of whether or not I can get that person to confess.'

Martha looked both excited and a little alarmed. 'It's not Lionel, is it?' she demanded, trembling slightly.

I moved towards the door. 'Is he aware that Edmund was his father?' I enquired.

She shook her head. 'No. I've never told him; I've never seen the need. Whether or not I *would* have done, had Edmund and I ever married, I can't say.' She sighed again. 'Maybe I'll tell him the truth one day, if the moment seems right.'

I thanked her for her time and patience, and left quickly before she realized that I hadn't answered her question.

'I'll let myself out,' I said. 'Don't trouble your maid.'

I made my way back to the Strand, more than ever convinced that I knew the identity of Fulk Quantrell's murderer.

This time I did see Bertram, although he failed to spot me. With a face like thunder, hot and sweating, he was returning through the Lud Gate and about to climb the hill. I didn't call out, but carried on along Fleet Street to the bridge, and across the Fleet into the Strand.

Paulina Graygoss answered my knock, but pulled down the corners of her mouth when I asked to see her mistress. 'You'll have to come back later,' she informed me tersely. 'The mistress is doing her domestic rounds. And there are still details of Master Threadgold's funeral to arrange. She and Mistress Alcina will be visiting St Dunstan's later, after dinner. You can wait till then, if you like,' she added grudgingly.

But I wasn't prepared to wait. 'Tell Mistress St Clair I would like to speak to her *now*,' I said, drawing a gasp of protest from the housekeeper.

'I'll do no such thing,' she declared roundly. 'I've never heard the like. What impudence! A common chapman to issue his orders to the lady of the house! How dare you!'

One of the doors into the great hall opened and Godfrey St Clair shuffled in, a silk-covered folio (presumably the sayings of Marcus Aurelius) clutched in one hand.

'What's the trouble, Paulina?' he asked, giving me an odd, calculating look that he tried, unsuccessfully, to turn into a welcoming smile. Then, without waiting for her reply, he advanced on me, one hand outheld. 'Master Chapman! I saw your approach from a window. I'm sorry to tell you that my wife is but just this moment taken with one of her very bad headaches, and is laid down upon her bed.'

Paulina Graygoss gave a startled exclamation of sympathy and at once ordered me from the house. 'You see now that it's impossible for you to see the mistress.'

Godfrey silenced her with a wave of his hand. 'On the contrary, my wife has agreed see you, Master Chapman, if you keep your visit brief and do not object to being received by her in her bedchamber.'

'Mistress St Clair was expecting me?'

'She . . . She thought you might be back . . . might wish to speak with her again.' Godfrey seemed ill at ease and his eyes refused to meet mine. 'I don't know why,' he went on, 'but it was after Mistress Jolliffe called on her a little while ago, just as we were finishing breakfast.'

'And she's willing to see me?'

'I've just said so.'

'In spite of her headache?' Paulina Graygoss demanded. 'I ought to go up to her, master, and mix her one of her potions.'

'No, no!' Godfrey shuffled his feet. 'It's . . . It's not as bad as most of her headaches,' he explained. 'And as for the potion, I've already mixed one for her and she's already feeling a little better. Besides, she's so much else to do, she feels she must talk to the pedlar, here, and get it over with. Then, perhaps, he'll go away and leave us in peace.' Godfrey turned back to me. 'So if you don't object to being received by my wife in her bedchamber, Master Chapman, I'll take you to her.'

I gave a bow and indicated that he should lead the way. The housekeeper detained me with a hand on my arm.

'You upset the mistress and you'll have me to reckon with,' she threatened in a low, furious voice. 'Receiving you when she's suffering from one of her headaches! Whatever next!'

'That'll do, Paulina!' Godfrey exclaimed impatiently.

232

'Come along, chapman, please. Mistress St Clair doesn't like to be kept waiting.'

I followed him meekly up the main staircase and was ushered into the room I had already visited twice before, but, for the first time, I entered through the main bedchamber door.

'I've brought the pedlar, as you see, my love,' Godfrey muttered, and withdrew hurriedly, closing the door behind him. His attitude was that of a man who, having reluctantly played his part, wanted nothing further to do with the matter. His nervousness was palpable – an unease that should have made me wary but failed to do so because, in some measure, it was Godfrey St Clair's natural manner.

Judith, fully clothed, was sitting up on the bed, but not in it. She had removed her shoes in order, I presumed, not to dirty the magnificent coverlet, while the bed curtains had been pushed right back to the head of the bed so that the story of Daphnis and Chloe was visible only as streaks of ochre and daubs of terracotta pink.

'Ah! Roger the Chapman!' she murmured, somewhat mockingly, I thought. 'Sit down.' And she indicated a stool set ready for me by the side of the bed.

She was certainly very pale, but otherwise gave no impression of a woman in the throes of a debilitating headache. A carved wooden cup with a silver rim, which stood on the bedside cupboard beside the candlestick and candle, appeared, from what I could see of it as I sat down, to be full to the top of some brownish liquid. She evidently had not yet swallowed the potion Godfrey had prepared for her, which, again, argued no great degree of discomfort. These signs and portents should have put me on my guard. But, I regret to say, they didn't.

'Well?' she invited, a little smile lifting the corners of her mouth. 'Do you know now who killed my nephew? And why?'

I didn't return her smile. 'I think so,' I answered.

'You only "think so"? I expected better of you than that.'

'All right,' I said. 'I do know. But I'll be honest with you, mistress. I've no real proof.'

At that, she laughed. 'That's not just being honest,' she said. 'That's being foolhardy. So! You've no proof unless the murderer confesses?'

'No. Only suspicions. And if the Dowager Duchess of Burgundy refuses to accept those suspicions—'

'Which she doubtless will!'

'Which, as you say, she doubtless will, then there is nothing further I can do in this matter.'

Judith nodded thoughtfully. 'On the other hand,' she said, 'suspicion, like mud, tends to stick and can ruin a life quite effectively. Although, of course, one still has that life, which must be preferable to a painful death. So I can't promise you that you'll get your confession, chapman.' She closed her eyes for a moment or two before suddenly opening them wide and turning them intently on me.

'Tell me, then,' she said, looking down her masterful nose, 'what made you first suspect me?'

I considered this. 'I think it was when you told me that your nephew had been murdered in Faitour Lane. This, of course, was perfectly true, but his body was later shifted by two of the beggars round the corner into Fleet Street and left outside St Dunstan's Church.'

'A very foolish mistake,' Judith commented harshly, plainly angry with herself, as well as with me for picking it up. 'So that's how the corpse came to be moved, is it? I did wonder . . . Go on! What else?'

'I found it odd that, after Fulk's death, you changed your will back again to its original form with such speed. Not much in itself, perhaps, but when I thought about it, it suggested to me a desire to erase Fulk from your life as soon as possible – a desire to right a wrong for the people you truly cared for: your husband, Mistress Alcina and Master Jocelyn. Even, perhaps, Lionel Broderer. As I said: a feeling, not evidence.'

Judith pursed her lips. 'No, not evidence,' she agreed. 'You've mentioned nothing so far that I couldn't refute. So? What more? Or isn't there anything?'

I sat up straighter on my stool and eased my aching

shoulders. 'You haven't asked me yet', I pointed out, 'why I think you killed your nephew.'

She laughed. 'Very well, then. Why did I murder Fulk, Master Chapman? Although I'm sure you've worked it out.'

'Because he was threatening you.'

'Indeed? And why would he be able to do that?'

'Because Fulk wasn't the first person you'd killed, was he, mistress? Twelve years ago you murdered your first husband. And I think – indeed, I'm almost sure – that if I were to dig beneath that willow tree in your garden, I should probably find his bones.'

There was silence, eventually broken by a deep sigh as Judith propped herself a little higher on her pillows. 'I think you're forgetting that Edmund Broderer was dragged from the river several weeks after he disappeared,' she reminded me.

'No, I'm not forgetting. But a body that's been in the Thames for that length of time would be almost unrecognizable. Except, of course, by his loving wife who identified him by the shape of his feet and some intimate bodily mark.'

The slightly tolerant smile had by now quite vanished and her eyes were like steel. 'You *have* been asking a lot of questions, Master Chapman,' she snapped. 'And, seemingly, getting a lot of answers. So tell me! Why would I have wanted to kill Edmund Broderer?'

It was my turn to smile. 'I wasn't sure until young Bertram Serifaber mistook Lionel for Brandon Jolliffe, and then I realized the likeness betwen them myself. And when I found young Roger Jessop, Nell's half-brother – you remember Roger Jessop, don't you? The young lad who used to work in your garden – and saw that he, too, bore a strong resemblance to the other two, I started to believe that they might all have been sired by the same father. This morning, therefore, I talked not only to Mistress Jolliffe but also to Martha Broderer. Both women were quite frank with me about their relationship with your former husband.'

'A lot of men have bastards,' my companion sneered. 'Men are like that: incontinent where their need for women is concerned. But their long-suffering wives don't murder them. They endure, like our poor Queen.'

'Maybe,' I agreed. 'But what if a woman's husband is proposing to leave her for his former sweetheart, his cousin's widow? What if he's talking of obtaining a divorce because of that wife's barrenness? What if this woman cannot bear the thought of being abandoned and humiliated for a woman she despises?'

'What if! What if!' Judith St Clair broke in angrily. 'It seems to me there's more "what if" about your suspicions than substance. And what makes you think Edmund is buried beneath my willow tree?'

'You're very fond of that spot. People have told me so. Yesterday, when you invited me into your garden to stand with you under the tree, I had the feeling that you were secretly laughing at me. Mocking me. Taunting me, perhaps, with the evidence buried beneath our feet. Call me fanciful if you like, but that is how it struck me.'

She gave a hard, artificial little laugh. 'I certainly do call it fanciful! Do you think anyone would be convinced by such nonsense?'

'Probably not. But someone might be more interested in the fact that young Roger Jessop, a child raised and nurtured by you from his earliest days, suddenly ran away because, after a series of odd mishaps and near "accidents", he grew to believe that his life was in danger. I wondered why that should be, until I learned from William Morgan and from you that he had been digging around the willow. The lad didn't find anything; his suspicions of anything, or *anyone*, being buried there weren't even slightly aroused. But you couldn't take the chance of letting him live.'

My companion was really angry now. She was also beginning to be frightened. But she wasn't as yet seriously alarmed. 'Is that all?' she sneered.

'No,' I said. 'There's the mystery of why you married your second husband, Justin Threadgold. Everyone I've spoken to, including his own brother and daughter, says that he was a violent, abusive man. So why, knowing this, did you agree to become his wife?'

'For Alcina's sake,' she whipped back at me.

'That's the impression you've always given to other people, and it seems, on the face of it, to be the only reason that makes sense. But you were rich and the Threadgolds were poor. Suppose, therefore, like Fulk after him, Justin blackmailed you. Into marrying him.'

'How could he do that?' Judith flung at me contemptuously, but I saw her lick her lips.

I gave her back look for look. 'That little room of the Threadgolds', above the fireplace, looks out over your garden with a clear view of the willow tree. Only, of course, there wasn't a tree the night Justin saw you and your sister and William Morgan burying your first husband's body. I don't suppose he guessed at once what you were up to, but when Edmund Broderer went missing, and his body turned up in such a state that only you could recognize it, he put two and two together. He probably claimed to have seen more than he did, but you weren't to know that. Or you daren't take that chance. The price of his silence was marriage. I wonder what death you were planning for him, if he hadn't died of natural causes.'

Judith laughed and abandoned all pretence. 'Oh, I'd have thought of something,' she assured me. 'Of course, I couldn't dispose of him immediately. It would have looked too suspicious. I had to wait a year or two. And then, as you say, my plans weren't needed . . . Well! Continue! What other proof of my guilt do you have to offer me?'

'You have twice had me assaulted by your loyal henchman William Morgan. At first, I was puzzled as to why such a loutish, insubordinate man should hold a privileged position in your household. Later, of course, I understood. He's your tame boarhound. You obviously instructed him not to kill me. My death would have been a great mistake, as I feel sure you agreed. You just wanted me warned off – to go back to Bristol.'

'Dear William! He's a man who knows the meaning of loyalty, unlike my nephew.' Judith spoke with venom.

'Ah, yes! Fulk! You never were enamoured of him, as everyone thought, but you had to play the part of his choosing. What happened? Before she died, did your sister tell him the truth of what happened that night when he was six years old? The night she helped you bury the husband you had killed, while Fulk was asleep in bed? Your twin had a reputation at the Burgundian court – did you know? – of winkling out fellow servants' more disgraceful secrets and using that knowledge against them. "Like mother, like son," I was told, and that seems to have been the truth.'

'I'd never have thought it of my own sister,' Judith hissed. 'My twin! She turned out to have been a viper who'd given birth to a venomous toad.' She leaned forward, her headache apparently forgotten, and gripped my wrist. 'You're right. Almost from the moment of his arrival Fulk made it clear that he knew everything, and intended to take full advantage of what he knew. I was to play the role of loving, besotted aunt and make a new will, leaving everything – *everything*! – to him, or he would tell Duchess Margaret the truth. Veronica was dead and he had been too young to be involved in Edmund's murder. There was only me left to take the blame.'

'Incidentally,' I interrupted, 'how *did* you kill Master Broderer?'

'I stabbed him with a carving knife that happened to be on the table with the remains of our supper, which he'd missed. Edmund came into the dining parlour after we'd eaten. He'd been drinking, but he wasn't drunk. Certainly not enough for me to disbelieve him when he told me he was turning me and my family out of his house to make way for Martha Broderer. I was so furious that, almost without knowing what I was doing, I seized the knife and stabbed him through the heart . . . Later, Veronica and William Morgan helped me strip his body and bury it at the bottom of the garden, by the river. (It was Justin who planted the willow tree over the spot. He thought it a joke.) Then I gave out that Edmund had never come home. People naturally assumed that he must have fallen in the river. So many drunkards end that way. Then all I had to do was to wait until a naked, suitably decomposed body was fished out of the Thames and claim it as my husband's.'

'But you made the mistake of keeping his things,' I said, 'including the gold-and-agate thumb ring that Martha Broderer had given him.'

Her eyes narrowed. 'How do you know that? Have you been in this room without my knowledge?'

There was no point in denying it, and we had gone past the point of fencing with one another.

'Twice,' I admitted.

'And you discovered the "fly trap"?' I nodded. 'How?'

I explained and she swore fluently.

'How did you murder your nephew?' I interrupted her.

'Oh, that was easy. I knew he was going to St Dunstan's that evening, it being the Feast of Saint Sigismund. I simply retired to bed with one of my headaches and, later, left the house by the "secret" stair, wearing a suit of Edmund's clothes and one of his cloaks. I went out by the garden door, over the wall into the alley, and from there to Fleet Street, where I waited outside the church until Fulk came out. There were too many people around to do it then, so I followed him into Faitour Lane' – she curled her lip – 'where he had business at one of the brothels. I had one of Godfrey's cudgels hidden under my cloak and I bludgeoned him to death with that.'

I shivered. 'You're a formidable woman, Mistress St Clair. And the wine you sent by Alcina to Martin Threadgold? What was that laced with? Poppy and lettuce juice? It must have been an easy matter then for either you or the devoted William to smother him with the cushion. You thought he knew something and was going to tell me, didn't you? William Morgan had overheard my conversation with the housekeeper.'

Judith suddenly let go of my arm and swung her feet over the edge of the bed, so that she was standing beside me. 'Let me show you something,' she said. 'Come! It's just over here.'

And like a fool, I followed her.

Twenty

When Judith St Clair said, 'There! There! Look!' I should never have been taken in. I, of all people, should never have followed the direction of her pointing finger.

It was a year, or maybe slightly less, since I had been cudgelled over the back of the head while obeying another duplicitous woman's instrucion to look out of a window. And there I was repeating the same mistake and peering at the floor of Judith's bedchamber because she told me to do so; because I was gullible enough to believe there was something there. I didn't see her open the 'fly trap'; I hadn't even heard William Morgan enter the bedchamber by way of the 'secret' stair. It was only when he grunted, 'Open the door wider, mistress,' that I realized he was behind me, and, of course, by then it was too late.

Far too late.

As I tried to straighten up, suddenly, nerve-wrackingly aware of what was happening, I was heaved forward, head first through the wall into the hidden cupboard, and even before I could gather my wits about me, the door of the 'fly trap' swung shut. And there I was, thanks to my crass stupidity, caught in the spider's web.

It was several minutes before I could even move. I had banged my head on the edge of the shelf as I fell, and had hit the floor at such an angle that I was completely winded. I also discovered, to my chagrin, that I was crying like one of my two young sons, but hastily attributed my tears to rage and frustration rather than pain.

At last I sat up, tenderly feeling my right ankle, which was throbbing, but found that I could move it easily enough

240

and therefore concluded that no lasting damage had been done. Only then did I address myself to the situation I was in.

Of course, I groped for the key, which should have been hanging from the shelf behind me, in order to open the door from inside. But the hook was empty. I would have been an even bigger fool than I had already proved myself to be had I expected otherwise. Judith St Clair had removed it before I was summoned to her bedchamber. She had planned everything with the faithful William Morgan before I arrived.

After Mistress Jolliffe's visit, she must have guessed I would come, and had probably expected me earlier. The sisterhood of women had ensured that Lydia would warn Judith that I was asking questions about Edmund and his relationship to both Brandon and Lionel. Judith could not possibly have known exactly how much I knew, nor what I had made of such information as I had, but she was not a woman who took chances. Her attempts to have Roger Jessop murdered only on account of what he *might* have discovered demonstrated that. So she had summoned William Morgan, her faithful henchman, and together they had laid the trap. No doubt some signal – perhaps 'There! There! Look!' – had been pre-arranged to bring the Welshman from his hiding place behind the door to the 'secret' stair.

It had been unwise to show my hand so plainly; lying there in the airless dark, I could see that now . . . The airless dark! I had been wondering what the murderous duo's plans were for me, but it was suddenly blindingly obvious. They need do nothing until the lack of air in the 'fly trap' suffocated me; then, at night, they could carry my body down to the river and tip me in. There would be no stab wounds, as there had been with Edmund Broderer, to indicate that I had met my death other than by drowning. If Judith insisted that I had left the house *after* talking to her, and William confirmed that he had shown me out, who would contest it? Not Godfrey, who was doubtless lost in the sayings of Marcus Aurelius. Not Paulina Graygoss and the maids, busy in the kitchen preparing ten o'clock dinner. As for Alcina and Jocelyn, they probably had no idea that I had ever been in the house that morning; I had seen no sign of either of them. I really was caught like a fly in a trap.

Keep calm, I told myself. Breathe slowly and don't use up too much air. Yet what was the point of that? Neither Judith nor William was likely to open the door for at least twenty-four hours, if not longer. They would make absolutely certain that I was dead before disposing of me.

My eyes were growing used to the gloom by now, and I stood up carefully to make a search of the shelf. But it revealed nothing that I had not seen during my previous visit, except for a paper folded and sealed. I turned this over once or twice, before noticing that it bore an inscription in a large, bold, confident hand. Even so, I had to squint a little to make it out, then recognized, with a painful jolt to my stomach, that it was addressed to me.

'Roger the Chapman,' it ran; and underneath was the message: 'Candle and tinder-box on the floor.'

I was on my knees almost before I had finished reading, feeling with my hands over every inch of those dusty boards until I found what I was seeking. Right up against the clothes chest my fingers encountered a candle in its holder, and a tinder-box. Carefully, I lifted them on to the shelf, reflecting that in this, at least, Judith St Clair had kept her word.

I put flame to wick and watched the golden light spread and glow, illuminating the narrow space. The 'fly trap' suddenly seemed a less menacing place, and in my relief I failed to notice that the candle was little more than a stump which could last only a very short while. I broke the paper's seal, flattening the thick parchment as well as I could, then held the candle close.

It didn't take me many seconds to realize that what I was reading was Judith St Clair's confession to the murder of her first husband, Edmund Broderer, twelve years earlier, and to that of her nephew, Fulk Quantrell. It wasted no words and offered no excuses, being short and to the point.

242

It merely stated that she, and she alone, had killed them both, and exonerated anyone else of being involved.

I read it through two or three times, wondering why she had not adduced some sort of explanation for the killings, both of which might be thought justifiable in certain circumstances. Then it occurred to me that, if this confession was ever read by anyone but me, I should somehow or other have managed to escape from the 'fly trap' and could supply all the explanation needed. But if I failed to get out, and everything went according to Judith's plan, the confession would be disposed of, along with me.

For a tantalizing moment I flirted with the idea that I might be able to free myself. What would Judith do then? Suicide? I remembered the poppy and lettuce juice potion she took for her headaches (those headaches that could be put to such good use when an alibi was needed). Taken in a sufficiently strong dose, could it kill? My guess was that it probably could.

I had a sudden heart-stopping memory of Bertram picking the inside lock of the 'fly trap' in the Threadgold house. With a trembling right hand, I drew my knife from my belt as, with my left, I held the candle closer to the centre of the door, where Bertram had told me the lock of these things was always located. At that moment, however, the candle guttered and gave up the ghost. Cursing fluently, I hunted around for the tinder-box and, having at last found it, attempted to relight the wick. But it was a lost endeavour: the candle had burned itself out.

I tried, half-heartedly, to use the tinder-box as a light, but it proved impossible, as the tinder was swiftly used up. I was back in the all-enveloping gloom and with eyesight that needed to adjust to the dark all over again.

'What now?' I asked myself.

I was sweating profusely, panic adding its toll to the heat of the cupboard. Then, with something akin to hope again lifting my spirits, I recollected Bertram, in similar circumstances next door, running his finger over the panneling until he could feel the inside lock . . .

243

Several agonizing minutes must have elapsed before I found this one – before a finger of my left hand travelled round a strip of metal so thin that I was at first unaware that I was touching it. With my heart pounding, pressing my finger to the spot, I once more drew my knife in my other hand and brought up the blade . . .

It was hopeless. I don't know how long I kept trying, using every trick of lock-picking that Nicholas Fletcher had taught me, and that had never failed me before. But in the end I had to admit defeat. I was growing short of breath, my head was swimming unpleasantly and my throat was parched. Unconsciousness threatened to overtake me and I was forced to sit on the floor, my chest heaving. This was it, then. This was death, which I had faced on so many occasions in the past, but always cheated until now.

Until now! The true implication of the words hit me with all the force of a blow to the heart. I should never see Adela again. I should never see my sons and daughter again. What would they do without me? Life was not easy for widows or fatherless children. Perhaps Adela would marry for a third time, once she had recovered from my loss. A picture of Richard Manifold rose up before me. He had wanted her from the start. A sheriff's officer, a sergeant, he would be a good provider, but somehow I could not bear the thought of him taking over my family as his own. I remembered the many times they had seemed a burden to me; my sense of freedom as I took once again to the open road and put the miles between myself and them. I remembered how often Elizabeth and Nicholas had driven me to the limits of my endurance, and how frequently Adam had inspired me with thoughts of infanticide . . .

But sitting there in the dark, feeling my senses being gradually overpowered, I vowed that if I ever got out of this dreadful trap alive, I would be a reformed character. I would treat each member of my family with the loving tenderness that he or she deserved. Even Margaret Walker, Adela's cousin and my former mother-in-law, would receive her share of appreciation and esteem.

I gave a gasp, a desperate sucking in of fetid air, halfway between tears and laughter, as darkness began to close in. Even *in extremis*, my old, cynical self told me that, if I did survive, everything would be exactly as it was before. But I hoped that, somehow, Adela and the children would know that I loved them, and had died thinking about them, their names on my lips . . .

But, strangely, it wasn't Adela standing beside me, looking down at my supine form, but Lillis, my first wife, who had died after our all too brief marriage, giving birth to our daughter, Elizabeth. She bent over me, smiling.

'Go back, Roger,' she said. 'Go back. It's not time yet . . . not time.'

The vision of her faded with her voice and she was replaced by my mother, who stood, hands on hips, regarding me in that exasperated fashion I recalled so well from my childhood – a kind of despairing 'what are we going to do with you?' look. She said nothing, but shook her head and warded me off as I tried to wriggle in her direction. She took a step backwards and was gone, and a small, dark man with weather-beaten features, stood there in her stead. I recognized him vaguely as my father, who had died when I was barely four, after a fall from scaffolding as he worked on the ceiling of Wells Cathedral nave. He had been a stone carver by trade and by name, and throughout the early part of my life, I had been known either as Roger Stonecarver or Roger Carverson (and a lot of other names, besides, far less complimentary; but we won't go into that). I couldn't remember much about him; he had made very little impact on my young life compared with my mother, and then he was gone. I had the vaguest recollection of finding my mother in tears on more than one occasion, and associating her grief with my father. But she told me, during one of our rare conversations about him, that, unlike a lot of men, he had never beaten her or used any other sort of violence towards her. So her sorrow must have had a different cause . . .

The visions faded as I briefly regained consciousness. I

became aware of a great weight on my chest, as though someone had placed a heavy stone there. I tried to push it off, but was unable to shift it . . . I was drifting now, down a long, dimly lit passageway, at the end of which was a peculiarly bright white light, and I suddenly felt very calm and peaceful, as though all my life I had been waiting to get to the end of that corridor and lose myself in that light. Indeed, so strong was the urge to complete this journey that when someone shouted in my ear, 'Roger! Roger! Wake up! Wake up!' I was angry and resentful at having been robbed of my goal . . .

I was suddenly awake. The 'fly trap' was open and Bertram was bending over me. The bedchamber beyond appeared to be extraordinarily full of people: men-at-arms, wearing the blue-and-murrey livery of the Duke of Gloucester, and Sheriff's officers.

'What . . . What's going on?' I murmured dazedly, and a voice I thought I recognized said, 'Thanks be to God. He's alive. Carefully, now! Carefully! Carry him out and put him on the bed.'

It was the Duke of Gloucester.

I would have struggled to my feet, but was told peremptorily not to be a fool and lie still. Someone – Bertram? – brought wine and held it to my lips while I drank greedily.

Meantime, all around me chaos reigned. Sheriff's men – there were probably only some three or four of them, but to my still disordered senses it seemed like a cohort – went in and out of the bedchamber as Duke Richard issued his orders. A bewildered Godfrey St Clair and an equally bemused Jocelyn and Alcina were summoned into his presence, but had little to contribute by way of answers to his questions. Paulina Graygoss and the two maids arrived, breathless and scared half out of their wits from the kitchen regions, but had equally little to say, except that William Morgan had disappeared. According to Nell, he had run into the garden and heaved himself over the wall into the alley as soon as the first loud, authoritative knocks on the outer door had heralded the arrival of officialdom. (''E buggered off out the garden an' over the wall as soon as 'e 'eard that there banging,' were her precise words, but we all knew what she meant.)

Judith, too, seemed to be missing, to the great distress of her husband, who found it impossible to comprehend what was going on, and was overwhelmed by the invasion of his house by the King's brother and various representatives of the law. I whispered to Bertram, who, following my instructions, slipped inside the 'fly trap', emerging a few seconds later with Judith's confession. This he handed to the Duke, who read it without comment, before passing it to Godfrey St Clair.

Godfrey's whole body was shaking so much that Duke Richard ordered a stool to be found for him, and, when this had been brought, he read his wife's confession with Alcina and his son looking over his shoulder. Of course, all three refused to believe it, but there was a desperation in their denials reminiscent of people spitting against the wind. There was no refuting, either, that the confession was written in Judith's own hand, no matter how much they would have liked to prove it a forgery. Even so, they would have continued to express their doubts, had not one of the Sheriff's men brought word that Mistress St Clair was to be seen sitting beneath the willow tree at the bottom of the garden, apparently either asleep or gazing out across the Thames. At this information, Godfrey gave a great cry and, oblivious to protocol, rushed from the bedchamber without so much as glancing at the Duke or asking his permission. He had guessed the truth, of course: Judith had taken her own life.

Duke Richard glanced at me with raised eyebrows. I told him about the lettuce and poppy juice potion that she took for her headaches.

'She must have seen Your Highness's approach along the Strand,' I suggested, 'and realized that the game was up. But, My Lord, how did you know where to look for me?'

The Duke, who could be extremely haughty if he wished, merely grinned like a schoolboy and perched on the end of the bed, smoothing the beautiful, embroidered coverlet with a long-fingered, appreciative hand.

'First things first,' he reproved me gently. 'Are you fully recovered after your ordeal? If so, I should be glad to know the details of these two murders. My sister, the Duchess Margaret, will be shocked beyond measure and and it will be hard to convince her of Mistress St Clair's guilt, in spite of her confession. I need to know all of the facts.'

So, I told him.

When I had finished speaking, I lay back against the pillows, exhausted, my recent experience in the 'fly trap' having sapped my strength. Bertram handed me another beaker of wine and, over its rim, I met his reproachful gaze.

'If only you'd kept me informed,' he chided, 'instead of trying to keep me in the dark all the time, you wouldn't have ended up almost dead meat.'

'I'm truly sorry,' I said contritely.

But my apology must have lacked sincerity, because the Duke laughed.

'And so you should be, Roger,' he told me. 'If it wasn't for young Master Serifaber's unshakable conviction that something had happened to you, and his insistence on speaking personally to me, you would certainly have died of suffocation.'

It appeared that Bertram, calling on Lydia Jolliffe, had been informed not only of my visit, but also of the fact that she had seen me returning along the Strand in the direction of the city. Indignantly, he had returned to the Voyager only to find that I wasn't there.

On some God-given impulse, he had decided to visit the Broderer workshop, where Martha had just arrived in order to give a hand with some of the beadwork. She admitted to having seen me and, under pressure, had reluctantly divulged the gist of our conversation. Bertram had then set off back to the Strand, convinced that I had gone to confront Judith St Clair and, as a much brighter lad than I had earlier given him credit for being, already beginning to get a faint inkling of the truth.

At the St Clair house, Paulina Graygoss, who answered his knock, had declared that I had called, but must have gone without her noticing, because she hadn't seen me since. She had referred him to William Morgan, who had confirmed that I had left. Something in the latter's manner, however, had aroused Bertram's suspicions and convinced him that the Welshman was acting under orders from Judith St Clair. Bertram, therefore, had made his way back to Baynard's Castle to seek out Timothy Plummer, but that gentleman, still swollen with self-importance in his role as chief guardian to the Dowager Duchess of Burgundy, had refused to listen to what he considered the merest conjecture. My fate could well have been sealed there and then, had the Duke of Gloucester not happened to ride into the outer courtyard at the very moment Bertram was leaving.

So anxious was Bertram by this time, that, nothing daunted, he had seized the Duke's bridle – and very nearly got himself killed by one of the Duke's squires for his pains. Fortunately, My Lord had intervened just in time; and, as soon as Bertram had explained his worries for my safety, had acted with speed and a fine disregard for the consequences, should Bertram's hunch have proved to be wrong. A messenger had immediately been despatched to the Sheriff, while the Duke himself had taken Bertram up behind him and, accompanied by three or four men-at-arms and two of his squires, ridden directly to the Strand.

It was during this frantic dash through the London streets that Bertram had recollected my telling him of the 'fly trap' in Mistress St Clair's bedchamber, and he had made straight for it as soon as he had been admitted by Paulina, his royal master hard on his heels.

'And so I hope you see, Roger,' the Duke said, still smiling, 'how much you owe to this astute young man.'

I had regained a little of my bravado – enough, at any rate, to grin impudently and say, 'My trust is all in Your Grace to reward him as he deserves, because I'm very sure I can't.'

'He shall become one of my personal bodyguards,' was

the prompt reply, leaving Bertram pink with excitement and gasping like a stranded fish. 'And now,' the Duke went on, getting to his feet, 'I must return to Baynard's Castle and seek an interview with my poor sister. As I said, this news will be a great blow for her, I'm afraid.' He addressed Bertram. 'Master Serifaber, you will accompany me. From henceforth, you will answer only to my household officers and not to Master Plummer, with whom I am seriously displeased. Roger!' He gave me his hand to kiss. 'Once more, I have to thank you for a job well done. I wish it could have had a different outcome, but you've done your part and solved the murder. I would repeat all my former offers to you, except that I know you won't accept them.'

'It's enough to know that I have Your Grace's gratitude,' I replied, and laughed when he gave me a quick, suspicious look from under his brows. 'Your Highness, I mean it, most sincerely.'

He nodded, his face clearing. 'My Scots cousin, the Duke of Albany, has been singing your praises to me. It would seem that he, too, has cause to be grateful to you.'

I said hurriedly, 'I think the less said about that, Your Highness, the better. Especially with so many officers of the law within earshot.'

'Perhaps so,' he agreed sardonically, but then pressed my arm. 'Don't step outside the law too often, Roger. Even I may not be able to protect you if you do . . . You'll come and see me at Baynard's Castle before you return to Bristol, I hope.'

I did, of course. As I have observed so often in the past, royalty's hopes are tantamount to commands. Also present at our meeting was that ebullient young man, the Earl of Lincoln, who threw his arms around my neck and hailed me as a genius. This extravagant and wholly undeserved praise was somewhat tempered by the discovery that Lincoln had had a substantial wager with his father, the Duke of Suffolk, that I would unravel the mystery within seven days, and could now claim his prize.

Neverthless, I could not doubt that his admiration was

genuine, and he assured me several times that he would not forget me. I groaned inwardly. I would much have preferred a life untrammelled by the esteem of princes, who were in the habit of regarding my time as their own. It was bad enough that the volatile Duke of Albany remembered me with gratitude, let alone having young Lincoln thinking of me every time he needed a mystery solved.

But there was nothing I could do about it.

It had been in my mind to remain in London for a day or two in order to renew acquaintance with my old friends, Philip and Jeanne Lamprey; but after my harrowing experience in the 'fly trap', my one desire was to return to Adela and the children as soon as possible. I had completely abandoned my original intention to walk back to Bristol, enjoying my own company and selling my wares as I went. Nothing now but speed would satisfy me; so I rode on the horse hired from the Bell Lane stables (which, when I thought about it, seemed the sensible thing to do: how else would the poor beast get home?).

The nag and I reached Bristol a week later (slow going, but I've already admitted I'm no horseman) on the feast of Saint Augustine of Canterbury. I returned my mount to the stables and walked the short distance to Small Street. As I approached my own house – mine by the generosity of the sweetest woman I have ever known – my heart swelled with pride and the anticipation of embracing my dear wife and family again. It would be no exaggeration to say that my heart beat faster with expectation . . .

I should have known better.

As I opened the street door, Elizabeth and Nicholas hurtled downstairs, screaming at the tops of their voices, in full cry after Hercules, who had someone's shoe betwee his jaws. Also joining in the chase was Margaret Walker's black-and-white mongrel, yapping and snapping like the fiend he was. In the kitchen, Adam was indulging in one of his tantrums, while from upstairs came the sound of Margaret Walker – she was still with us, God save the mark! – banging with her stick on the bedchamber floor. Adela – looking, not surprisingly, overwrought – appeared in the passageway, saw me and said, 'Oh, you're back. I wish you'd control that animal of yours.'

I leaned against the door jamb and, suddenly, began to laugh. I laughed until the tears ran down my face, and in the end I wasn't sure whether I was laughing or crying. But one thing I knew for certain:

I was home.